HEIRS OF A BROKEN LAND
BOOK 1

PRINCESS OF LIGHT

MARIE BILODEAU

Cover by Deranged Doctor Design

Editing by Jessica Torrance

Map by Kerri Elizabeth Gerow

AUTHOR'S NOTE

Thanks for picking up *Princess of Light*! As you might already know, this was my first novel, originally published in 2009 and now re-released with extra glitter. It's been an amazing author journey since, and I'm excited to celebrate how it started, with this epic fantasy trilogy.

I hope you enjoy!

Marie

xo

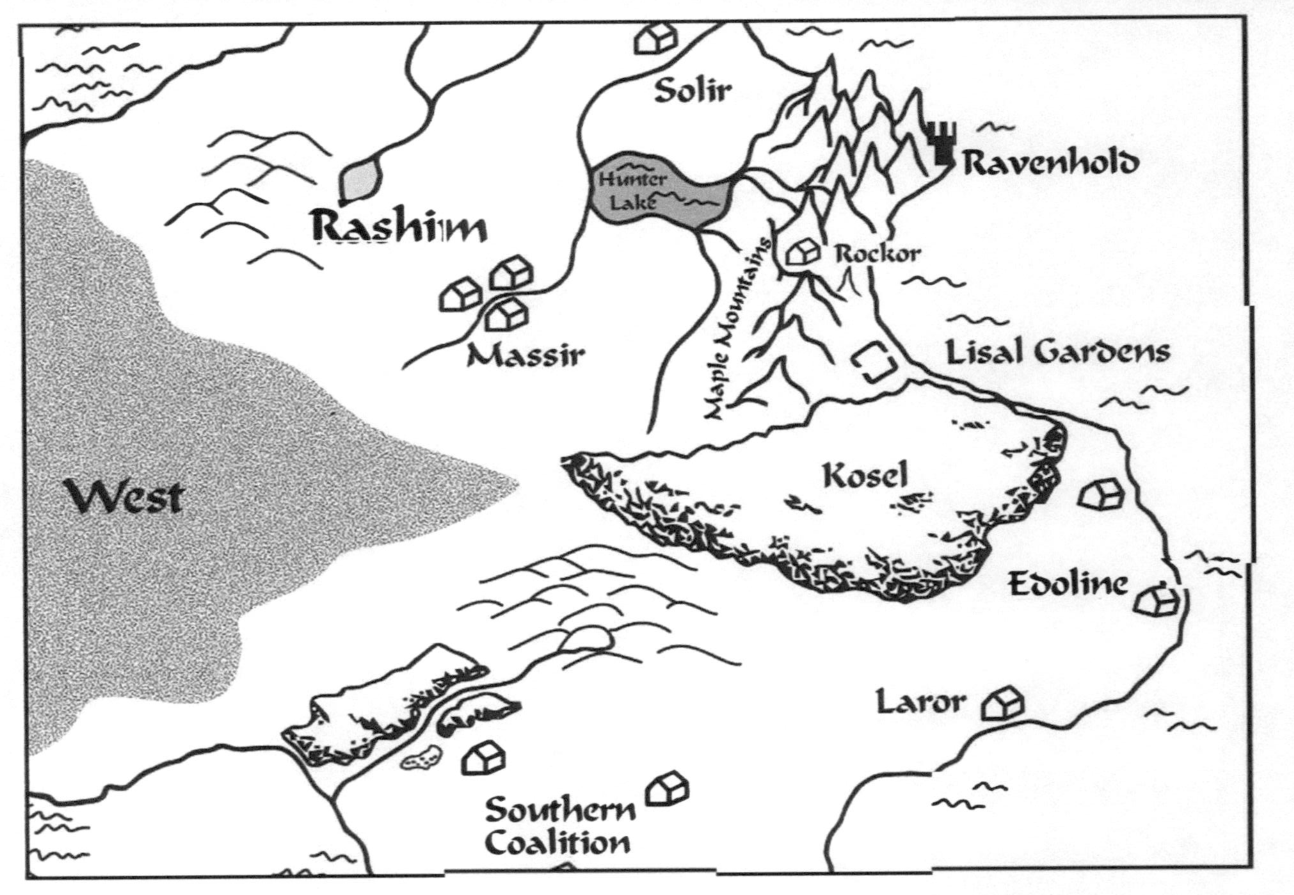

Solir
Rashim
Hunter Lake
Ravenhold
Rockor
Maple Mountains
Lisal Gardens
Massir
West
Kosel
Edoline
Laror
Southern Coalition

Cassara shifted her right leg, careful not to make any noise, wincing as the blood flowed back into the numb limb.

If Klar would hurry up and do his rounds, I wouldn't be having this problem! She exhaled more sharply than intended, her hand rising to her mouth.

Klar turned around, his gray hair and eyes reflecting the light of the lantern he held. Cassara tried to melt between the pillar and the statue, hoping the darkness would be enough to engulf her. Had she known Klar, the captain of the guards, was on duty tonight, she would never have attempted this. He was entirely too watchful and quick to act. She vowed to make her informants pay.

The guard approached the single wooden door, plainly but elegantly decorated, that stood across from where she hid in the shadows. He examined the door intensely.

Cassara held her breath and feared she might pass out from the lack of air.

Klar gently tried the handle, finding the princess' room well secured. If he decided to open the door now and found the princess missing, everything would be lost and Cassara would have to return to her prison.

Deciding that interrupting the princess' sleep was not necessary, Klar moved on, casting wary glances at the shadows all around him. Cassara was grateful that the hallways of the royal manor of Edoline were kept dark during the night, providing her the stealth she needed.

The guard vanished around a corner and Cassara quickly slipped out from hiding. A small bag was secured to her waist and her skirt flowed around her ankles. She wrinkled her nose at the stale smell down the corridor, wishing she could open every door and window to get rid of the scent of rotting wood wafting down from the attic.

Grazing the stone wall with the tips of her fingers, Cassara walked past two other doors, her steps muffled by the faded carpet. A lone torch flickered from an adjacent hallway further down, but she did not need its light to navigate, using her knowledge of every detail of the stone wall and its sparse decorations to guide her.

Reaching the last door in the hallway, Cassara glanced around one more time to make sure she was alone before reaching into her hair and pulling two pins free. Her long blond tresses cascaded down her back. Holding the handle of the door, she placed the pins in the lock, twisting one to the right while keeping the other firm in the center. The door opened in one swift motion. The scent of sweet cherry blossoms embraced her and Cassara smiled as she entered the room, closing the door and locking it again behind her.

A small candle illuminated the bedroom, its wick flickering as it reached the last of the wax. A bed, only big enough to hold two children, was close to the open window. The only other pieces of furniture in the room were a bookshelf, a desk and a wardrobe. A small figure shifted under the blankets, and Cassara cursed herself for being too loud. The last thing she needed was for the young prince to wake up.

The wind caressed the trees in the orchard outside, blossoms flying into the room, the dancing petals like a soothing lullaby. Soon the young prince's breaths were once again long and smooth.

Cassara smiled and put down her bag, quickly removing her skirt to reveal the pants she wore underneath for ease of movement. The disguise had served its purpose a few other times she had been caught and had simply pretended that she could not sleep and was going for a walk in the orchard. No one truly believed her, but no one questioned her either. They simply kept a closer eye on her.

Free from her skirt, Cassara tied her hair back again, and donned a small jacket to ward off the cool night air. The candle flickered once again and died, the wick's smoke leaving the smell of an extinguished flame in its wake. Cassara crossed to the desk, carefully slid the top drawer open and pulled out a fresh candle. Jayden hated sleeping in the dark and she didn't want him to have to wake up to it. Besides, hiding her clothing under his bed was easier when there was some light.

She quickly lit it and, as she bent down to hide evidence of her passage, her amulet slipped from under her shirt, catching the weak light and reflecting it. Cassara quickly covered the cool metal and tucked it back into her shirt, glad to see the light had not disturbed the prince's slumber.

Satisfied all signs of her passage were taken care of, Cassara headed for the window. The great cherry tree that graced Jayden's window had been a blessing on more than one occasion. She expertly grabbed a branch and let herself swing towards the thick trunk as she reached for another branch.

Cherry blossoms glided around her, marking the end of a season. She climbed a few more branches and let herself fall to the ground, the blooms scattering about her feet. Moonlight graced the land, the few clouds in the sky shying away from the moon.

"A perfect night," she whispered as she began walking away from the manor, her boots having traveled this path countless times before.

She cast a final glance back to make sure no one was looking in her direction. Aside from Jayden's small candle, a single light was visible, in the king's chambers. It was the only room on the second floor, a wooden addition clumsily built onto the original single-level stone building. Through the white curtains she could see the king pacing slowly, his body following the same tired rhythm it had for many years.

Grasped by the familiar regret that always clutched her whenever in the presence of the king, Cassara turned away from his restless sight, concentrating instead on her destination. This escape would do her a world of good.

The path Cassara chose to reach town was always through the orchard, which was not the quickest path, but by far the most beautiful. The trees danced in the wind all around her, apple blossoms clinging when the cherry blossoms were already falling. The wind carried with it the fresh smell of the sea, crisp and refreshing, soon to be joined by the sound of waves striking unmoving earth.

Cassara freed her hair from its restraints, letting it join the blossoms on the wind.

"This is more like it!" Cassara laughed, no longer afraid of being overheard and stopped.

"Quite," a voice said from behind her.

Cassara turned around, adopting a stern look as she faced the man who was following her.

"Thanks for warning me that Klar was on duty tonight, Kaden."

"Was he?" The old guard responded, a smile on his lips, his wrinkled face showing the years that the laughter in his eyes denied.

"You can be bothersome, old man." She smiled at him. "You know that, don't you?"

Kaden brought up his hands defensively. "I only do it

with your best interest in mind, princess." He ended with a bow.

Cassara raised an eyebrow.

"Besides," Kaden said, standing again with some difficulty. "Carsyn wanted to get some rest tonight and I like to make sure he gets little of that."

"Carsyn!" Kaden shouted towards the shadow of a tree, to be answered by a grunt. "Get up, you're on duty tonight!" Another grunt followed.

"You can just leave him here," Cassara said. "In fact, why don't you both stay here and rest. It's not like I'll be in grave danger in our little kingdom."

"It is our duty, my Lady," Kaden said, simply bowing his head. "Carsyn, get up or I'll gut you where you stand, well, sleep." Cassara smiled. She had been hearing Kaden speak that threat for over sixteen years, now.

"I'm coming, I'm coming," the gruff voice said from the shadows as the other old guard struggled to his feet and joined them.

"Fine night for a walk, princess," Carsyn grumbled as the three resumed walking along the coast, Kaden and Carsyn staying a few steps behind, a position they had assumed when she was just learning to walk and had kept ever since, despite her protests for them to join her.

"We should not stay late tonight, my Lady. The prince of Rashim is calling on you tomorrow," Kaden shouted over the sound of the surf.

Cassara sighed and slowed her steps, allowing the two

guards to catch up to her. She slipped her arms into both of theirs, making them keep pace with her.

"Tell me honestly, Kaden. How desperate is my father to marry me off?"

Kaden sighed and lowered his head, shaking it. Carsyn answered before his superior could, however, a slight smile playing on his lips. "The king is very desperate to be rid of his disobedient younger daughter, my Lady. He fears that she may find herself in a situation where she becomes no longer marriageable."

Cassara felt her face grow red and elbowed the old man in the ribs, almost sending him to the ground. Carsyn coughed and wheezed out a laugh, before growing serious again.

"I believe, my Lady, that your guards are getting old," Carsyn said with a sigh. "And that your father would like you to be happily wed before they retire."

"Which they will not do as long as your safety is in their hands," Kaden said softly.

Cassara squeezed his arm and continued walking, the two guards silently falling behind her again. Since she'd turned sixteen four months ago, her father had decided it was imperative to find a good match for her, whether to a lord of a prosperous land or to a prince of a wealthy kingdom, it hardly seemed to matter. As long as it was a good match and his youngest daughter was gone, leaving his only son to occupy the throne of the small forgotten kingdom of Edoline.

She looked up past the orchard and onto the

farmlands. Edoline boasted one manor that housed an ancient royal family, and one village. The rest of the kingdom consisted of farmland. Edoline was so small that certain lords of Graydon oversaw more property than her father ruled.

The fresh smell of the sea was overtaken by the memory of the rotting pillars of her family's manor, of the sparse decor and the slowly dwindling supply of candles. Her older sister, Altessa, had struck a good match a year ago by marrying a noble lord's son from a neighboring country. Those were the last riches Edoline had ever seen.

Cassara reached up and touched some apple blossoms, the velvet of the petals cool against her palm. The few citizens of Edoline worked together to gather the food and to collect outside goods, but it wasn't enough. But could the entire future of the kingdom really depend on one good marriage?

The kingdom of Rashim was the richest of Graydon, despite its reputation for strict and unforgiving rule. It couldn't hurt to at least meet with this prince.

"It's the least I can do for my father," Cassara whispered, haunted by the sight of him pacing back and forth in his room.

The eventual meeting slipped from her mind as soon as she heard the laughing voices up ahead in the village. Since it was the only village in Edoline, it was known simply as that, the village. Cassara smiled and quickened her pace, ignoring Kaden's plea for her to stay close.

The inn rose up ahead, and Cassara felt as light as a

falling blossom as she entered into its smoky interior, to be greeted by shouts of welcome.

Cassara waved and smiled as she headed for the chair that Barlos, the innkeeper, was hurrying to place on the small stage. Cassara reached into her bag and felt around for her flute, the wood soft and comforting.

She pulled it free, and the room quickly hushed as the inn's patrons sat down and prepared to enjoy what had become one of their sole entertainments. It was predicted that it would be a dry summer with weak crops, and rumors of a new war with the West were brewing, so Cassara knew that her people needed all the entertainment they could get.

Kaden and Carsyn walked in, out of breath, and the patrons moved aside to give them room to approach the front. Barlos made two of his patrons change seats so that the guards could sit close to the princess. Kaden thanked him, and Carsyn as he offered her as withering a stare as he could muster. She smiled back.

Cassara held the flute in her hands, her practiced fingers slipping into place with ease. Closing her eyes, she let the music come to her at its own pace, the sound of her flute filling every corner of the inn.

She let herself be carried away by the music, every note invoking a memory or a desire, every melody an ache that had lived within her ever since she had finished carving the instrument with her own hands. An ache that only seemed to grow with time, even as the memories grew dim as she kept telling herself that time healed all wounds.

She played until all memories vanished and she was left with only hope—hope for her people, for her kingdom, and most of all, for herself. She did not know how long she played, losing herself entirely until the music stopped coming to her, the melodies vanishing as her fatigue grew, and she ended on a mournful air, holding the final note until it died with her breath.

She opened her eyes, realizing that tears had fallen down her cheeks and that silence had fallen in the room. Several of the men and women, all people whom Cassara knew, had tears glistening on their cheeks in the candlelight as well. The only ones who were not paying attention were her two guards, Kaden's chin resting on his slowly rising chest, Carsyn's head fully fallen on the table.

Cassara felt heat rise to her face. She offered them an apologetic smile.

"That was supposed to be cheerful."

The tension broke with her jest and talking and laughter filled the inn once more. Well, at least she had fulfilled her goal of making them laugh.

"When will we see you again, my Lady?" Barlos asked as he approached her, bowing his head respectfully.

"Soon, I hope," Cassara said with an unconvincing smile.

If she were soon to be wed, it might never happen again.

Barlos merely nodded. "Shall I room these two for the

night?" he indicated the two guards with a quick motion of the head.

"Please. Kaden will be furious for falling asleep on duty, but I think my guards have well-earned their rest." Cassara was surprised at the sadness she felt in her voice. Was she already bidding farewell to her land and her people?

"I'll send two of my men with you," Barlos said, looking around for some free staff.

Cassara placed her hand on his shoulder. "Thank you for the offer, but I'm sure I'll be fine. Besides," she added in a whisper, "I think I would prefer to walk alone tonight."

Barlos seemed uncomfortable at the suggestion, but he nodded nonetheless, bowing awkwardly as he returned to the bar.

Cassara tucked her flute away and exited the inn, the patrons lowering their heads respectfully as she passed by. They knew her well, the youngest daughter of King Alexavier, but still they did not approach her or speak with her in the same way they did amongst each other.

She did not know if it was because they were intimidated by royalty, even if that royalty played music for them, or if it was simply because they did not want to get attached to someone who was obviously just passing through their lives. As she stepped into the fresh night air and avoided the main road to cross through the orchard once again, Cassara could not decide which reason made her feel worse.

Or more alone.

<hr>

THE CLOUDS COVERED THE MOON, leaving Cassara with little light by which to navigate. She cursed silently for letting herself get caught in her music and not leaving earlier. But it had felt so good to be free, if only for a moment. The sea shimmered as the clouds parted from the moon once more, only to be quickly covered again.

Cassara walked silently, brooding over the day's events. It was getting harder and harder to escape the manor now, since her father had doubled her security. If it wasn't for Kaden's and Carsyn's help, she knew she would never escape to visit the land and play her music for her people.

Of course, the only reason they agreed to it was so she wouldn't run away on her own, making their lives difficult. She kicked a rock and watched it roll before her.

Her planned escapes were best for everyone concerned, really. She was still able to do what she loved, and her guards still knew her whereabouts. When they didn't fall asleep, anyways. And she knew that were she ever to run away, something she never seriously considered doing, Kaden and Carsyn would be made to pay, and they were like family to her.

All they needed was a good retirement, which they refused to take as long as she was under their care. She exhaled loudly into the night and filled her lungs with the fresh sea air.

The sound of her breath filled her ears before she slowly released it. At that moment, her ears felt empty and ached for sound. No cricket sang. No owl broke the night with its haunting cry.

The wind had died down, so not even a leaf rustled, and no wave struck the cliffs. The apple blossoms were eerily still as they caught what little light the moon offered.

A pungent smell overtook the air, sending a shiver through her entire body. Her steps faltered as her stomach lurched.

Cassara looked back towards the village. She was halfway to the manor.

She cast another wary glance about her, trying to convince herself the smell came from the sea. Perhaps a whale had perished. But she knew that it was not the season for whales to be migrating, nor was there any wind to carry the smell so quickly and efficiently.

Cassara hastened her steps. The orchard was starting to feel like uncharted territory to her.

The sound of a twig breaking shattered the stillness. Cassara stopped and looked towards the dark trees. The weak moonlight revealed nothing.

"Kaden?" she whispered, trying to summon the courage to continue walking.

It can't be Kaden, you fool! He's too slow to catch up to you!

She bit her lower lip and forced herself to keep

moving. Another noise broke the night, this one louder, like a growl. But it sounded nothing like the few wolves that frequented the area near the borders of Kosel.

Her hands numb, she fumbled for the dagger she kept at her waist, at Kaden's insistence. The weight felt inadequate in her hand but she was still grateful for the presence of a weapon.

A figure moved within the woods, barely ten feet from where she stood. She backed away quickly, towards the cliffs, before thinking better of it. The air around her turned cold, and Cassara wished she could be anywhere but here, alone at night.

The growl grew louder and the creature came closer. Something suddenly burned against her chest, and Cassara touched her mother's amulet. Her heart raced below it, the metal warm on her flushed skin.

"Come out!" Her scream fell weakly into the night. "Come out and face me!" She screamed again, this time with more force.

As if she had recited the words to some great spell, three creatures emerged from the woods. Something in their clunky walk, crooked posture and guttural sounds led her to believe these were not mere thieves. Cassara gasped and dropped her knife as the moon broke free of the clouds.

If they had been human at one point, some force had robbed them of any grace and warmth. Their faces bore human features, now twisted and grotesque. Skin tight against bone and muscle, tattered clothing clinging to them, veins dark red and blue, pushing against the greying skin. Their movements were not quite human, like something else moved their limbs. Hands like claws. Teeth like daggers.

Despite all of that, it was their eyes that terrified her the most. Deep black, bottomless wells riddled with grief and deep yearning. But hatred as well, and in that instant Cassara knew that she could not fight these creatures.

She had to run or she would die. Her chest burning more intently, Cassara was running before she had even realized her feet were moving, toward the manor. Her breath became ragged and fear robbed her of it while pushing her to go faster.

She heard something behind her, but dared not look back. More twigs snapping, feet falling on the earth, grunts. They were chasing her! How could these creatures even be capable of running with their misshapen bodies!?

A creature knocked into her. She kicked it off and began running again before she fully fell. The second one came shortly afterwards, and this time her luck did not hold out. She stumbled hard, her left arm folding under her body, her face scraping the earth and her legs flying above her.

Strong, leathery hands grabbed her and turned her onto her back, pinning her down. Cassara's head swam but she forced herself to stay conscious, the smell almost more than she could bear. One of the creatures was on top of her. Its teeth, still surprisingly white in contrast to the rest of its body, were sharper than any wolf she had ever seen. Cassara fought weakly as dizziness overcame her, but her limbs were paralyzed by fear.

It was going to eat her!

The creature's head lowered towards her. There was no hint of victory flickering in its eyes, only the same look of pain. A sound escaped Cassara's lips, a useless protest against the destiny fate had provided her this night.

Teeth met her neck and she screamed more out of fear than pain. In that instant, the night sky exploded with light, and Cassara wondered if the moon had come from the shadows, or if she was joining her mother in the Afterfate.

A scream jerked her back to her senses, and she realized that the creature had fallen off of her and was writhing in agony. Cassara sat up, searching the origin of the strange light, a light that kept the other two demons at bay.

Looking down, she saw a glow coming from her chest. Slowly, warily, she reached inside her tunic and pulled her mother's amulet free.

The metal that had been dull all her life suddenly glowed brilliantly white. It was warm, but it did not burn her. Its light reached deep within the orchard, casting dark shadows as far as the manor.

But the other two creatures seemed unaffected by the light, except for needing to crouch and cover their eyes protectively. Summoning what little courage her bewildered mind had left, Cassara resumed walking towards the manor, holding the amulet protectively in her hand.

She only took a few steps when, without warning, the light vanished. Cassara stopped and stared at her amulet. Couldn't the light have flickered first and given her fair warning?

She looked up to see the two creatures already straightening, their teeth bared for the kill or to avenge their fallen comrade. Her legs would not move.

Maybe if she stood her ground, the amulet would stop them a second time. But her arm refused to remain extended. Her whole body tingled with deep fatigue and no more power emanated from the metal.

She forced her knees to stay straight, refusing to let them buckle below her and leave her prostrate on the ground, ripe for the picking. She was still a daughter of the House of Edoline and if she was to die in battle, she would at least try to face death standing.

The two creatures surrounded her, taking their time, apparently feeling that she would not try to escape. Cassara tried to keep her head high, but tears were soon clouding her vision and she closed them, concentrating on at least remaining standing.

She realized she had stopped breathing. Sweat poured down her back, and every sound became her enemy, every small sensation against her skin foretold incoming death.

The smell of the creatures grew stronger. She knew they were now right beside her, and she was about to die, alone, in the orchard of her youth.

Then someone screamed: "Get down!" A flash of light broke the darkness.

Kaden? No, it was a woman.

"I said get down!" The woman screamed again. Cassara felt her knees easily give way as she threw herself to the ground, willing to trust this last chance at life. She looked up, to see one creature fallen, and a woman wielding a sword expertly against the second one. The sword flashed with light every time it met the creature, which soon lay dead, the smell of charred flesh slow to spread in the windless night.

Stunned, Cassara remained seated, looking up at the woman, who was cursing softly. She was tall, which was about the only feature Cassara could make out in the dark night.

"Ruined my last good shirt," the woman grumbled as she approached Cassara. She struggled to get to her feet to thank the woman properly.

"Thanks," she said, her voice barely more than a squeak. The woman nodded and offered Cassara her water skin, which she accepted gratefully, drinking deeply.

"You know you're bleeding, right?" the warrior said casually as Cassara handed her back the skin. Her hand automatically went up to her neck, feeling the warm blood in the shallow wound. She could deal with it back home.

"What were those things?" Cassara asked, looking back at the corpses of the creatures, her hand shaking as she pointed to them.

"Eloms," the woman said as she cleaned her blade and sheathed the sword on her back.

"Eloms?" Cassara repeated, not recognizing the term.

The woman nodded. "Where do you live?"

"The manor, up ahead," Cassara said, not caring if the woman knew she was the princess. Edoline was not worth anything to anyone, and so neither was its royalty.

The woman's eyebrows shot up. "The royal manor? What's your name?"

Cassara was too tired to care if the woman intended to kidnap her after all. At least she was fairly sure the warrior wouldn't try to eat her.

"Cassara Edoline," she said, a twinge of pride returning to her voice. It might be a small kingdom, but it was one to be proud of nonetheless.

"That explains a bit," the woman said, looking contemplative.

"And your name?" Cassara snapped. She didn't enjoy being taken at a disadvantage by so many events in her own land. Surely she had the right to know what was happening! The warrior grinned at her, apparently amused by Cassara's outburst.

"Avarielle," was all the woman offered. "You can head home, now. You'll be fine."

Without another word, Avarielle walked away, towards the cliff, the moon breaking free of the clouds once more, its light reflecting on the tall woman's auburn hair. Cassara watched her walk a few steps, tempted to follow her and find out more about these Eloms. But one look at the burnt, twisted bodies that had almost eaten her made her consider otherwise.

Without further hesitation, her legs feeling numb and clunky, Cassara did her best to continue walking.

By the time the moon clouded over a few moments later, she was running.

2

"Wake up, my Lady," Emala's voice broke the silence, followed immediately by light as the curtains were tied back. Cassara grunted and rolled over, stuffing her face in a pillow. Her cheek burned as the soft fabric rubbed against it.

Cassara sat up, stunned by its roughness. Then she remembered the events of the night before, the creatures' dark eyes haunting her still. She raised her hand to feel the roughness where she had fallen.

"What's wrong?" Emala asked as she hurried to her mistress' side. The older woman's face flickered from concern to anger in a single instant.

"You were out again last night, weren't you?" Emala asked, her eyes scrutinizing the scratch on Cassara's cheek. "I might have known! Who else would have had a bath during the night, and for what other reason?"

Cassara shook her head to fend off the woman's angry

gaze. Emala continued: "You know you shouldn't do this, not anymore, not as your father's trying to find you a husband!"

Emala took a deep breath, her face losing some of its redness. Her eyes flickered and suddenly they were filled with concern again.

"You weren't attacked, were you?" She turned from red to white.

"No," Cassara answered calmly, still amazed after all this time at Emala's ability to jump from thought to emotion in a split second. On any other morning it might have amused Cassara, but today she simply found it disorienting. Her mind was still groggy and she needed time to think on what happened last night.

Emala shook her head and moved to the small vanity bearing Cassara's older sister's rejected cosmetics. Choosing a lighter tone, Emala compared it to Cassara's fair cheek. Her eyes lit with victory.

"Perfect. It's sunny today, and we want you to look your best for the prince!" A smile broke out on the maid's face, the wrinkles on her still-young skin a testament to an emotionally charged life. Although only ten years older than Cassara, she could easily have been mistaken for her mother.

"Prince?" Cassara barely managed to say through a yawn as Emala applied the cold makeup to her sensitive skin. She was glad she had had enough forethought to wear one of her light scarves around her neck. Emala would have fainted at the sight of the wound.

Another disapproving glance. "Yes, of course, princess. Prince Dayshon of the Kingdom of Rashim. He hasn't much time, since an emergency council was called this morning by the Circle. But he's still staying to meet with you, and here you are, sleeping the morning away. You've only got an hour, at most!"

"What emergency meeting?" Cassara asked while grabbing her brush and beginning to brush out the multitude of tangles. The golden braid she had quickly thrown together after her bath had apparently been too quickly thrown together.

Emala ignored the question, instead concentrating on Cassara's sparse collection of fine dresses, all much past their prime and long out of fashion.

"Blue should do," the woman said happily, holding out a dress Cassara despised. No woman should ever have to fit into anything that was smaller than her.

"Emala, what meeting?" Cassara asked again more forcefully, wincing as she tugged at the knots in her hair.

"The one that will take him away from you soon! He's such a nice young man, too. Only a few years older than you, I'd say!" Emala answered, obviously more interested in Cassara's wardrobe than politics.

What meeting? Could it have anything to do with these Eloms? Cassara thought, her brush strokes slowing.

She jumped as a knock came at the door. Cassara was up and almost at the door before Emala caught up with her and covered her with a robe.

Cassara threw the door open. Emala sighed heavily behind her.

"Captain," Cassara said as Klar appeared before her. She was glad the wound on her face was already covered.

"My Lady." He bowed at the waist. "A woman is here to see you."

"And you felt the need to tell me this personally?" Cassara snapped, annoyed at all the interruptions that were happening. She needed time to sit alone somewhere and think.

If Klar was offended, he did not show it.

"She seemed dangerous to me, so I approached her myself," Klar said, his upper lip twitching as he looked at Emala's annoyed look, the blue dress still hanging from her arm. "And the rest of the staff seems preoccupied with other matters."

"What does this woman look like?" Cassara asked.

"Tall, short red hair. She says she has something to return to you."

"Thank you, captain. She is a friend, but thank you for your concern." He bowed and took his leave, suspicion still in his eyes.

Let him think what he will, Cassara thought, closing the door.

Emala's tension seemed to break as she clearly imagined Cassara would now get ready. It returned immediately as Cassara crossed the room and quickly threw on a simple beige dress.

"You can't wear that to meet the prince!" Emala gasped.

"Of course not, but first I'm going to meet my friend," Cassara said as calmly as possible. "Help me tie this at the back, please," she said, placing herself in front of Emala, who was turning a shade of purple.

"Emala, I'll only be a moment, and then I promise I shall meet this Prince Dayshon and let him sweep me off my feet and carry me to his large and rich kingdom to bear him many heirs," Cassara said in one breath. "But first let me take care of this."

Emala grunted as she finished tying the dress. Cassara turned to face her and hugged the woman.

"Knowing my friend is waiting will bother me, my dear Emala, and I wish to be at my best for his highness." Cassara was surprised to see Emala soothed by her words. Were she in her place, she would have hit her upside the head and forced her into the too-small dress.

"Very well, my Lady," Emala said, bowing slightly. Then, her voice taking on the strict tones of a mother dealing with a disobedient child, she added: "But if you're not back here within ten minutes, young lady, I'll have the guards drag you back."

Cassara did a quick mock bow to the maid before slipping from the room. Klar had not specified where the woman would be, but she guessed it would be in the main courtyard, located at the front of the manor.

Cassara descended the steps with little grace, grateful that her father was not a witness to what he would certainly call a "plain and immodest display of rebellion." She opened the main door and walked into the courtyard, the prospect of meeting the prince in her current attire tugging at her mind.

She spotted the tall warrior woman from the previous night.

Her mind was still haunted by dark creatures and moonlight.

"PRINCESS," Avarielle greeted her with a small nod of the head, not bothering to rise from under the tree that shaded her. Cassara returned the nod, approaching the warrior warily.

The sword that had flashed into the night was strapped to her back in an old scabbard. The sword was the only visible weapon aside from a long knife attached at her waist. She was plainly dressed and Cassara doubted the woman had cleaned herself in at least a week. Her hair shone red only in direct light and was short and slightly uneven. Cassara guessed it had been hacked off with a knife and not scissors.

The woman, Avarielle, did not seem concerned or intimidated in the least by her surroundings. Kaden and Carsyn were nowhere in sight, but Klar and another guard, Gragor, stood watch nearby, their weapons plainly displayed in an obvious attempt at intimidation. Avarielle paid them no heed, although Cassara doubted they had escaped her attention.

Avarielle seemed to grow amused by the intensity with which Cassara scrutinized her, and she came lazily to her feet. The two guards came closer.

"I guess it's hard to get a moment's peace around here?" she asked casually, beginning to walk among the courtyard's trees. Cassara followed, annoyed that the woman showed such little respect. The trees were old and tall, but they had been planted apart so that the guards could always keep an eye on the royalty. She saw Klar and the other guard separate and follow on different sides.

Ignoring Avarielle's earlier question, Cassara asked, "What are Eloms?" Her hands rose to her shoulders by instinct, and she was disappointed to find no shawl with which to ward off the late spring air.

"You certainly don't waste any time with questions, do you?" Avarielle grinned.

Cassara shrugged and lowered her voice. "Thanks again for last night. But what were those things?"

"Do you really want to know?" Avarielle asked, stopping so suddenly Cassara almost walked into her. She turned and looked down into Cassara's eyes. The princess forced herself to stand her ground.

"Yes," she whispered, with none of the fire that seemed to burn in Avarielle.

"Good." Avarielle seemed relieved. "There's a large nest on the cove, and I need your help to destroy it."

Cassara's mouth opened once, then twice, but before she could speak, a young voice interrupted them.

"You're from the West, aren't you?" Cassara turned in horror to see her little brother, Jayden, standing there. Klar hovered nearer with each passing second. Cassara hoped he hadn't heard them. From the look of wonder in Jayden's eyes, she doubted he had.

Cassara was about to reproach him for sneaking up and for being so rude, but Avarielle spoke first.

"Why do you say that?" Avarielle asked, diverting her full attention to Jayden.

"Because when I was a kid," Jayden said, and Avarielle took on a serious air, obviously trying not to laugh. Jayden continued, his voice growing authoritative as he was being taught to be, as future king of Edoline. "I heard stories of the red-haired demons of the West. So I saw your hair and I figured you must be one of them."

Cassara's eyes grew wide with shock, but Avarielle's laughter broke the tension. She wiped tears from her eyes before speaking.

"You have a good sense of deduction, young prince," she said, giving him an exaggerated bow. "But you should be careful who you call a demon," she ended with a wink. Jayden seemed taken by her, and he smiled up at her, losing his grown-up persona and becoming a twelve-year-old boy again.

"You should get back to your lessons, my prince," Klar said, and Cassara noticed his hand was on his sword and he was substantially closer. Avarielle ignored him.

"Maybe you can tell me stories later," Jayden said, his eyes wide with the hope of hearing tales of the wild, barely charted lands of the West.

"I promise I'll tell you the best stories you've ever heard," Avarielle said, and Jayden left, pleased with the encounter.

Cassara grabbed Avarielle's arm and began walking with her, away from Klar. The warrior did not protest, a wide grin still on her face. Although Cassara was curious as to Avarielle's origins, she felt there were more important matters at hand. Cassara could learn of her origins later, when she fulfilled her promise to Jayden. Hopefully after Cassara had a chat with her brother about diplomacy.

"First, I'm so sorry. He obviously shouldn't have told you those stories."

Avarielle shrugged. "Seems to me he probably just shouldn't have heard them in the first place."

Cassara flushed and bit her lips, then nodded. The warrior examined her as though she had all the time in the world, which only made Cassara more nervous.

"You're right." She paused. "About that, anyway." She forced words out through her dry throat. "I mean, you want me to walk into a nest of those things?"

"Yes."

"You're joking, right?" Cassara laughed nervously.

Avarielle shook her head. "Your magic works against them, so you should be fine. Besides," she added, raising an eyebrow, "surely the princess of such a fine kingdom has been trained to defend herself against possible assailants."

Heat rose to Cassara's face.

"I can defend myself against human assailants," she said, fighting to keep her voice low so that Klar would not overhear. "But those things weren't human." She then took a step closer to the warrior, closing the gap between the two. "And this kingdom may be small, but it *is* a very fine one."

Avarielle kept her eyes locked on the princess'. Cassara was beginning to wonder if she had gone too far. She had seen the woman's fighting skills last night, and knew this was no mere mercenary. Could Klar come to her aid quickly enough? She wanted to look about to see where he now stood, but did not want to be the first to break eye contact.

After a few moments, Avarielle grinned and laughed. "You'll be fine! Just stay angry like that. Believe me, magic answers better to emotion than cold logical appeal, no matter what the Circle wants us all to believe." She practically spat out the last few words.

She continued without giving Cassara the opportunity to speak. "Meet me two hours after sundown tonight, where we met last night. Be very quiet, and come armed."

Avarielle reached towards her sword. Cassara heard Klar hurrying near, drawing his own weapon. The warrior did not slow her movement as she pulled free a dagger. Cassara felt heat rising to her face. It was hers, the one that she had lost last night.

"Klar, calm down," Cassara said to him, holding up her hand. Klar stopped, as did the other guard who was approaching from behind the trees. They did not sheathe their swords.

"A gift of friendship," Avarielle said as she handed the knife to Cassara, performing a perfect curtsy in the process.

"Thank you, friend," Cassara said, forcing herself to smile as she followed Avarielle's lead. She hoped Klar would not recognize the dagger as hers.

"Until next time," Avarielle said, locking eyes with Cassara for only a moment before walking out of the courtyard. She did not once acknowledge the guards or their drawn weapons.

"An odd gift," Klar said as he approached.

Cassara did not turn to face him, knowing he would see the lie on her face.

"But a practical one, captain," Cassara said. "Now if you will be so kind as to excuse me, I have to get ready to meet the prince."

"Perhaps I could store this...gift in our armories, my Lady," Klar said before Cassara could take another step.

"Thank you, captain," she said, beginning to walk away at what she hoped was a normal pace. "But I will take care of it. It's on my way."

She fumbled to keep the knife low, so that Klar wouldn't see it again and recognize it. If he knew she had left the manor last night, he would surely tell the king, and then Cassara would be shipped off to the nearest

Lord's son before she could even breathe a word of explanation.

"But the armory isn't on the way to your room," Klar called after her, his voice gruff in the quiet courtyard.

"I know the way to my room, captain," Cassara replied coolly. "But I wish to take some fresh air before I meet this prince."

She did not look back, but she knew that Klar was not fooled by her poor act.

So be it, Cassara thought as she walked away, knife clutched tightly in her white hand. There were more important things to worry about now than Klar's suspicion.

All she needed was one more night, and she would know all that Avarielle knew of these Eloms.

She hoped she would live to tell her father.

***

THE SECOND COURTYARD was even quieter than the first. Cassara carefully looked around her before entering it. She was pleased to see that Klar and the other guard were no longer following her, apparently deciding that with Avarielle's departure, she was now safe from harm.

This courtyard, the Courtyard of Travelers, was the one she loved the most, though she visited it the least. Flowers were scattered about the grounds, various shades already beginning to bloom, others waiting for the warmth of summer before appearing. A small fountain stood at the center of a pond in the back of the courtyard, a beheaded horse regurgitating water from its stone neck. The head had been carried away years ago, and that had been the only attempt made to beautify it.

Rocks leading to a now overgrown gap in the fence could still be seen through the tall grass, the old road that Cassara had traveled so many times with her mother, during happier times. Cassara felt her grip on the knife loosen. She wished she had her flute with her, and that she could simply sit here and play all day until the sun had set for two hours.

She walked towards the fountain on the familiar path.

She stared at the horse, glad she did not have to entertain anyone in this place of memories. The courtyard was now mostly kept as a memorial. Visitors were shown to the Courtyard of Stars, by far the most beautiful in the manor.

As Cassara looked away from the gurgling fountain, she saw an outline in the cedar fence. Someone was standing there, observing her.

"Who are you?" Cassara asked, her grip tightening around the knife. The figure did not move.

"Show yourself or I shall call the guards," Cassara said, hoping she sounded and looked threatening enough. After facing the dark, misshapen creatures last night and waiting to face them again, Cassara felt little fear at the sight of this figure. She hoped that would not be her downfall.

The figure took a few steps forward until it reached

the sunlight. A woman stood before Cassara, wearing a simple white robe adorned only by a crimson circle above her heart, perfectly matched to the color of her cloak. Her hair contrasted the robe, the raven locks tied back only by a leather band. "It is a pleasure to meet you, princess," the woman said, nodding her head in respect. It seemed very few people knew how to properly curtsy of late. Since the woman was from one of the most powerful organizations in Graydon, Cassara was not about to point out the lack of manners.

"A pleasure to meet you as well," Cassara said, wondering how the woman had known she was the princess. Wearing a simple robe and carrying around an unsheathed knife were not exactly the marks of royalty.

"I did not realize my father had visitors from the Circle today," Cassara said, studying the woman closely. She couldn't be more than a few years older than Cassara, yet she seemed so cold. Could her presence have anything to do with the meeting that had been called?

"Your father was kind enough to grant me a last-minute audience, since my presence was not announced."

Cassara nodded. The woman was examining her very closely. Cassara shifted her feet and wished she could put the knife down, since her hand was becoming too clammy to hold it well.

"I shall leave you, then, and wish you the best of luck," Cassara said, feeling heat rise to her head, as though a small fever had been kindled. She took a deep breath and forced a smile, feeling the heat already dissipating.

"Very well," the woman responded, giving her a small nod.

Cassara walked away. At this rate, she would never reach the prince in time. The sun was almost directly overhead and he had urgent business to attend to. She hoped he would be gone and she wouldn't have to stop breathing to fit into the blue dress.

"Until our next meeting, may your steps be steady," the woman whispered, barely loud enough for Cassara to hear.

"And may your thoughts be heavy," Cassara whispered back the traditional Circle saying. She turned around to make sure that the sorceress had heard her reply and would not believe her uneducated, but the courtyard stood empty, the only sound the gurgling water bleeding from the horse's neck.

THE CLIFF FACE spread before her, majestic, mysterious, and filled with darkness. Avarielle squinted her eyes as she looked up, a vain attempt to block out the midday sun.

Every crevasse represented a lurking danger, every dark patch an Elom waiting to attack. Her left hand rested on her long knife, her right hand itching to hold the reassuring weight of her sword, an urge that she resisted. The magic of her blade would only confirm what she already knew—a large nest was in the area, midway across the cliff, deep within a cave she hoped was only accessible through the entrance she was currently staring at. It was the largest nest she had ever encountered, and she intended to bring a princess, of all people, into it.

But she had little choice. Times had been changing of late. Eloms were settling closer to villages and were increasingly bolder in their attacks. Last night had only confirmed what Avarielle already knew. They weren't cautious anymore. They'd kept coming even after one of their own had been killed by the princess' magic, a magic she hoped could help her this night.

To think, Avarielle thought, looking towards the entrance of the cave. *There was a time when they were impossible to find except through my magic, and even then, I had to hunt them down to kill them.*

Avarielle sighed and shook her head. She needed to clear her dark thoughts and get some rest. She had traveled for two days without rest, and using her magic last night had robbed her of the third day she could have otherwise enjoyed.

Pulling her gaze away from the cave entrance, Avarielle climbed the cliff and planned their entry for the night, when the tide would be too high to take this route.

"Elihor!" Avarielle swore as sharp rocks dug into her palm, causing her to bleed. The noise was lost as the surf hit the cliff below. She wondered how the fair, soft-skinned princess would handle the climb.

Another worry for tonight, Avarielle thought as she pulled herself up by the orchard, the white flowers shining in the sun, casting deep shadows between the trees. A perfect place to nap.

I hope she knows what she's doing. Avarielle wasn't sure the princess had even known how to use her magic last night, but she was gambling that she would this night. She guessed the princess wouldn't have accepted otherwise. At least she hoped.

"Eli, who cares about the princess!" she mumbled as she entered the orchard. "I hope *I* know what I'm doing!"

She fell ungracefully under a tree, inhaling the apple blossoms' soothing aroma, her skin cooling in the shade. The soft grass beckoned her and she heeded its call, unsheathing her sword and holding it in her right hand as she lay down.

She felt the familiar warm sensation of magic course through her arm. Avarielle raised her head slightly, knowing she would see nothing, knowing that the magic was only responding to the Eloms hiding in the darkness below her.

From where she was, she could easily see where they would come up from the entrance, and they never came up until well past midnight, when the sun's rays had been cooled from the land.

"There is only one exit," she whispered, looking towards the overhang, repeating the words several times. *I've checked this place several times today,* she thought as her fingers stroked the pommel of her sword.

It was still a long time before she slept.

THE COURTYARD OF STARS loomed before her, the vision holes installed on top of the manor visible above the tall edge. Each of these holes was a gateway through which to view the most important constellations, hailed as a feat of astronomical science 472 years ago, when the monarchy was formed in Edoline and the manor expanded in an attempt to make it look regal. By far the greatest attribute was the main vision hole which stood at the North End of the manor, where at midnight exactly, gazers standing on the center markings of the courtyard could see the most important constellation of all: the Lost Lovers.

On nights Cassara could not escape the manor, she would spend hours on various markings in the courtyard, playing her flute, following the celestial dance as the various clusters journeyed through the sky. Today, however, she lingered at the threshold of the courtyard, the knife in her hand heavier with each passing second.

She had originally intended to pass through the secret passage hidden in the cedar hedge of the Courtyard of Travelers, but she did not want to reveal its existence to anyone, especially not to an outsider from the Circle. Her mother had shown her the way when she was very young, and she doubted many others knew of its existence. She intended to keep it that way. Of course, this now meant that her only alternative to crossing this courtyard was to go back and face Klar, giving him the chance to positively identify her knife, which would undoubtedly result in her being shipped off with the prince that very afternoon.

And the warrior Avarielle would be left waiting for her in the dark, counting on a magic Cassara was not certain she could deliver. She hesitated in indecision and doubt. Perhaps immediate marriage wouldn't be so difficult to withstand. Before she could even begin to convince herself, images of the Eloms flooded her mind, and this time, instead of fearing them, she clung to them.

Cassara took a deep breath filled with the scent of cedar. The prince would have more than likely been left here to wait for her. Were she to encounter the prince, would he even recognize her, dressed as she was, carrying a knife in her hands? Her grip on the knife loosened and a grin played on her lips. He might recognize her afterwards, but that would only encourage him to run back to his kingdom and never mention the princess of Edoline again. And then she could reach the armory and be rid of the treacherous weapon.

She followed the main stone path. Usually, she would take the time to admire the smooth symmetry of the courtyard and its diverging stone paths, which lead to marked areas where gazers could quietly look up towards the constellations. But today she often looked over her shoulder, fearing Lady Fate would grasp her in her unforgiving grip.

The wind was softly blowing, leaves dancing in the wind, their sound masking whatever little noise she made. Her tension lessened with each step. The courtyard seemed empty and she hoped the prince was already gone. The sun directly above her marked the middle of the day, the time of his departure.

Movement caught her eye and Cassara looked up. A man entered the courtyard from the other end of the manor. Cassara drew herself up, analyzing the man walking towards her. He was plainly dressed in riding clothes, his sandy hair slightly tousled by the wind. No royal mark.

Good.

Still, even if he was part of the prince's entourage, he shouldn't simply be walking around the two private courtyards. The outside courtyard was where he should stay.

"Good day," Cassara said as she approached him, nodding in greeting. She wasn't passing for a princess and there was no need for formalities between two servants. She couldn't help but smile. She was enjoying this.

The man stopped strolling and looked up, his gray eyes silver in the high sun and as piercing as the blade Cassara gripped. He looked her over quickly, his eyes resting on her golden hair for a moment before he locked gazes with her, a grin playing on his lips.

"Beautiful day, isn't it?" he replied.

"Quite. But I'm afraid this area is reserved only for the royal family and their guests."

One of his eyebrows shot up inquisitively. She felt herself blush.

"And the royal family's servants, of course," she added,

stumbling over the words. She wanted to kick herself. So much for being subtle.

"Of course," the man said, obviously amused. Her blush deepened.

"I believe Prince Dayshon's escort must be gathering at the front of the manor now, since it is midday," Cassara said, forcing herself to look at him. She pointed back from where she had come. "If you go through the next courtyard, a passage will lead you to the front."

The man nodded and proceeded to walk towards the middle of the Courtyard of Stars, away from where Cassara had just indicated. She felt her blood pulsing, annoyed she still held the knife, annoyed this man was stopping her from quickly hiding her tracks. And annoyed that she would be punished for not meeting with the prince.

"That's not the right way," she called after him as she followed.

"This place is amazing," the man said, reaching the stone with the depiction of the Lost Lovers. "I hear that you can actually see the constellations at night, perfectly aligned with these vision holes!"

He paused, looking up. When he spoke again, his voice was filled with regret. "I wish we were staying longer so that I could witness it."

Cassara stepped on the stone and looked up at the sky with him. "It is beautiful. But perhaps you could return later and see it, if your master will allow it."

The man smiled at her, and suddenly the afternoon

seemed warmer. Cassara reached up to push a stray strand of hair from her face, distracting her from his smile. The knife flashed in the sun as she quickly lowered her hand again.

"Do princesses in Edoline always travel with unsheathed daggers in their hands?" the man asked, smiling.

"How do you know I'm the princess?" Cassara asked before she could think better of it. She winced. Some politician she would turn out to be if she couldn't think before speaking. Maybe it was for the best that she wanted to remain here, in Edoline, away from the world's troubles and woes.

"Perfect hands, smooth skin, clean dress, and," the man continued, pointing at her hair, "the cascade of golden hair that is legendary even in Rashim."

"My Lady," he said, executing a perfect bow.

Cassara wanted to say something commanding to him, something that would put the man in his place and get him out of her way. But seeing him bowing to her in a place he should not be, both standing in the most famous place, well, the only famous place in the manor, while she stood before him in a plain dress holding an unsheathed knife, made her lose whatever pretense of royalty she could have otherwise mustered.

Instead she began laughing, not gently, her entire rib cage shaking with laughter, which she tried to smother with her hand. The man looked up and his laughter soon joined hers.

"I'm sorry," Cassara said as soon as she could speak, quite a few minutes later. "This situation just struck me as very amusing. I suppose I'm not quite the princess someone like your prince might have envisioned."

The man grinned. "I suppose not, although you would have to ask the prince himself."

She winced at the thought. "To be honest with you, I had hoped to forego the encounter."

"I had assumed as much," the man replied. "May I ask you a question?"

"Only if I can ask one of you afterwards." Cassara replied, quick to seize the opportunity.

The man asked without hesitation, as though he had been meaning to ask her all along, regardless of her answer. "You've refused many suitors in the past few months, some of which would have been perfect matches. Why is that?"

Cassara smiled and slowly gestured at the courtyard around her. "I'm not ready to leave this yet. Someday, I will be. But not yet."

She gave a quick laugh. "I love my land and its people. If your prince ever asks you why, you may tell him it has nothing to do with politics, for to be true, I know very little of politics. It has everything to do with my home, and although Edoline is small and boasts only one village and some farmland, to me it's the most beautiful place in the world."

The man looked at her, a smile on his lips. "I love my land too, and so I understand you very well, my Lady."

The longing in his eyes made her understand that he too missed his land. Rashim was a three-week hard ride away, and from what she had heard the prince had been traveling for a year now, getting acquainted with all of his kingdom and its surroundings, to prepare himself for when he would be king. Edoline had probably not even been an original destination, because of how small it was.

Cassara reached out and touched his arm in sympathy, quickly withdrawing her hand as he looked at her with surprise.

"Now for my question," Cassara said, trying to play down her impulsive gesture.

"Go ahead," the man grinned. He probably expected her to ask a thousand questions about the prince: his look, his attitude, his riches…She was pleased to see surprise flicker in his eyes as she asked her question.

"Why was a Council meeting called in a month?"

The man's smile vanished, replaced instead by something she had not often seen in her life that could only be admiration. She kept her gaze steady.

"And you say you know nothing of politics, my Lady," he said, bowing to her again. This time, she did blush.

"I know nothing," she answered. "But I am willing to learn."

The man hesitated, apparently debating how much he should tell a young princess from a land with little to no political power.

"I don't know much," he began slowly, gathering his words. "But I do know it involves the Circle of Magic. In fact, they called the meeting, something they themselves have never been known to do."

Cassara nodded at every word, wanting to know more. He hesitated again.

"I don't know much," he repeated. Cassara nodded impatiently. "But I think it has to do with Elihor."

Cassara stopped nodding, and the man studied her reaction. She was careful to give him nothing that he could report to his prince.

Elihor. The land of darkness. The land of the damned, of the lost, of the murderers. A place that none had reached in a thousand years, and none ever should, according to all of the writings in the world. A place of death.

Eloms. Dark creatures. Cassara suddenly felt lightheaded. What if the creatures of darkness had come from Elihor? Surely that was impossible. The wall had been a steady boundary for a thousand years. Why would it begin to fail now?

"Are you alright?" the man asked. She noticed he was closer to her, holding her arm, his eyes filled with concern.

"I'm sorry, I should not have frightened you so."

Cassara smiled at him and steadied herself. His grip fell away, the warmth remaining on her arm a comfort to her.

"Cassara!" She heard Emala's voice break through the manor. She winced. Her father wouldn't be able to scold her before Emala tore her to pieces first.

"I have to go," Cassara said, beginning to walk away. "I must try to meet your prince or my father will have my head!"

The man gave a short laugh. "Don't worry, my Lady. I'll convince him to stay to meet you. I believe he would like you!"

"Please tell him to meet me here in a few minutes!" Cassara waved farewell to him, very ungracefully running towards the manor. Emala found her on the way and berated her the entire way back to the room. Cassara kept the knife in her hand, hiding it in her vanity once in her room, before Emala expertly began dressing her.

Its presence, although unseen, was a comfort. Why did she ever think she could join Avarielle in her quest when the very mention of Elihor had almost made her faint?

3

By the time Cassara was stuffed into the dress, the sun was at its highest peak in the sky. Emala opened the door and waved frantically for Cassara to walk through.

Cassara took a deep breath, wondering if her ribs would be permanently deformed by the blue dress. If by chance she should lose one of her blue-pearled slippers, she would never be able to bend down and place it back on her foot, so tight was the dress' grip on her waist.

She supposed she should consider herself lucky. Her father had simply requested she walk the prince from the Courtyard of Stars to the front, where his men would be waiting. After speaking to the servant, she wanted to see them on their way, so that he could reach his home. She realized with regret that she had never asked his name.

"Shoulders straight, cheeks rosy, hair well-placed," Emala listed off as Cassara walked by her. The checklist had been a weekly activity for the past three months, ever since Klar had caught Cassara sneaking off to the village. Being a woman, she was now too much of a liability to be allowed to roam free.

"Ribbons tied, slippers holding, princess not breathing...perfect!" Emala squealed in delight. Cassara grunted.

"Remind me to...find someone else...for your position," Cassara said, exaggerating her pauses.

"Oh, you do love drama, Cassara," Emala said, calling the princess by her first name as she usually did when the two were jesting.

"Easy for you to say," Cassara said as the two began walking down the hall. "You're not the one being suffocated by this thing!"

"Oh, it's not that bad. Besides, if this suitor does as well as the others, then you'll be out of that dress before the sun lowers even a tiny bit in the sky. You're lucky your father didn't just decide to ship you off. Still soft, that one."

Cassara gave a short laugh. "Yes, of course, he's quite soft. As soft as a brick." She shrugged. "But maybe this prince will at least be handsome. Do you think we could loosen this just a bit?"

"No. And hurry. He's probably leaving already! Or gone. The king will have my head!"

"Good. Then I will burn this dress and never mention its existence to my next maid."

Emala twisted her features into what Cassara guessed

was supposed to be deep hurt. The two burst out laughing. Cassara stopped quickly and caught her breath.

"That hurt," she said, wincing.

"The price of love. He's here to woo you, princess, not make you laugh."

Cassara sighed and kept her pace steady, the smell of magnolias from the Courtyard of Stars reaching her as she planned which excuse she could give her father for not marrying this prince.

THE SORCERESS ENDED her meeting with the king, where she had asked for shelter while she remained in Edoline for the next few days, or however long was necessary. The king had of course agreed, but only after many questions on her current Circle activities and her personal knowledge of Edoline. It had proved an annoying delay, but at least it seemed the Circle's might was legendary even in this remote little kingdom.

Shirina headed to her room, led by a guard who kept casting wary looks her way. On one side was the brick wall of the manor, but on the other tall pillars and cedar hedges blocked off the two middle courtyards.

Something caught her attention up ahead, and she looked up to see the princess, wearing an uncomfortable-looking blue dress, walking into the famous Courtyard of Stars. She was obviously displeased with the situation, even from this distance. A maid watched her go before walking away, shaking her head and mumbling as she crossed Shirina. She did not once look up.

The sorceress watched the princess' golden mane vanish into the cedar fence as she followed the guard down another hallway, one leading into the depths of the manor. Enough light infiltrated the manor that no torches were needed during the daytime. Not that it mattered to Shirina.

She was trained to see as well in darkness as in light, just as she was trained to see the magical potential in others, to prepare the Circle for the upcoming Harvest. Cassara had been a surprise. Her magical potential seemed low at first glance, nothing for the Circle to be concerned with. But she had recently used a strong magic, its residue clinging to her like a fine white powder. Even more surprising was the fact that when Shirina had scanned deeply, the princess had somehow blocked her.

It seemed that the little kingdom of Edoline produced more than just crops. It had also produced a princess with the potential to become one of the Circle's strongest sorceresses. Had the Circle noticed her eight years ago during their last Harvest, she would have easily been taken. But now, older and at the perfect age for a political marriage, acquiring her would prove to be more of a challenge.

But Shirina was satisfied that she had done all that she could. The offer had been made to the king, who would pass it along to his daughter. He had been polite when listening to her, but Shirina sensed he was not enthralled with the Circle's practices. And the guards didn't seem thrilled either, two others following not far behind.

Shirina doubted she would see Cassara wandering the dark halls of Ravenhold any time soon.

The guard stopped, waving her into a small room. A slight smell of mold mixed with dried flowers met her. Shirina walked in, not bothering to acknowledge the guard, closing the door behind her. The princess was just an interesting addition to an important journey, anyhow. Whether she grew old bearing royal babies or casting spells was of no consequence.

What mattered was her current mission: to capture the sword before its wielder was killed and it vanished forever. Shirina did not look forward to seeing the mad woman again, but this night, knowing where she would be, she would confront her and she would not fail.

It was the Circle's bidding and therefore her will.

THE PRINCE STOOD with his back to her. Cassara approached him quietly, careful not to misstep on the stones for fear of losing a slipper. His hair was pale brown, his shoulders seemed unable to slouch, and he was finely dressed in rich reds and deep golds. There was no mistaking him.

She was close enough to touch him when she decided his shoulders seemed *too* proud and his garments *too* fine. Being the heir to the most important throne in Graydon must have made him too egotistical to bear. She would get rid of him quickly, a simple feat considering the sun was already beginning its slow descent into the western sky.

"Your highness," Cassara said as she performed a perfect curtsy, grateful the dress allowed her at least that much movement. "Welcome to Edoline."

"I've already been greeted, thank you," the prince said, turning around to face her. Cassara immediately recognized his eyes, filled with mirth, and his grin. He was the servant from earlier!

She quickly straightened.

"You're not the prince," she said, smoothing out her dress, already feeling relief that she would not have to meet him.

"How do you know I'm not the prince, princess? Have you observed me closely enough to know?"

Cassara was about to retort when small details began catching her attention. He was too well-built to be a simple servant. He was definitely military of some sort, something the heir to the throne of Rashim would be. The fine expensive clothing fit him perfectly, made to his size, including his broad shoulders. And it would easily explain why no one had stopped him from wandering in the Courtyard of Stars. Why hadn't she thought of this earlier? Guards were posted at each entrance at all times to ensure privacy.

Had the knife really been that important at the time? Frantically, she tried to remember their entire conversation. Had she said anything incriminating? She decided the earlier encounter wasn't necessarily to her disadvantage. He should be easier to get rid of now.

"I'm afraid I was at a disadvantage," Cassara said, giving him a slight smile. "You have no legendary golden hair through which I could identify you."

Prince Dayshon laughed warmly, bowing to her as he finished.

"A pleasure to properly meet you, Princess Cassara."

"And you, Prince Dayshon." She curtsied again, fighting for her balance in the awkward dress.

"Are you well?" he asked, concerned.

Cassara blushed. "Quite, you simply took me by surprise."

He looked at her again. "You seemed more comfortable in servant's clothing, princess."

She smiled wryly at him. "Simple clothing does not have a tendency to stop the air from reaching my lungs."

He laughed again, offering her his arm as they walked towards the front of the manor. Cassara felt relief, but she was not sure whether it was because the prince was leaving soon or because she felt more balanced while leaning against his arm.

"Since I would hate for our first official meeting to end with you passing out, I will be brief," he said as they crossed the first cedar hedge. The headless horse gurgled nearby.

"I've asked your father for your hand in marriage."

"What?!" Cassara shouted, whirling around before she could think better of it. She lost her footing and her breath, and would have fallen had Dayshon not caught her and sat her on a nearby bench.

"My mother always used to say women would fall for me, but I doubt that's quite what she had in mind."

Cassara looked into his eyes. He knelt in front of her, hand still on her arm. Would it be so bad to be held by those arms, be greeted by those eyes every day? And to bring prosperity to her kingdom by such a strong union?

She took a slow, deep breath. *Eloms.* She at least needed to help Avarielle rid her land of them. She remembered the feel of the magic, her amulet warm against her skin where it rested above the line of her dress. She had the power to help her people, and so she would use it.

Before she could speak, he implored to her.

"Think about it, Cassara." She looked up at him, surprised to hear her first name without title escape his lips. The courts of Rashim were reputed to be stuck on ceremony, and a first name during a first official meeting seemed casual.

Or desperate to be heard.

"I need to find a suitable fiancée, and I need to do so soon or my parents will do it for me. I suppose that's common practice in Graydon," he said, giving her a quick smile. "And the princess they've chosen is beautiful, rich, but more arrogant than most of Graydon's royalty combined."

He paused, choosing his words carefully.

"You need to find a fiancé soon, or your father will also

choose one for you. You would only need to accept now, and then we can set the date of the marriage to be as far as a year from now, if that's what you desire. You wouldn't need to come to Rashim until a few weeks before that day. Your name is not unknown to my parents, and they would be satisfied to know that I am to be wed to royalty, and since we're the most important kingdom in Graydon, we're not too worried about a political alliance at the moment. Not that I'm saying Edoline isn't important!"

He paused, taking a breath, making sure he had not insulted her. She couldn't help but smile gently as she saw such vulnerability in his eyes.

"You love your land, and you could always come back and visit it, as often as you'd like. I promise I would never try to stop you."

He searched out her eyes again.

"You must be desperate to find a wife," she said casually, wishing her pulse would slow down and he would remove his hand from her arm. The dress seemed tighter than before.

He gave a quick laugh. "This journey was partly for that very purpose, which is why I decided to come this way once I'd heard of your father's wish to see you betrothed. And you were right earlier. You're not at all what I expect of a princess, and I've met enough princesses to be an expert on the subject by now. And, to be honest, that's partly what draws me to you."

She shook her head, but she did not know if it was to refuse him or to shake herself back to reality.

"You don't have to answer now," Dayshon said, finally removing his hand. "But please consider it. It would be a wonderful opportunity to learn about politics."

After some consideration, he added, "And to get to know each other better, not as prince and princess, not as two servants, but rather as Dayshon and Cassara."

He stood up, offering her his hand to help her up.

Cassara stared at the hand, callused from many hours of swordplay. She hesitated, feeling as though the simple act of taking it represented a sealing of her fate.

One year before the wedding. A lot could happen before then, and that year would buy her the time she needed to finish the business she had here. It would end the courtings, and appease her father.

One year. It was the best offer she had been given, from the only man she had liked in all of the men that had come streaming through on their way back to the door. The only offer that was even remotely appealing.

And no amount of time would ever be enough.

She reached out and took his hand.

"He was a handsome one," Emala said as she peeled the blue dress off of Cassara.

"I wonder if these clothing marks will ever come off," Cassara said, passing a finger over one of the grooves etched in her skin.

"And he was so polite! I think the king truly liked him, too."

"Maybe with a good hot bath they'd come out."

"And his smile could have made me swoon! And he did smile at you, princess! I saw him from where I was watching. What teeth!"

"I suppose if I had decent help more concerned with me than the prince, I could have a hot bath," Cassara said, looking at herself in the mirror.

"Oh, but he was a good-looking man!" Emala continued as she pulled out some scented bath salts from Cassara's vanity. From the scent, she guessed her maid had chosen roses and lavender. Love and healing. How extremely wonderful.

"I'll draw you a bath in the first bathing room, my Lady. Give me about ten minutes, and then I'll be back," Emala said, bringing the good bath salts with her as she exited the door.

"But he was so handsome!" Cassara heard her maid say even through the closed doors.

Cassara sat at her vanity, feeling nothing when she had always imagined she would feel joy. She had all but accepted Prince Dayshon's marriage proposal, and yet she sat here, looking at her dull reflection in her dull mirror in her dull room. She could accept in a few days, and then they could wait one year for the wedding to take place.

Why had a year seemed like such a long time when she was younger, and now it seemed so short? She picked up her brush and passed it through her hair in a clumsy motion, pulling out a chunk of hair in the process. She looked at it: the golden hair that had managed to gain her a fame she did not need nor crave. Could it be that during all of those months, trying to fend off suitors, she had actually only managed to reel in the one man she could not say no to?

Cassara forced herself to smile in the mirror, something her mother had taught her when she was a child. Smile until you feel like laughing. Then cry later, in private, if you have to. But at first always smile and try laughter as the true remedy to your sorrow.

She smiled, but did not feel like laughing. Nor did she feel like crying.

A soft knock came at the door. Cassara rose, tying her bathrobe around her waist tightly. For a brief moment, she hesitated, frightened that it would be Prince Dayshon, come to take her away without waiting. She was not convinced she could resist.

"My Lady, it's Kaden," the reassuring voice came at the door.

"The king wishes for you to meet him in the front courtyard." She heard him shuffle outside the door.

"Thank you, Kaden. I'll be out in a moment."

Cassara placed her hand on the wooden door that separated her from the man who had been more like a father to her than the king had ever been. Ever since she was a child, Kaden had watched over her. As other guards came and went, he remained. Only he was growing old and tired, but he had taken an oath to protect the youngest daughter of Edoline, an oath he did not intend to break until another took it.

Another, like a future husband.

She removed her hand and began putting on her simple brown dress.

It seemed her bath would have to wait.

THE COURTYARD at the front of the manor was really only an extension of the orchard itself. Apple and pear trees were scattered about the grounds, a few paths spread amongst them leading to plain but sturdy fountains. The manor's beauty lay within its first two inner courtyards. There was a third inner courtyard in the back, ending where the cliff began. But, due to erosion a few years back, it was now rarely used. It had become too dangerous, especially for Jayden, who was blessed and cursed with their mother's sense of adventure.

Cassara still spent some nights there, playing her flute gently to the sound of the waves.

The sound of the surf seemed far, surreal, lost somewhere between the sound of her feet on the rocks and the leaves dancing in the trees.

Kaden and Carsyn, who had followed her in silence from her room, remained at a respectful distance, recognizing in her the need for silence. The jesting and comradeship they shared on the nights she escaped the manor was not needed here.

She spotted her father on a bench near a fountain and headed towards him. Klar was not far behind, and Kaden and Carsyn took up similar positions, near enough to see but not close enough to hear.

"Father," Cassara said as she approached him, curtsying. Her father looked up at her, and the sun amplified his age. Each white hair stood out from his once-dark head and each wrinkle dug deep shadows into his flesh. But his eyes held the same strength they always had.

He did not look directly at her. He had not since her mother's death.

He did not ask her to join him on the bench, so she knelt on the grass before him, waiting for his judgment.

"Klar tells me you had a visitor, today," her father began, taking her by surprise. He was not one to skirt around an issue, which was the main reason Edoline was still a kingdom and not simply a province of a bigger power.

"Just a friend," Cassara said, her voice calm and steady. The meeting with Avarielle seemed so far away now that it was lost within the sound of the surf.

Her father merely nodded, his eyes unfocused.

"Your mother was like that. Always making friends wherever she went." His eyes came into focus, and for the first time in many years, he looked directly at Cassara. She steadied herself by putting a hand on the grass. When she was a child causing mischief, she would always look down when he looked at her. But now, she refused to. Let him see the woman she had become, independent and unafraid.

"Just like your mother," he said softly, a slight smile on his lips. Another rare sight.

"Prince Dayshon has asked for your hand in marriage," Alexavier said, suddenly rising. Cassara rose with him, placing herself at his side as they walked slowly.

"He's a fine man and I've only heard good things, but the decision is yours, Cassara." King Alexavier looked forward, deep in thought.

"What other decision can I make?" An edge crept into her voice. She certainly hadn't been the one to choose to begin seeing suitors.

Her father did not turn to look at her as he answered. The winds grew stronger. Behind them, the three guards followed. Cassara took a deep breath in an attempt to soothe her rising temper. So far, she had been able to convince her suitors or, failing that, her father that the match wasn't good. But she wasn't sure how to convince her father that marrying the heir of the most powerful kingdom in Graydon was a bad idea.

"Something else of interest occurred today," her father continued as though Cassara had not spoken. Cassara, sensing hesitation in her father's voice, gave him her full attention

"I met with a sorceress from the Circle, and she said that you could join them, if you'd like. It is a hard life, Cassara, but she believes that you could even become one of the Elite."

The words washed over her like a great wave. An Elite. One of the highest ranks a sorceress could attain in the Circle, arguably the strongest organization in Graydon. Theirs was the duty to protect the Wall of Loss, to protect the children of Graydon and its dwindling magical heritage.

It was seen by most as a sacred duty, even though those that sustained it were often met with fear and suspicion. *Just like by me*, she thought, feeling shame at the suspicion she had felt towards the sorceress today.

"The Circle would allow you to develop whatever powers you may possess to their full capacity," her father continued, obviously struggling with the words. "But it would also remove some other possibilities, such as having a family."

"I have a family here," Cassara said, immediately wishing she hadn't. They hadn't been much of a family since her mother's death, and her father knew it as well as she did.

"You remind me so much of your mother," Alexavier said, turning to face her, passing a soft hand on her cheek. He broke contact and resumed walking, and she was left to follow again, wondering where her father's odd state of mind would take her.

"I know that the glory of the Circle must hold some appeal to you, simply because it held some for your mother. She was asked to join them too, you know, at a later age than you, even. But after much thought, she refused, and we were wed."

He paused.

"We were happy, you know. I know things haven't been the same since she died, and Lady Fate might have seen fit to bless her with a longer life had she chosen another path, but I do believe that she wouldn't have traded this life for any other."

He paused for a longer time, taking several deep breaths before continuing. He did not mention her mother again, but he had done so more on this day than he had in all the years since her death.

"Choose, Cassara, but choose wisely. Either path is difficult, and both will bring reward. Think of the legacy you will leave this land." He turned to face her.

"And not just Edoline, daughter, but all of Graydon."

His eyes spoke the words that he dared not, of how he loved her, and how he wanted to hold her, but how he feared losing her too, the daughter who most resembled his beloved wife. He leaned over and kissed her forehead gently, a simple brush of the lips against her warm skin. But it was enough. He turned around and headed back to the manor, leaving her amongst the trees, trapped by her indecision.

The power of anyone is choice, Cassara. And that is something that only you can give yourself.

Her mother had been right when she had told her that long ago, when Cassara could not decide on the pattern to give her flute, a pattern that would be carved into it for what seemed like forever back then.

She would have to make a much more important

decision soon, between independence and marriage, duty and love, life and magic.

She would have to choose soon, but not before the next sun had risen, for this night should hold the rest of the answers she currently sought.

Or so she hoped.

<hr>

THE SUN SET in the western sky, its slow descent accompanied by a few passing clouds that took on the sun's pink and purple accents. Time seemed to crawl by as Cassara sat alone in the broken courtyard at the back of the manor. She sat on the trunk of a weeping willow, half-fallen over the cliff, only its strong roots keeping it in place, its spidery branches falling towards the water and dancing with the strong winds.

Like me, Cassara thought as she let the notes escape her flute and join the sound of the waves breaking upon the rocks. She leaned back on a branch, watching the clouds pass by, calm and free.

She turned her flute upwards and played for them, their slow rhythm tugging at her notes. She closed her eyes and let the songs carry her far away, and when she opened them again, the sun was casting its final light.

With the darkness came silence. Cassara lowered her instrument, looking into the starry night. The moon was only a sliver, which would make her escape easier. In one hour, she had to be out of the manor, were she to meet

Avarielle in two. She wondered why two hours after sunset had seemed ideal to her.

Oddly enough, she felt no fear, only cool acceptance. She still felt numb from the day's events. So many choices, so many *good* choices, had suddenly crept up on her.

"One thing at a time," she softly said to the surf.

"Emala awaits you in your chamber, my Lady," she heard Kaden say as he walked up beside her, his head coming up to her knees, so large was the willow.

"What would you do, Kaden?" Cassara asked, looking down at him, finding comfort in his dark eyes.

He looked up at her and smiled gently, as a father would to a child. She felt safe again. It did not matter to her that he was old and barely able to keep up. He was still Kaden. Trustworthy, wise Kaden.

"I would choose, my Lady. And I would never look back."

He held up his hands, and she let him help her down. "Never look back, Kaden?" she asked when they were face to face.

"Never, Cassara. That's when regrets will cling to you, no matter what you chose."

She nodded and took his arm as they walked out of the courtyard, to where Carsyn waited by the door.

Had the surf not been striking the rocks with such ferocity, they might have heard the cries rising from below.

AFTER ONE HOUR in the darkness of her room, Cassara quietly began dressing. She slipped on her riding pants, to allow her greater ease of movement than a skirt. She threw on a white shirt and covered it with a small brown jacket, to ward against the night air.

She secured the knife to her waist and brought a small bag with some medicine and supplies with her. She wished she knew what exactly a "nest" entailed. The more she knew, the more prepared she could be. Out of habit, she placed her flute in her bag, its familiar shape reassuring.

Her hand rose to her neck, making certain the chain of the amulet was well secured. She slowly pulled on it until the amulet was free from her shirt. Its silver, untarnished since Cassara's mother had given it to her over ten years ago, reflected the moonlight streaming through the open curtains. She examined it carefully. The crescent shape was smooth, without flaws, a gold sphere inserted in the lower, wider portion of the crescent. For Cassara, its beauty lay not in its workmanship, but in the words her mother had spoken when she had given it to her.

"This was the sign of Edoline, long ago, Cass. Keep it on you always. When you feel the warm metal against your skin, know that I am not far."

It was the last thing she had ever given her. But never had she mentioned it was a talisman of magic, never had she mentioned that it would protect her. Idly, Cassara wondered if her mother had even known. Cassara gently slipped the amulet back into her shirt, intent on keeping her meeting.

She hoped her mother's magic would protect her this night, as well.

She threw on a bathrobe to cover her clothing in case she should be seen. Though she truly doubted she would be. Klar had kept watch last night and most of today, and so he should be asleep and one of the other guards would be on watch. She had convinced Kaden and Carsyn that she did not intend on going anywhere this night, and their tired eyes told her they were more than happy to believe her. It was becoming increasingly difficult for them to follow the whims of their young ward.

Cracking the door open, she peered down the corridor. No light illuminated it. Perfect.

She closed the door behind her, quietly treading on the carpet, using her instincts and memory to guide her. Her hand skirted the corridor, the stone cool to the touch.

She neared the second door when the darkness was broken by a voice.

"Who goes there?" A guard, Merlo, she believed, shouted. Her breath caught in her throat as she fought to slow her heartbeat.

Why wasn't he using a torch? Had all of the Royal Protectors of Edoline developed such an innate sense of sight that they required no more light?

"It's Princess Cassara," she replied, keeping her voice low and steady.

"May I assist you, my Lady?" he replied, suspicion tinging his words.

Wonderful. It seemed that not just Klar was on the lookout now.

"I'm fine, Lieutenant. Unless you intend to help me go to the lady's room?"

"Ah, I'll resume my watch," he said, stuttering his reply as she suppressed a grin. She heard his weapons clanking, guessing he was bowing to her, and then his footsteps moved away from her, down another corridor.

Cassara steadied herself, taking a moment to breathe. Curse that Klar! He was entirely too efficient in his post. He must have been the one who'd warned Merlo to keep an eye on her room. She hoped he would not follow her. After all, she had not heard him sneak up on her the first time.

She estimated a full minute had passed before she dared move again. Would the Lieutenant simply go warn Klar? The guards' barrack was located within the manor, and was quick enough to access from here. She hoped that would not be the case.

It's out of my hands now, she thought and resumed walking down the hall. *What matters now is keeping my meeting and protecting my family.*

She passed her older sister's room, empty since she had married Sir Anesh Bestian of the bordering country of Laror, effectively securing Edoline's position, since fear had been growing for some time of an invasion.

A good match, she thought, pondering her sister

Altessa's choice, and the indecision that must have preceded it. Maybe she would have the chance to go see her to discuss her own choices. Cassara's steps were lighter by the time she reached Jayden's room, feeling for the first time today like she had a plan. It wasn't much of one, but speaking with Altessa, who was blessed with their mother's wisdom, would surely make her decision easier.

She entered the room quietly, the soft candle burning in the night. Slowly she removed the night robe, glad to be rid of the heavy garment. She went on her knees and hid it under Jayden's bed.

"Cassara?" the young voice asked, heavy with sleep.

"Yes, Jayden? Go back to sleep."

"You forgot your stuff this morning, but I hid it better for you," Jayden said, ignoring his sister's request and sitting up in bed, rubbing his eyes.

"Thanks, Jayden," Cassara said, cursing herself silently.

How could such a large detail have escaped her?

"Can I come with you?" Jayden pleaded, his big eyes and tousled hair shining in the candlelight. She smiled at him.

"Not tonight, but someday soon, we'll both go down to the village together." Jayden's lips immediately turned into a pout. Cassara suppressed a smile. Jayden had been to the village many times, professing his boredom before they had even left the manor. But Cassara's midnight escapes seemed adventurous to her little brother. He was still too young, almost five years younger than her, the only child to barely remember their mother, for she had died a few short years after his birth.

Still, he would be turning twelve in a few months, and she preferred to keep him near for when he began causing endless mischief. At least if he snuck out with her, she could keep an eye on him.

"I promise some day soon," Cassara said as she tucked him back in, kissing his forehead, to be rewarded with a look of disgust.

"Promise?" he asked as she headed for the window.

"Promise," she said, holding out her fist solemnly to seal the promise. Appeased, Jayden closed his eyes and was soon breathing heavily.

Cassara shook her head, envious of his undisturbed rest, before grabbing the first branch of the cherry tree, the last blooms falling around her as she climbed to the ground.

SHIRINA STOOD in the manor's shadows, watching the princess of Edoline run into the darkness of the orchard. There was no confusing her for anyone else, her hair reflecting the moonlight. Shirina waited for a moment before following, her dark cloak effective in warding the night air as well as blending in with the shadows.

The princess vanished into the trees of the orchard, the moonlight kept at bay by the still clinging white blooms. Shirina slightly increased her pace, instinctively calling her magical senses to life. The princess' magic left an easy trail to follow for those gifted with the Sight.

Up ahead, weaving through the trees, she could clearly see the trail of magic, wild from its misty appearance, and powerful from its clarity. Whatever magic this girl possessed, Shirina was becoming more convinced that it needed to become the Circle's.

She felt another magic nearby, one familiar and dangerous, and increased her pace to catch up with the princess. Eloms lurked here, and she was heading straight for them.

Seeing the princess walking up ahead, Shirina slowed again, keeping an eye on her, but not announcing her presence.

Perhaps if she met Eloms, the princess would make her magic known.

And Shirina could, somehow, claim it as the Circle's.

4

The darkness grew thicker within the orchard, and Cassara slowed her pace, casting wary glances at the shadows around her. She was nearing the area where she had been attacked the night before, which did nothing to calm her.

Her only comfort was the amulet, which lay against her skin, as cold as the night air. Last night, the amulet had only reacted when the Eloms were near her, and she guessed that it had reacted to their presence. As long as it remained cool, she felt fairly confident she was safe.

A twig snapped behind her and Cassara whirled around, clutching the hilt of her knife, her heart pounding. She took a deep, silent breath, her eyes darting back and forth in the darkness. She reached for her amulet, which was still cold against her clammy skin. A few more silent moments passed before she dismissed the noise. She continued following the path, but cast more glances over her shoulders.

Every shadow became an enemy, every noise a creature waiting to attack her, every falling blossom a potential threat.

The day had been eventful, but not so much that it should have impaired her from thinking clearly. Why had she been more concerned with princes and the Circle than this night, which would see her in grave danger?

Cassara shook her head. This was folly. Avarielle could easily take down enemies with her sword, but what did she have? An amulet she didn't understand and didn't know how to wield? A dagger at her waist, which had already proved insufficient last night? What would save her now? Her legendary blond hair, perhaps?

The sound of the surf increased, and she knew that she was nearing the area. Her stomach somersaulted with every crashing wave and her breath grew shorter each time the tide pulled away from the cliff. She imagined the sea, the moon reflected in it, and for the first time in her life, wished to be nowhere near it.

She took a step back and was about to turn around when a hand shot out from the darkness and clamped her mouth, the other firmly grabbing her waist and dragging her back into the shadows. The knife and the amulet were forgotten as Cassara reached up, frantically trying to pull at the arm holding her mouth, wishing she could bite the flesh.

This is it, her mind kept screaming at her. This was how she was going to die. Alone, in the beloved orchard of her youth, no one knowing the sacrifice she had been willing to make to save her family. Her mind jumped from memory to dream, to hope and grief all in a second, and she wondered if she would be made to suffer, and if she would be missed.

"Can you be quiet?" the familiar voice whispered in her ear. Cassara nodded as much as she could.

She was set free, and Avarielle moved up beside her. "They're out early, tonight," the warrior whispered, looking ahead into the darkness, her sword still sheathed. "They're becoming bolder," she added as an afterthought.

Cassara simply nodded, not daring to make a noise for fear of drawing attention to herself. Without warning, Avarielle moved forward. Cassara scrambled to follow her.

"I don't think I can do this," Cassara whispered when she reached the warrior. Avarielle motioned for her to be quiet. Cassara folded her arms in an attempt to make them stop shaking.

Avarielle pointed, and Cassara followed the finger, her breath catching in her throat as she saw an Elom barely ten feet from them. The warrior stopped by a tree and remained crouched, the sword still in its scabbard. Cassara wanted nothing more than to see the sword in Avarielle's hand.

The Elom lingered where it stood and despite her

desire to flee, Cassara could not look away from the creature. She found herself examining its movements more closely. They seemed more calculated than last night. Whereas yesterday they lacked grace, today they seemed blessed with stealth and ease of movement.

The creature's head turned and it looked directly at them with a cold, thoughtful look where yesterday there had been only pain and grief. Cassara's instincts took over and she stepped back, tripped on a root and crashed to the ground.

She heard Avarielle curse before her war cry pierced the night. Suddenly, Cassara was blinded by light. She tried to scramble up, but another Elom charged at her from behind. Cassara barely had the time to raise her hand to protect her head before another flash broke the night and the creature fell dead at her feet. She jumped up and became light-headed, grabbing a tree for support.

"Are you alright?" Avarielle asked as she came to her side, her features pale.

Cassara forced herself to stand without support.

"I'm sorry," she muttered, feeling like a foolish, useless girl.

"Don't even worry about it, it's my fault," Avarielle said, shrugging.

Cassara managed to smile as she pointed at the Elom that had fallen by her feet.

"Thanks for saving me."

A look of confusion crossed Avarielle's features as she

looked towards the corpse. In an instant, her look changed to anger as she pulled her sword free.

"I didn't do that," Avarielle offered as explanation, placing herself in front of the princess. Cassara stood, as rooted in place as the trees around her. She looked at the still-smoking corpse, wondering who could have done this. Who had such power, and what did they intend to do?

"Were you planning on simply strolling in there, Avarielle?" A voice shot out from the darkness. Avarielle did not relax her stance.

Before them, a dark-cloaked form emerged. The woman who had spoken was short and graceful, all but her chin and dark hair hidden under her hood. Cassara recognized the way the woman walked, the way she stood perfectly still and the focused stare.

"You're the woman from the Circle," Cassara said, her tension not lessening a bit.

The woman nodded and lowered her hood.

"My name is Shirina," she said, her eyes as calculating as before. "It is a pleasure to meet you properly, Princess Cassara."

The sorceress then performed a perfect curtsy, which struck Cassara as very odd, considering the situation. She began to feel a measure of control.

"A pleasure to meet you," Cassara said, nodding her head.

"Don't be so sure of that," Avarielle threw back at Cassara, turning her head only slightly, keeping her other eye on the sorceress, her sword still held defensively. "That witch is a harvester, and if she bothered saving you, that means she's after you. Don't trust her, Cassara."

Whatever little control she had gained quickly slipped away. The sorceress gave a short, dry laugh.

"Am I the one trying to get her killed? Bringing her into a nest, Avarielle? Does that strike you as being in her best interest?"

Avarielle's sword rose, as did the sorceress' hand.

"Stop!" Cassara shouted, the sound breaking the night. The two looked at her. She felt heat rising to her face. "This will serve no purpose but to get you killed, and probably me as well. Solve it on your own time," Cassara said, anger pouring through every word. "There's too much at stake here to worry about your petty differences." Cassara paused, meeting Avarielle's look of surprise and Shirina's bemusement fully. She did not back down, did not shy away. Her little brother slept quietly at home, and she was here to make sure that he could continue to do so.

"Look," Cassara continued when the two made no attempt to interrupt her. "I'd be happy to hear both of your woes after this, but right now my kingdom is threatened by creatures of which I still know nothing about."

She hesitated a moment before resolutely meeting Shirina's glance. "But I do know that the Circle has called its first meeting in all of history, and it has to do with Elihor."

She was satisfied to see Shirina's bemusement vanish into surprise.

"How do you know that?"

Cassara shrugged. "That doesn't matter. What matters is that you both seem to know what's going on here, so I don't intend to let you kill each other before I get the answers to my questions and before I'm certain that my family is safe."

Avarielle shot a look at Shirina, who simply kept looking at Cassara.

"What magic do you possess?" the sorceress finally said, her voice cool and calculated.

Her hand instinctively reached for the amulet, which was still cold to the touch. She suddenly realized that it had never become warm, never warned her of the danger, nor protected her against it. She bit her lower lip, fighting back the urge to cry. She was stuck in a land filled with dark creatures with two bitter enemies as her companions. Cassara suddenly wished she could take back everything that she had said and simply plead to be brought back home.

She let her hand fall again. It was too late for that now, but maybe she could ensure her safe return home some other way. Those Eloms needed to be dealt with, and since she couldn't do it alone, and Avarielle didn't seem to think she could do it alone, there was only one alternative.

Cassara met Shirina's look.

"If you'd like to find out, why don't you help us?" Cassara asked, surprised that her voice was steady.

Avarielle shot her a look of disbelief.

"You can't trust her, Cassara," Avarielle growled.

"Swear on the Circle that you will neither harm nor impede Avarielle and I, and in fact you shall do everything in your power to make sure that we are safe."

Shirina remained perfectly still, her eyes flashing for an instant with what could only be interpreted as amusement.

"I swear it, on the Circle, but only for tonight," she said. She looked at Avarielle, adding, "Although I'm certain many of my brothers and sisters would argue that this oath is against my earlier one."

She looked towards Cassara, pointing to Avarielle with a quick motion of her head. "How do you know you can trust her?"

Avarielle sighed heavily and walked towards a tree, leaning against it.

"Because it's my prerogative to do so," Cassara said. "And because she's already proven she's trustworthy." She cast a glance at Avarielle, who as looking off into the distance, hoping she would not regret her words.

"You're right," Shirina said. "It is your prerogative."

"The two Eloms must have been guards, although I've never seen such a thing," Avarielle whispered, gaining their immediate attention.

"The Eloms don't have the intelligence for that," Shirina said in a sneer.

Avarielle shot her an angry look. "How do you explain the fact that the rest still seem to be in the nest, then? Or that apparently one of them distracted us while the other one was sneaking up behind us?" she finished, pointing at the charred remains, not thanking Shirina for her contribution.

"They did seem different than last night," Cassara said, crossing her arms protectively over her chest. "They were more graceful, and their eyes were...they were very different."

"How so?" Shirina asked, apparently more interested in the princess' opinion than Avarielle's. Cassara looked at the charred remains, longing for the warmth of the amulet.

"Yesterday they seemed filled with pain and grief," Cassara said, wishing she didn't feel so young and useless. "But today, they seemed to be calculating, and cold."

"What does that mean?" Avarielle asked of no one in particular.

"Why do you care?" Shirina shot back. "Aren't you just here to kill them?"

Avarielle was about to reply when Cassara shot up her hand, effectively gaining both of their attention. She was at once surprised at her bold move and even more surprised that they had acknowledged it.

"Enough," she said, wondering how long it would take for them to realize she was useless and leave her to rot. "We'll figure this out later, but right now, we need to stop this nest before it spreads."

Avarielle reluctantly agreed and Shirina simply

nodded. Cassara was relieved that neither one of them corrected her, but at the same time terrified. She had only guessed that the nest would spread, but now, through their quiet acceptance, she was certain of it.

"This way," Avarielle whispered, taking the lead and walking low to the ground into the orchard, towards the cliff. Shirina waited for only a moment before she raised her hood back in place and followed. Cassara was the last to follow, her feet leaden on the grass.

Up ahead, storm clouds covered the moon.

LIEUTENANT MERLO WAS HALFWAY through his shift when the slightly opened door caught his attention. It led to the broken courtyard, the one by the cliff that used to be so beautiful before erosion had claimed part of it. Merlo fondly remembered sneaking in there when he was just a boy to try and catch a glance of the beautiful queen, who favored it after the Courtyard of Travelers.

But when Jayden was born, the broken courtyard had been locked for fear the young heir would fall. After the queen's tragic accident, the Courtyard of Travelers had also been left in a sad state of disrepair, too central to close and too filled with memories to repair.

Merlo approached the door carefully, a firm grip on the pommel of his sword. Although chances were that it was only two foolish young lovers come to sneak into the courtyard, Merlo had not become Captain Klar's right hand by taking chances.

He could only hear the surf. He unsheathed his sword, the small hairs on the back of his neck rising. His instincts told him that something was wrong. He hesitated by the door, wondering if he should warn the captain and the others, but feared that might lose him some respect. He would scout first, carefully, and warn the others if necessary.

Gently he nudged the door further ajar, just enough so that he could pass. He squeezed his large frame through, bringing his sword up defensively.

Staying by the wall, he moved quietly, one slow step at a time, his eyes seeing very little in the darkness. He knew the manor well enough to navigate it, but the darkness out here seemed thicker than inside. He felt a chill. His stomach turned. Something was definitely wrong.

This is foolish, he thought, deciding it would be wiser to retreat and come back with help, or at least a torch. He could wake up Gragor, the new guard. It would be a good training exercise, and he wouldn't see Merlo's nervousness.

All he had to do was reach the barracks, which were not far. He was almost at the door when he spotted movement from the corner of his eye. He turned, sword drawn, his feet placed defensively apart.

The alarm! he instinctively thought, turning again as something else moved at the other end of the courtyard.

Whoever was there was quick. Merlo steeled himself, knowing he would have to fight his way out, knowing that he had to ring the alarm and wake up Klar and the royal family.

Just outside this door! The alarm was just outside this door!

Merlo retreated quickly, looking all around him, every shadow now his enemy. He made it inside without a single encounter, and he slammed the door shut behind him, reaching for the rope that would ring the alarm bell as he did so.

His hand met air. He looked up in disbelief. The rope was gone. There was nothing there. A sound caught his attention and he looked down the corridor, sword drawn. Sweat poured down his face as he tried to focus into the darkness.

Something fell on his head, and he looked down, confused to see the rope of the bell at his feet. Understanding gripped him as he looked up. Something moved in the darkness, clinging to the rafters.

Pain shot up his leg and he was down in an instant. He stared in disbelief, his mind numb with shock. Both of his legs were lying uselessly under him, broken.

The alarm! He grasped the useless cord.

A noise caught his attention and he sluggishly looked up. He was dead before he could scream.

THE SURF HAD ALMOST REACHED the cavern's entrance by the time the three women neared it. The waves struck the cliff hard, fueled by storm winds. Cassara swore she could hear cries mingling with the surf.

"The water is higher than I'd hoped it would be," Avarielle said, shouting to be heard over the waves. The warrior was leaning over the edge much further than either Cassara or Shirina dared.

"How do you plan on getting down there?" Shirina asked, her arms crossed as she hugged her cloak closer to her body. Such a human gesture somehow seemed out of place on her.

Avarielle turned to face them, a large grin plastered on her face.

"Climb," she said casually as she began to lower herself over the cliff.

Cassara heard Shirina exhale, but did not turn around to look at her. Instead, she approached Avarielle to see which ledges she was using. She went down on her knees, and approached the drop. Her two hands firmly gripping the edge, she moved forward, until her head and shoulders were clear of it. Her palms began to sweat and she was glad she had worn leather gloves. Her stomach turned. Heights were much more pleasant when one didn't plan to fall off of them.

"Just follow me closely and do what I do," Avarielle said, looking up at Cassara. "You'll be fine. Now turn around, and catch that little ledge with your foot. I'll make sure you're on the right one."

Cassara nodded, swallowing even though her throat was dry. Swinging around slowly, she let her right leg fall, looking for the ledge. She felt Avarielle's hand direct her foot, and soon was secure enough to lower her second foot onto it.

She looked up. Shirina was still standing there.

"This isn't so bad," Cassara told her, hoping to create some bond with the woman, or at least pierce through her armor.

"I'll make my own way," Shirina said coldly, not moving.

Cassara looked at her, wondering how she would manage to climb down, considering the dress she was wearing, visible now as the dark cloak billowed in the winds. She wanted to say something, but the sorceress seemed in deep concentration, with a look that did not invite conversation.

She heard Avarielle say something and turned to look at her. As she did so, she caught a glimpse of the watery depths below and jerked her head back up. She clutched the cliff, hugging it fiercely with her body, the growling surf making her dizzy. Those were not welcoming waters and they would be her doom were she to fall in.

"Just concentrate on climbing," Avarielle screamed up. Cassara nodded, wishing the words were more comforting, more along the lines of "don't worry, you can't fall."

She took a deep breath and looked down again, this time following the rock so that she did not have to look at the waters. The next ledge Avarielle pointed to was close enough. Cassara bent her knees and gripped the edge of the cliff with her fingers as her foot reached it. Once again, Avarielle's hand was there, making sure Cassara's footing was firm.

She took one more look at Shirina, who did not even seem to register them anymore, before lowering her second leg. She clung to the rocks, feeling like a trapped animal in a very small cage.

She followed Avarielle's lead, having no choice but to trust the warrior who seemed intimately familiar with the cliff face. Gripped by fear, she concocted a thousand different scenarios, from her death on the cliff to her death at the hands of the Eloms. The only similarity between all the scenarios was her horrible and unpreventable death.

Angry winds slammed into Cassara, her face thrown into the cliff face, reminding her of last night's wound. She bit her lip, tears welling in her eyes. Her hands were frozen despite her gloves, and her grip on the rocks felt increasingly uncertain. Avarielle screamed something at her, and Cassara chanced looking away from the cliff in front of her.

The high winds forced her to fight with each breath to capture enough air. Her hair was breaking free from its braid, the strands whipping her face and sticking to her damp skin.

Avarielle stood beside her, motioning her to follow onto a small, narrow path that led directly to the cave, with which they were now thankfully level. Casting one more glance at her, Avarielle turned around and concentrated on walking the small path, her body plastered against the cliff.

Cassara looked away from her, gulping a few deep breaths before taking a first nervous step. The cave now in sight, she wanted to run towards it and jump in, but logic and fear held her back.

Another small step and Cassara felt her confidence rising. She thought she heard Avarielle scream back encouragement, but the howling winds swallowed the words.

The surf was rising, goaded on by the winds, and in another step, the waves skirted the ledge, the waters dangerously close to the cave's entrance. Cassara paused and closed her eyes again, realizing that her wet feet were quickly growing numb. Another scenario entered her mind, which involved drowning in the cave, helpless to escape, her body lost for all time.

Avarielle reached the cave and motioned for her to come, the warrior's arms extended to help her in the last few steps.

Only a few more steps and I can grab her hand.

Her hands and feet moved automatically, negotiating the ledge, too numb to show any grace. She had almost reached Avarielle when sheet upon sheet of rain plummeted from the sky and pummeled her. The surf struck high, crashing into her knees, her left hand losing its grip, her entire body falling back towards the water.

Frantically she tried to reach out, to grab the rock, but it was too smooth and wet and her hands were too numb. Unable to restore her balance, Cassara made one final desperate move, throwing herself towards Avarielle, her arms reaching out, hoping the warrior would see her coming through the thick rain.

She fell, first sideways, and then towards the water, already partly caught by the surf when strong hands caught hers and pulled her clear, the surf pushing her the rest of the way into the cave. Cassara sat up and gasped for breath, frozen by the waters.

"Are you all right?" Avarielle asked, sitting by her, rubbing her arms to try to restore some warmth into them. Cassara found the strength to grin.

"Do we have to do that again?"

Avarielle gave a short laugh. "Up is better, trust me." Cassara nodded and swallowed hard.

"Let's go," Avarielle said after a short time, pulling her blade free. Cassara grabbed her arm to stop her, the warmth making her fingers ache.

"What are we going into?" Cassara asked, feeling foolish that she had not asked before now, when they stood at the threshold and could not very well turn around.

"I'm not sure," Avarielle said, shrugging. "But keep that magic of yours ready."

"Comforting," Cassara mumbled, wishing the amulet would be warm again, wishing she had never come, that she could be back home, warm and dry in bed, without a care or worry in the world, safe from harm.

She followed Avarielle closely, afraid to lose her in the darkness, trying to walk quietly despite her wet and still-numb feet. The cave inclined up, and Cassara felt for the first time that night that fate was gracing them. At least they wouldn't drown in this cave.

They reached the top of the small incline, Avarielle so quiet ahead of her that if she couldn't see the warrior's outline, she would have believed herself alone. Suddenly, Avarielle turned around and raised her blade. Cassara stopped, rooted in place, her hands grasping her knife.

"It's me." Shirina's voice broke the darkness, and Avarielle reluctantly lowered her sword after a few moments.

Cassara walked up to the sorceress, who had been concealed in the shadows.

"How did you...?" Cassara asked, staring at her, unable to finish the question.

Shirina gave her a wry smile. "I *am* a sorceress."

"You could have taken her with you," Avarielle said angrily to Shirina, pointing at Cassara.

Heat returned to Cassara's face.

Shirina took a step towards Avarielle, their faces only a few inches apart.

"It was your idea to take a princess along, and besides, she chose to follow. I am not her nursemaid." Shirina was the first to break eye contact with Avarielle and she walked away further into the nest.

Avarielle shook her head and mumbled a few choice words, casting a quick glance at Cassara and winking before following the sorceress.

Cassara stared for a few moments, feeling useless and unsure, but left with few options, she followed them into the darkness.

5

Klar woke up with a start, uncertain who or what had jerked him awake. At first, he only opened his eyes, keeping his breathing steady as he listened carefully.

The storm outside was the only noise that reached his ears, but his warrior's instincts told him something was wrong.

The door to his small room, a privilege as captain of the guards, was still closed, so Klar took the chance to rise quickly, dress and don his weapons. He perched by the door for a few moments, listening for any sound. Still, nothing out of the ordinary reached his ears.

Merlo was on rounds tonight, by far his best man, but that gave him little comfort. The last time he had felt so certain of incoming attack, slaughter had ensued. He closed his eyes, taking deep breaths, fighting back the memories. He was no longer part of that war with the western provinces; he was in Edoline now, peacefully serving its king. This was his salvation.

Klar reopened his eyes, the memories repressed deeply once again. Slowly he opened the door, his hand relaxed on the hilt of his sword.

The corridor facing his room was calm. Klar decided to make his way towards the king's chambers, to ease his current fears. Trik and Gort were both guarding the way to the second floor tonight, and Merlo was guarding the lower section, including the prince and princess. Klar wished he could be in two places at once. But the king was his priority.

He turned down a second corridor, adjacent to the Courtyard of Stars. The manor was dark and humid, the rain not yet strong enough to leak inside. A light flickered up ahead from the short corridor that led to the second floor, where the king had spent most of his nights pacing since the tragic death of Queen Alayna.

Klar turned down the corridor, Trik and Gort greeting their captain with a grin. The two still stood at their post, obviously bored. Nothing seemed out of the ordinary.

The two guards stared at their captain, his nightly checks not out of the ordinary. Trik's face was set in a constant grin. His marriage to his sweetheart was taking place in two more moons and it was now the only thing on his mind.

Klar nodded at them and had convinced himself he was growing old and delusional when a scream echoed down the hall, from the direction of the guards' barracks.

It was followed by another, and then the bell rang through the manor, once, twice, before it fell as silent as the screams before it.

"Eli of blood," Gort swore, grabbing his sword. Trik's grin vanished. He now stood deathly pale.

"We have to help them," Gort said, taking a step forward.

Klar blocked him.

"No," the captain said, pulling his sword free, amazed at the calm he felt. Just like during the wars. "Our first duty is to protect the king."

Gort met his eyes defiantly, but stood his ground, knowing the captain's words to be true. Klar turned his back to them and they formed a line, three drawn swords reflecting the light.

A grunt down the hall. Something was coming fast. It was joined by another, and another, until whatever it was stopped nearby, just outside the light. The smell of rotten flesh and fresh blood filled the hall. Trik inhaled sharply, holding his breath a long time before letting it flow out of him slowly.

"We hold our ground, and push them back," Klar said, not liking the defeat this one breath conveyed.

"Then we regroup with the others and we eat breakfast as the maids clean up!" Trik laughed nervously and Gort snorted. They were both able warriors, but Klar doubted it would be enough.

The enemy moved forward, cold, calculating eyes shining before the body came to light. He heard Trik gasp and Gort swear. The grotesque creature came towards them, its tongue flapping around its lips and fangs as if preparing for a feast.

"Hold your ground," Klar commanded, his voice soft and low.

They shuffled their feet, but held. More creatures walked into the light, each as deformed as the last. They mostly stood on two legs. They might have been human, once. But that time had come and gone, buried under gray skin patched with dark veins and deep pools for eyes.

Klar watched them come, his vision narrowing as he concentrated on every movement of the creatures, waiting for them to strike. Time slowed as he waited, noticing every detail, from the fresh blood on some of their limbs, to the deadly claws which served as hands.

They paused a few paces from the three guards, a look of triumph shining in their eyes. Klar could feel Trik's rising nerves and Gort's desire for revenge for whichever of their comrades had been killed. They were still too young for this horror and he knew they would break under the pressure long before the creatures attacked. Looking into the monsters' eyes, he knew that they also knew this, and chose to give his men a fighting chance.

"Edoline!" he shouted, his sword coming down for the first blow as he quickly closed the gap between him and the creatures.

"Edoline!" the two other guards shouted, closely following him, their swords striking in almost perfect unison. The front rank of the creatures fell, but it was quickly replaced by another, and another. No matter how many they struck down, more came.

"Let them block the way with their bodies!" Klar shouted at the two guards, who now bled from several cuts. Gort's left arm hung uselessly by his side. Still, they redoubled their efforts at the idea of a plan, the bodies amassing even faster.

The wall of twisted and deformed bodies was halfway to the ceiling when a creature leapt over it and landed near Trik, slashing him across the chest. Trik looked stunned for a moment before dropping his sword and crumpling to his knees. The creature raised its bloodied claws for the final blow, but Klar quickly downed it, screaming through his exhaustion. He grabbed Trik and threw him back against the door leading to the king.

Gort leapt to his side, covering him as he regained his battle posture. The two were all that stood between the monsters and their fallen comrade. And their king.

No more creatures jumped over the pile. Both guards were breathing heavily, Klar ignoring his wounds, the old familiar aches returning to his bones.

"What are they waiting for?" Gort asked, his eyes wide with anger and fear, his sword moving sporadically from side to side. Klar put his hand on the hilt of Gort's sword and steadied him.

"They're coming for a final attack, all at once," Klar said calmly. He had used this technique before, many times, and had always been amazed at its effectiveness.

Gort nodded, his posture changing, his back becoming straight again, his hands steadying, his eyes focusing.

"It was an honor, captain," Gort said.

"The honor was mine," Klar whispered back, hoping the king would somehow escape, hoping Cassara and Jayden would see daylight again, before he pushed these thoughts far below, where they would not slow his hand nor cloud his instincts.

A shrill scream pierced the manor. Claws scraped the floor beyond the pile of bodies.

They braced themselves for the final attack.

IN THE BLACKNESS, Cassara fought to keep her footing, the vague outline of Avarielle guiding her. Unable to see where she was going, Cassara kicked a rock, only to see the warrior turn around and give her what she was certain was a stern look. Once again, she could feel herself blush, but did not lower her gaze.

They resumed walking and Cassara carefully picked her path, grazing the cavern wall. She wondered how Shirina and Avarielle could have such a clear view of the cavern, when all she could discern were vague shadows, half of which she suspected were created by her frightened mind.

She suddenly smelled stale blood and Avarielle stopped abruptly in front of her, Cassara colliding into her.

"They're near," she whispered, and Cassara nodded, not caring that the warrior wasn't looking at her.

The stench of blood deepened, infiltrating every pore, before receding again as they continued walking. Cassara couldn't help but wonder what carcass they had stumbled upon in the dark.

Or corpse, she corrected herself, wanting to draw her dagger free for protection, but afraid of accidentally running Avarielle through. Still, her hand clasped the hilt, its cold metal feeling inadequately small.

She reached instead for her amulet, pulling it free of her shirt, the metal even colder than the knife despite having been against her skin all day. She turned it around in her hand, trying to focus on it as much as she concentrated on her steps, unable to conjure any heat or sign of life.

Blood filled the air again as Avarielle stopped, Cassara not far behind. Then suddenly Avarielle swung her blade inches from Cassara's face. She plastered herself against the wall as light flashed and a creature fell, dead on the ground, its eyes illuminated for just a brief moment by the magic that had killed it. She reached for her dagger instinctively, letting the amulet drop, when a cold hand reached out from beside her and dragged her down.

A strange song resonated and light sprang forth, revealing the Eloms that surrounded them. Cassara screamed as she came face to face with one. Kicking wildly, she managed to throw it off of her, but another creature cut off her escape.

She jumped up and struck out with her dagger, amazed she could still hold it while her hands shook so much.

"Cassara!" Avarielle screamed, cleaving the creatures encircling the princess before three others appeared and she was left with no choice but to confront them.

One of the Eloms jumped towards Cassara and she slashed it with her dagger, almost losing her footing as she did so. Vast shadows exaggerated each of the monster's movements in the unnatural light. She struck out as another came close.

"Help her, Shirina!" Avarielle screamed as she went down, cursing as a creature bit her. Cassara could no longer see the warrior.

The sorceress was not far from her, cloaked in shadows, her eyes cold and calculating as she observed Cassara.

So much for oaths, Cassara thought as she tried to dodge another hit, but the creature proved too quick. A claw tore the skin of her left arm. She bit back a scream as the blood gushed from the wound.

The amulet! She reached for it, dropping her dagger in the process, but it was still cold, as useless as her discarded dagger. A creature jumped at her and she went down under its weight, knocking the breath out of her as her head resonated with the sound of stone on bone. She threw up her arms to defend herself, the left one throbbing from the wound.

The creature opened its jaw, white teeth leading to a

black abyss, the smell of blood pouring from its mouth onto her. Its head lowered, and she gave one last effort, wishing the amulet to life.

Then the creature was off of her, fallen to the side, half of its head gone. Cassara pushed herself up to her knees, spots blinding her vision. She reached for the amulet, but it still lay cold around her neck.

Confused, Cassara looked around, and noticed Shirina was standing near her, hand lowering, robes as clean as when they had first met in the courtyard.

"You could have helped her earlier." Avarielle stormed towards them, nicks and cuts covering what could otherwise have been beautiful features. "Is this how important oaths are to you? She could have easily been killed!"

Cassara resisted the urge to cover her bleeding arm.

Shirina shrugged, unfazed by the warrior's onslaught. "I kept my word," she said simply. "And it was still your idea to bring a princess along."

"But not you," Avarielle said angrily, still clutching her sword.

"If I had not come," Shirina said, her voice gaining a new, dangerous edge, "she would already be dead."

Cassara stumbled to her feet and approached the two, hoping to diffuse the situation.

"Is this all of them?" she asked as smoothly as she would ask for another cup of tea.

Avarielle did not immediately answer, keeping her

eyes on the sorceress before thinking better of it and crouching to clean her sword on a fallen creature.

"It seems to be," she said reluctantly, looking around as if counting.

"It is," Shirina said with no trace of a doubt. "But it isn't very many for a nest."

Avarielle stood back up and sheathed her sword, shaking her head.

"When I found this place yesterday, it was dangerously full. I don't understand where they could have gone. Eloms gather, they don't break apart."

Shirina nodded in agreement. Cassara's gut wrenched, a deep fear growing within her. She tried to figure out where they were, but found it impossible, the darkness having destroyed any chance at orientation.

"Maybe we should have a look at where this leads?" Cassara said slowly, finding the words difficult to articulate, dread numbing her tongue.

Avarielle nodded, following Cassara's eyes towards the deeper section of the cave. If the warrior knew where they were, she gave no indication and did nothing to ease Cassara's fears.

This time, Avarielle took the lead, followed closely by Cassara. Shirina took a moment to end her spell of light before following.

Darkness reigned again, but Cassara didn't care this time, keeping up with Avarielle, not worrying about the noises of kicked rocks on the cavern floor. The warrior, as if sensing the princess' anxiety, moved faster. Soon the darkness began to fade as dim light infiltrated the cave. Cassara realized she could hear thunder and rain.

Overarching all of these noises was the sound of the surf pounding angrily against the rocks. Before her, another entrance to the cave came in sight, and she heard Avarielle inhale sharply. Cassara walked ahead of her, stumbling on the rocks and not caring, her arm aching as she fought to remain standing. Lightning struck again, and this time, Cassara saw what Avarielle had already seen when last the thunder had rolled.

A dangling plant covered the entrance and it took only a moment for Cassara to recognize it.

A weeping willow. The branches belonged to a weeping willow! She stopped for a moment at the entrance of the cave, the small branches of the tree thrown wildly against the entrance. She stood at the edge, the world stopping as it waited for another lightning strike. When it struck, Cassara was already looking up, recognition collapsing on her like a cliff.

She remained motionless, gasping as the lighting vanished and the thunder washed over her, the sight burned in her mind despite the darkness. She would recognize that tree anywhere. It was the very tree that she had perched on as she played her flute and watched the shadows of this evening stretch into night, where Kaden had come to fetch her.

Whatever path you choose, never look back. His words came back on the wind, and she closed her eyes for a moment, trying to fully understand, her mind unwilling to grasp what it already knew.

"Cassara," Avarielle whispered, before the lightning struck again. The warrior was still standing where she had stopped, grief marked on her features.

Cassara registered it but did not acknowledge it. Instead, she looked at the sorceress, who stood passively to the side, a dark shadow against a dark wall.

"Get me up there," Cassara said, her voice a low, menacing command.

"I can't," Shirina said, her voice conveying no emotion.

"I know you can teleport, Shirina," Cassara said, walking towards her. "Now do it. Now."

"I can only teleport to an area I already know." The words were softly spoken, and Avarielle reacted to them before Cassara had even fully understood them.

"You mean you'd already come down here," Avarielle growled, slowly walking towards the sorceress. "Did you know of this exit?"

Shirina hesitated for only a moment. "Yes."

The words broke over Cassara like a thousand angry waves.

"How dare you!" she screamed, releasing hot, angry tears. "That's my family up there!"

Shirina did not look at Cassara, but only stared at the branches of the willow.

"That's not why I came here," she whispered.

Avarielle walked towards her, but Cassara ignored her, running towards the opening instead. Maybe someone was still alive. Maybe the amulet would respond to their needs when it had failed to respond to hers. If she scaled the cliff quickly enough, maybe she could make a difference. Succeed in what she had set out to accomplish this night. To protect those she loved.

Lightning struck, and in the brief flash of light, Cassara reached up and grabbed a rock, hauling herself up as her feet struggled to find footing. She barely registered Avarielle pushing her up.

The branches of the willow quivered in the winds and struck her, over and over again, little whips slapping her, hitting her open wound, her arm aching as it continued to bleed. Cassara ignored the pain as she ignored the willow, focused only on reaching the surface, so close and yet so far. The cliff was slippery but the willow offered some shelter from the angry winds. Cassara was soon grasping its bark and hauling herself up onto its great trunk.

She pulled, screaming at the pain in her arm, stumbling off the tree into the broken courtyard, the rain falling around her in sheets. She tried to run, but fatigue and mud only made her stumble until she reached the door, broken down and marked by scratches. She saw Merlo's twisted corpse, surprise etched on his features, but she did not stop to close his vacant eyes, breaking into a tired run instead, not stopping even as she heard Avarielle scream her name.

She ran down the hall, not bothering going up to the king yet, knowing her father would be protected, knowing he would be safer than anyone else.

I promise I'll bring you with me someday. The words danced around her mind, taunting her to despair, her feet stumbling as the ground became difficult to see through her tears. The smell of blood was everywhere, clinging to everything, and Cassara doubted she would ever feel clean again after this night.

She ran past her room, the door a wooden wreck, running past Altessa's untouched door, until she reached Jayden's room and ran through the broken door, not caring that the wood scraped her thighs, leaving splinters in her skin. Here she did stop, at first not knowing what to do, now that she had reached her destination. Her hands flexed uselessly, her eyes darting at the blood splattered around her. The sheets on the bed, once white, were now red. The candle still burned, but it had fallen to its side.

She walked towards it and picked it up, gently setting it straight again, not flinching as she noticed the body of a guard, now unidentifiable, on the floor beside her little brother's bed. She fell on her knees and raised the sheets, but saw nothing underneath.

Jayden, where are you? Clumsily she stood back up, barely noticing Avarielle as she ran past her, feet numb and body aching. Maybe Jayden was with her father. He would be safe there. Surely the creatures had not managed to reach the king!

Hope gave her the strength to increase her speed, scrambling up the pile of creatures in front of the stairs to the second floor, slipping on their blood several times before making it across, plummeting to her knees ungracefully, black blood mixing with the red.

Klar was slumped against the wall, sword still in hand as if waiting for the chance to attack one last time. Trik and Gort lay nearby, and Cassara crawled on her knees towards the captain of the royal guards, the man who had devoted his life to their protection. She took the time to close his eyes, his skin still warm to her touch. She looked at him for a moment, wondering what his final moments had been like, feeling ill at the sight of the dark blood on the sword he still clutched.

Tearing her eyes away, she turned towards the door, rising slowly and passing through its broken shell, no longer hurrying, no longer feeling the need for speed, knowing whatever had happened was past and none of her actions could now change it.

The stairs creaked in protest as she walked on them. Long had the king meant to fix the old stairs, but the queen had always loved the sound, and so he had left it, even after she had passed, every step somehow bringing him closer to her.

A cold draft blew down the stairs, whipping through the broken door of her father's study, the sound of the rain clear enough to indicate windows had been shattered.

She reached the landing and pushed what remained of the door out of her way, the creaking hinges barely holding it up. Two lanterns illuminated the room. Cassara recognized every pillow, every chair, every sculpture, even though she had not been in here for many years now.

Nothing had changed. Everything was as her mother had placed it.

She let her eyes wander slowly across the room, taking in every small detail, letting her world hold together for one final moment before her eyes rested on the broken form of her father, king of Edoline. She took a step forward, wanting to reach him, to hold him, but she did not want to see his face. She did not want to see if he had been afraid, or in pain, or worse, simply accepting.

Instead, she let the events of the day crash into her, one by one, and she fell to her knees, tears streaming down her face, her head arched back as sobs wracked her body.

The smell of blood clung to her, reminding her of only one truth, the only truth that mattered after this night.

Her family was dead.

And she had been powerless to protect them.

6

The mists clouded her vision for what felt like an eternity, although she knew only a moment had passed.

Slowly they receded, the fresh scent of a thousand flowers striking her as light invaded her world anew. She remained perfectly still, having learned after years of practice that teleportation left her disoriented for a few seconds when she was already exhausted. Taking a deep breath, she allowed herself a moment of peace as she stood in the light of the Lisal Gardens. The magical light was always present and nurturing the rarest flowers in Graydon, some of which were reputed to have come from Elihor itself, before the time of the Great Loss. A great stump of a tree adorned the heart of the gardens, planted by Graydon himself over a thousand years ago. Saplings still grew from its decaying bark.

Lisal was a small outpost run by the Circle, one of the

many places in Graydon used for teleporting. Due to the draining nature of teleportation, only very few of the Circle could travel long distances. Shirina was one of their best, but after using attack magic in the cavern that night, Lisal was as far as she could make before resting. Day would rise in a few hours, and she intended to reach the Circle's Covenant before the sun set again.

"Welcome back to the Circle, child," Grasky, the short and round keeper of Lisal greeted her. She smiled at him and walked slowly towards him, keeping her steps small and manageable.

"It is a pleasure to have returned," Shirina said, grasping his two extended hands in greeting.

"Were you successful in your mission?" Grasky asked as they began walking through the flower garden, a thousand colors washing the last of the cavern's darkness from her mind.

"I'm afraid not," Shirina said, thinking on the night's events. "But something urgent has occurred and I need to consult with the Lady Tangia as soon as possible."

Grasky made a noncommittal noise beside her. Shirina looked at him from the corner of her eye, but did not pry. He was leader here, and even if she was one of the Circle's Elite, it was not her place to question him. She would speak to the Elders soon, starting with her mentor, Tangia, and see what she could find out. Eloms that seemed capable of thought and planned attacks were more dangerous to Graydon than either Avarielle or Cassara seemed to realize. Shirina wondered how different the night would have gone for Cassara had Shirina known beforehand. Well, it was no use thinking about it now. What was done was done.

"You haven't received news of the Circle of late, have you?" Grasky spoke slowly, his pace reminiscent of a duck's waddling.

"I have been pursuing the Grayloft for the past few months," Shirina replied carefully. "Her magic is stronger than anticipated, and she has managed to avoid detection and capture on several occasions. Why, what news is there from the Circle?"

Grasky took a few more steps before speaking again. "Tangia was arrested for treason," he said, keeping his eyes on Shirina to gauge her reaction. Shirina did not show the shock, surprise or grief that she felt at hearing the news. As Tangia's main pupil, she knew that she too would be observed as a potential traitor.

"May I ask why?" Shirina asked, fighting to keep her voice steady. Tangia was extremely loyal to the Circle and would not have betrayed them. Had she been framed? Who would have done it? Due to her strong opinions, she was disliked by many Elders, but they certainly respected her. Without her, the last Harvest would never have taken place, and the Circle would be even weaker than it was now.

"It happened a few nights after you had left on your last hunt," Grasky answered, his voice free of opinion or emotion. She considered him a friend and so understood his caution. She supposed few knew who would be arrested next, now that an Elder had been caught for treason.

"She received orders and refused them." He hissed the last words. "The next day they threw her in Siabala's Rage."

Shirina fought to keep anger from overrunning her better judgment.

Siabala's Rage!

It was the worst, harshest prison in all of Graydon, built long ago before the worlds were separated. Demons haunted your mind, fires burned your flesh slowly, and water only came to you when you were closest to death. The land of the damned never let you die, never let you rest, for once in Siabala's prison, you were his forever. And Tangia had already been there for at least a month, and perhaps already beyond Shirina's help. She wanted to strip the flesh from that cursed Avarielle Grayloft for having evaded her for so long. She should have ignored her promise to the princess last night and captured Avarielle when she had the chance.

"It seems harsh for refusing an order," Shirina said, her voice wavering, wishing she could simply teleport to Siabala and free her teacher. Instead, she continued walking by Grasky, the colorful flowers a cheerful insult to her pain.

"The order must have been very important," Grasky said, stopping and turning to face her. He hesitated, looking from left to right, ensuring they were alone.

Grasky did not possess any magical powers and could not sense intruders or surveillance, but Shirina could.

"We are alone," she said.

He kept his eyes locked on hers for a moment, fear flickering in them, before he looked away and nodded, mumbling something to himself.

"I heard some disturbing news since you left," he whispered, Shirina's reassurances not enough to convince him of their safety.

"A woman came to the Elders before Tangia was exiled and, although no one speaks of it, many believe she was responsible for her fall. And Tangia wasn't the only one sent to Siabala, either. Four more Elders were also sent, and now only six remain." He paused, looking around nervously again before pulling a parchment from within his robe. "These are your orders, Shirina. I'd follow them, if I were you. Some Elites rose to defend the Elders, and they were slaughtered, every last one of them. And those that questioned quickly vanished. Just accept these, do them, and you'll live happily."

He gave her a nervous smile. "You might even become an Elder now, if you play your cards right."

Shirina gave him a withering look. "That is not a position I am interested in," she said coldly as her fist closed around the parchment.

"Very well," Grasky said. "You know where your rooms are, Elite. Please make yourself at home. Until our next meeting, may your steps be steady," Grasky said as he walked away, his voice showing comfort in the old Circle saying.

"And may your thoughts be heavy," Shirina replied, knowing her thoughts would be very heavy, but not in magic as the saying was meant to imply.

She stood in the garden for a few moments, choosing her best options. If Grasky was correctly informed, something the Keeper of Lisal prided himself on always being, then the Covenant was not a safe place for her, especially since her allegiance to Tangia was strong and well known.

Tangia. Siabala's Rage had never been breached, and although Shirina was powerful, she doubted she could break in and free her teacher. Her heart ached as she realized her helplessness.

Why did you refuse the Circle, Tangia? Shirina slowly unfolded the parchment, the invisible magical seals fading away at her touch. The order was simple, straightforward, and confused Shirina further. Why would Tangia be against this? It was something she herself had considered doing but a few hours ago.

Shirina frowned and burned the paper so that it could not be found or read. She was missing a vital piece of information and she needed to get it. Since neither Tangia nor the Circle could help her right now, her only option lay in following the orders and seeing if they would lead her to some answers. But she would do this her own way.

Comforted by having a plan, Shirina began walking

through the gardens, the colorful flowers blurred by visions of burning fires and crashing lightning.

THE SKY WAS clear but no birds could be heard from the orchard on the day Alexavier, King of Edoline, was buried by the manor, beside his beloved Queen Alayna. The few remaining guards, including Carsyn and a wounded Kaden, bore the king's simple wood sarcophagus, royal markings painted on its side by village artisans. Slowly they walked down into the crypt, followed by eleven simple coffins, all the Royal Protectors of Edoline who had died protecting their king, gaining them the right to follow him in the Afterfate. Captain Klar was the first to enter, his coffin slightly more elaborate, his name mentioned once, the other guards all nameless, already forgotten, carried down by villagers.

Cassara hugged her shawl closer even though the sun beat down on her. Emala placed her hand softly on her shoulder, muttering something as she continued shaking her head in disbelief. It had been three days since the attack, and still an air of disbelief clung to all of Edoline, like a thick morning mist refusing to dissipate with the light of the sun.

The princess looked away from her father's sarcophagus, focusing instead on what remained alive around her. She shed no tears, and had not since the night her father had died and Jayden had vanished.

Carsyn and Kaden looked weary, but they held their heads high, having only survived because of their discovery of Cassara's escape and their quick attempt at finding her. Emala, her faithful maid, had hidden when the bell had rung, and doubted any Eloms had come her way. The crowd was thick for Edoline, and Cassara thought that everyone from the village was here. Barlos, the innkeeper, caught her eyes once, and nodded solemnly. She returned the gesture and looked away, focusing on the speaker, Sir Anesh Bestian, her brother-in-law and new king of Edoline.

"But it is in loss that we bring forth new change, and in that change we should be stronger than ever..." His arms rose above his head as he unnecessarily bellowed the words, her sister standing dutifully beside him, hands gripping a handkerchief. Her eyes were also dry.

The coffins had all vanished and the bearers retreated from the dark crypt, eyes solemn, tired and frightened. Edoline was still not safe even though there had been no new attacks.

"Now go in peace," Bestian finished the ritual, lowering his hands and head respectfully. Beside him, her sister's head remained high and defiant. Curious, Cassara stared at her, until their eyes met and Altessa offered her a weak smile.

Cassara was the first to look away, focusing instead on the people leaving, their steps hesitant, as though even the sun could no longer protect them once outside the manor. Not that the manor itself had proved a great defense.

The final bearers exited and the crypt door was shut. The last remaining mourners stood around, Bestian the first to break away, followed by the guards, until all that remained were Cassara and her sister, both dry-eyed, both mourning deeper than tears could tell.

"The king will see you now," the dark-clad guard said, his uniform still bearing the insignia of Laror. Bestian had brought well over one hundred guards with him when he had arrived just this morning. He promised his new subjects, the five hundred citizens of Edoline, that fresh troops would soon arrive to ensure their safety. She wondered if many more would make a difference, without magic to aid them.

She nodded at the guard, longing for the days when she had known all of their names and had shared laughter with them. Of the thirteen guards that remained, most were wounded or had been offered honorable discharges. They had all accepted, except for Kaden and Carsyn. Cassara had yet to thank them for their unwavering loyalty.

"Thank you," she said as she passed by the two unknown guards, walking up the creaky stairs, navigating around the carpenter already at work fixing them, as per the new king's orders. Anger boiled within her. He had been here a day, a single day, and this foreign man who had proclaimed himself king was already changing the very heart of Edoline, first by beginning to build fortification walls around the village and initiating a curfew, and then by removing the sounds, smells and sights that marked the royal manor's history.

She reached the landing, where the door had been removed. A few of the carpenters were leaving the room, familiar faces from the village nodding or grinning shyly at her. In their hands they held her parents' possessions.

"I hope you intend to keep those," Cassara said to Bestian, his back turned to her.

"Of course. They are part of this kingdom's history, are they not?" His reply was laced with sarcasm. Cassara had never liked the man who had claimed Altessa as his wife but, never having been in a position to spend much time with him, she had let the matter drop, deciding his charms must be mostly hidden. As he turned to face her and their eyes met, she knew that her first impressions had been correct, and that they had little chance of ever getting along.

She was surprised at how angry she felt. One word, although illogical, danced around her mind like a swarm of locusts: *Usurper.*

"Sister," Bestian said, a false air of sympathy defacing him further. He could have been handsome, she supposed, even with his long nose and bushy eyebrows, but whatever physical beauty he held was marred by his personality.

Reaching her, he placed his arm around her shoulder, forcing her to walk with him towards the still-broken windows of her father's study. She resisted the urge to move away from his sickly-sweet stench of roses and cinnamon.

"Times are changing, sister," he said again, and Cassara wanted to slap him. She had a brother already, and he might still be alive. Hope wavered in her chest. "Times are changing," he repeated, shaking his head as in mourning.

She took this chance to disengage from his embrace. "Congratulations on becoming king," she said, performing a perfect curtsy. "I know that our kingdom can only prosper under your leadership." The words splashed like acid in her throat.

He smiled, obviously pleased with her subservience.

"Come now," he said, after some time, "we are family here, and you need not bow to me in private."

Only in public, she thought, bitter. Never had her father made her bow, and she had only done so out of respect.

She kept her feelings in check and simply nodded.

"When do you intend to send a search party for my brother?" Cassara asked sweetly, seeing the smile fade on his face.

"Very soon, Cassara, but that is not for you to worry about, not with such important matters to tend to," he said soothingly. Cassara knew he would never send anyone to look for the true heir. Not now that he had secured the throne of an actual kingdom and not just of a province of Rashim, as Laror had been since its treason in the Western Wars.

"What important matters?" She found her anger

difficult to contain. It was bad enough that he would condemn her brother to death and destroy her family's home. What else did he have planned?

"It has come to my attention that Prince Dayshon, heir to the throne of Rashim, has asked for your hand in marriage." Victory flashed in his eyes for a brief moment as he saw Cassara's anger turn to cold realization. He was getting rid of her. He was sending her away from her beloved Edoline.

"Since it's a good union, I've sent word through the Circle that you would accept, and that you would leave immediately to meet him."

"Immediately?" Her throat felt dry.

"Well, as soon as your maid is done packing your personal things. An hour at most. I'm sending a dowry with you and your two guards will escort you and keep you safe." He said the last items as though they were great favors on his part. Two guards. Her two old, tired guards. Were they to be attacked by Eloms, they would all perish, unless of course she could actually make her magic work. She automatically reached for her amulet, the metal still cold against her skin.

"Oh, and that will have to stay," Bestian said, waving towards her amulet.

Cassara's grip tightened around the crescent, her mouth forming a protest that was silenced when Bestian thumped his foot once on the ground and the two guards came running up the stairs, holding pikes in their hands. Her hands went cold.

"It is the symbol of the queen, Cassara, and therefore no longer yours to bear." His voice was smooth, like that of an older brother speaking to his poor, confused little sister. She wanted to hit him. The guards shuffled behind her.

"Bestian," she pleaded. "My mother gave me this." She swallowed hard. "It is nothing but a tired old relic, meaningless to anyone but me. Please, allow me to keep it."

He moved briskly towards her, the guards closing in behind her. "Sister, do not make me ask again." The words were plainly, almost dismissively spoken, but the fire in his eyes made her shiver. What kind of man was married to her sister? She wasn't certain she could survive without the amulet to protect her, but she knew beyond a doubt that she would not live past this day unless she handed it over now. *It's not like I can actually wield its magic, anyways.*

She reluctantly removed the amulet, her hand colder than the metal. The light bounced off of it as Bestian grabbed it and threw it in his pocket, his eyes shining with victory.

"I do not want you to sleep another night in this place of nightmares, sister," Bestian said, false concern dripping from every word. He put his arms around her shoulders again and turned her around, walking her towards the guards, her footsteps heavy and awkward. She wanted to push him away, but doubted the guards would hesitate to spear through the princess of a minor kingdom for their leader.

She was only an accessory now.

"You are free to visit at any time, of course," he said, obviously believing she would never return to Edoline.

"Take the princess to the courtyard. She'll be leaving us soon." Before she could protest, as little help as she thought that would do, the two guards had flanked her and were all but pushing her down the stairs. Reaching the bottom, she straightened herself and regained her footing, looking coldly at the two guards.

Her voice dripped acid. "I can find my own way to the courtyard, thank you."

She walked at her own pace towards the entrance of the Courtyard of Stars. If she could not keep her freedom and her home, the least she could do was keep her dignity.

Still, the guards followed her until she was well past the cedar fence.

IT WAS one of the slowest and longest hours of Cassara's life. Idly she wandered within the two inner courtyards, the guards on either gateway leading her to believe she would not be allowed to pass. At least they stayed out of sight, leaving Cassara with some peace as she bade farewell to her home.

Still feeling numb, she sat by the beheaded horse, debating whether or not to sneak back in using the secret passage. She chose against it, deciding it would buy her little time and would probably reveal its presence. The fact that Bestian did not know of its existence was a small victory she enjoyed.

Slowly she took out her flute, remembering what it had felt like to carve it and discover every small nick in it, whether voluntary or not, all now well known and loved. A lump rose in her throat at the thought of her mother, and she let her sorrow create the first note of her melody, filling the courtyard with soft music. She had not played this song since the day her mother had died. It was the last song she had taught Cassara: the Traveler's Song. It had been by far her mother's favorite, as she had always dreamed of leaving Edoline and seeing the world.

On the day she was to do so, however, when Jayden was but a tot and the physicians recommended fresh air away from the sea to help her heal, her horse reared and she had fallen, never to rise again. Until now, the Traveler's Song had been too riddled with pain and memories for Cassara to play it again. But today, as she was about to leave Edoline, as her mother had always dreamed of doing herself, Cassara played the melody effortlessly, remembering the young and vibrant woman her mother had been.

And the strong man her father had been, and her brother could have grown up to be. The thought of Jayden, the greatest injustice of them all, brought tears to her eyes, and she let them flow freely, warming her cheeks as she finished her song.

"I've missed hearing that music," she heard a voice say softly behind her. Cassara turned around and saw her sister standing by the cedar hedge. She too knew of the secret passage. Altessa came around the fountain and sat by her sister, hugging her fiercely.

"He has no right to do this, Cassara," she whispered in her ear, drying up the rest of Cassara's tears.

"But he can do it, Altessa." Cassara gave her sister a slight smile, trying to lighten the mood. "Tell me, is he always that charming?"

Altessa gave a short laugh. "He used to be charming, believe it or not." She waved dismissively. "Will you be all right?"

Cassara shrugged, not trusting her voice. The familiar chirping of the birds, the sound of the crashing surf and the smell of the salty sea mixed with the blooms of the gardens seemed surreal and distant.

Altessa's hands clenched in her lap. "But we must make the best of it." Cassara's head shot up in surprise. Altessa reached out and grasped Cassara's hands between her own.

"Think about it, Cassara. By marrying into the most powerful kingdom of Rashim, you will gain access to endless resources." She paused, eyes filling with tears. "Cassara, as queen you'd get your own military unit. You could mobilize them and, and maybe find Jayden!"

"Altessa, I..."

"He's out there, Cassara, I know it." Her voice trembled. "Why else would his bod...would he not have been found? Everyone else is accounted for." The tears vanished from her eyes as quickly as they had come. She repeated the words more slowly, her voice gaining strength of conviction. "He's out there, Cassara. I know it."

Cassara felt the warmth of her sister's hands and gazed into her blue eyes. Altessa was right. But was leaving her beloved land the only way to save Jayden? She blushed at the selfish thought and broke away from Altessa's eyes. Rashim would be an adventure to her. She had to see it that way. An adventure, and she would eventually find her brother, and she would take him to Rashim and share that adventure with him, too.

He would like that.

"He's strong," Cassara whispered more to herself than her sister. "He's surely survived."

"And you will survive too," Altessa gently said, pulling the previously hidden amulet free from her neck and handing it to Cassara. She hesitated to take it.

"Bestian insisted you should have it, as queen of Edoline," Cassara whispered, wanting nothing more than to take the amulet.

Altessa shrugged. "Mother gave it to you, Cassara, and since Edoline was a matriarchy generations ago, I always saw it as a sign that she chose you to be her heir, whatever that now represents in this patriarchy."

Cassara opened her mouth to argue. That was ridiculous. Altessa was the oldest and by far the wisest. Seeing the argument in her sister's eyes, Altessa raised her hand to quiet her.

"It doesn't matter anymore, does it? The power is not ours to wield, and we are too few in Edoline to fight or for the world to bother with," she said sadly. "The point is, the amulet is yours and I will not take it from you. And no one, whether my husband or the King of Rashim himself, will convince me otherwise."

Altessa smiled gently, running her hand over Cassara's cheeks. "Times change, Cassara, and Edoline is being swept along with the rest of the world. But know that although everything else may change around us, my love for you never will. You're my sister, and no power in this land will change that." Cassara swallowed hard, wanting to tell Altessa the same, but not trusting her voice. She hoped her eyes conveyed the message.

"Time to leave, my Lady," Cassara heard Emala whisper from the entrance. Altessa shoved the amulet into Cassara's hand before it could be seen, and she hugged her fiercely before she could be thanked.

"Live well, little sister. We'll meet again, soon enough, all three siblings," Altessa whispered, vanishing into the hedge again before Cassara could say goodbye.

"Cassara?" Emala said gently after Altessa had left, the maid long aware of the princess' secret passage.

Cassara nodded and walked towards Emala, taking a deep breath before crossing the threshold of the Courtyard of Travelers and stepping away from her home.

Only Carsyn, Kaden and Emala joined her. There was no fanfare, no farewell, no good wishes. She thought she saw Altessa standing at the second-floor window, but decided it could not be her, the woman only resembling her sister. The mystery was lost from her mind as her carriage crossed the orchard, the blooms falling around her like a thousand tears, the petals trod upon by the horses the only sign of the passage of the last princess of Edoline.

THE WOMAN SAT at the desk, letting her memories guide her as she stared with her astral eyes around the room, remembering the minute details that the eye could no longer detect, like the writing on the walls that Alexavier had painted over, without a second thought or glance.

Alexavier. It was odd to think of him as dead, so long had he been a strong, immovable presence. Until Alayna had passed away, leaving him a broken, lonely shell. Delora sneered as she ran her not-quite-opaque fingers over the centuries-old wood covered by coat after coat of wax, sending back an old, gnarled reflection of her hand. She stopped for a moment, wondering if Alayna had ever noticed the same reflection, before her attention was drawn to the door.

"My Lady Delora," the intruder said, executing a perfect bow, his fear only betrayed by the slight shifting of his feet as he stood tall again.

"Bestian," Delora said, rising lazily to her feet. "It seems you've had an eventful day." She smiled at him and was pleased to see the fear intensify in his eyes, even though he faced only a magical image of her. She had made sure on their first visit that he understood her powers were still complete despite her body's different location. He cleared his throat.

He spoke quickly, feverishly, as though by speaking he could wake from the nightmare he had so willingly helped her create. "Altessa's little sister is gone and my wife has the amulet you requested, Lady Delora."

Delora allowed herself a momentary smile. She didn't want the children dead, for they were really just innocent pawns, as she once had been. By keeping them out of harm's way, she could protect them. Except, of course, for Altessa, but Delora felt little regret. She had become too perceptive and cunning, and in her eyes gleamed the same wisdom that had once graced her mother. But for now, she needed her alive, as much as she needed the man who stood nervously before her.

"The Southern Coalition will leave Edoline alone, Bestian," Delora said soothingly. "This I guarantee. They fear the demons that lurk in the night and kill kings. And Laror will soon be able to claim its independence and absorb Edoline, making it a stronger power than before the Western Wars."

Delora smiled, pleased to feel his greed mix with the fear of losing his home. It drew her to him as a bee to a waiting flower, offering her the perfect grounds to spread her pollen and claim control.

"Do you want the amulet now?" Bestian asked, sounding eager to please her. *Or eager to be rid of me,* Delora thought, observing him closely.

"Not yet," she said, pleased to see his shoulders drop. "One of my...friends will come claim it within a week."

Let him know that I shall return, she thought, certain he would try nothing as long as he feared repercussion. Besides, she needed the amulet hidden for a while longer. The oldest Edoline daughter would do, for now.

"I trust you and your wife to keep it safe, Bestian," her words fell like thick honey, not meant to soothe him, but rather to trap him. She saw recognition flicker in his eyes, followed by hopelessness, which darkened his features like sunset's shadows.

Satisfied that her control of Edoline was now complete, Delora closed her eyes for an instant, long enough to cast her spell, but not long enough to allow Bestian to gather some courage and plant a knife in her belly. Although merely an image, she could still feel the pain and might even truly be wounded.

May your steps be steady, she thought as the mists gathered before her vision, seeing Bestian crumple to despair on the floor before her mind had fully left the room to rejoin her body.

She had less than a month to prepare for Rashim and she intended to be ready. And there was still the boy to deal with.

And may your thoughts be heavy.

7

When she was just a child, eight years old at most, Cassara had asked about the forested barrier that stood between Edoline and its northwest neighbor. Her mother, who sat on the horse behind her, gave a short laugh, saying it had taken her until she was fifteen to even care about anything beyond the borders of this realm.

The trees, as it turned out, did not simply create a border. They encompassed the entire neighboring country, a mysterious area called Kosel. For the next hour, on their ride back to the village, her mother had delighted her with tales of this mysterious land. No central government was known to exist, the entire land owned by an old reclusive family who didn't seem to care what the inhabitants of the region did, as long as it didn't bother them.

Justice was dealt swiftly by the population, which was

spread across small villages nestled deep within the woods. Nobody seemed to know how many villages existed within Kosel. From its shadows and secrets emerged legends and tales that delighted generations of the surrounding countries. Heroic warriors gone to die within its woods. Evil sorcerers lying in wait as their powers grew. Cursed maidens stoically waiting for their lovers to bring a cure. There were more to choose from than Cassara could possibly count.

Only one old road ran through Kosel, from the edge of Edoline to Rashim and, traveling down it, Cassara wondered where these legends came from. Trees. That was all there was. Many trees surrounded them, mostly maple, cedar and pine. Always trees and the occasional bush.

She would be hard pressed to imagine a more boring country.

Cassara turned her attention back to the task at hand, concentrating on the amulet she held. She focused and reached out with her mind, imagining energy from her mind passing her eyes and reaching the amulet. Within a few seconds, warmth emanated from it and it gave a soft glow. Cassara smiled and lost her focus, the amulet's magic vanishing immediately.

For the past week she had secretly practiced in daylight when Emala grabbed one of her frequent naps. The amulet's glow would be too noticeable at night. Her progress seemed painfully slow, but at least now she could summon the magic when she needed it. The problem was, that was all she could do. Her goal was to create attack magic, but she could make no fire spring forth as on the night she had first encountered Eloms. She needed more time and concentration to truly master the power, this she knew. There always seemed to be something stopping her, either her own failure to concentrate adequately or Emala's untimely waking.

She settled back into the cushioned seat, the fresh smell of pine trailing in on the breeze. Looking around the wooden carriage and its few luxuries, she supposed being unable to summon fire might not be such a bad thing. Patience, she suspected, would be the key to her success.

But what a slippery key it was to grasp.

"How long have we been on this road, Emala?" Cassara asked, waking her maid from her light slumber. It would be nice to hear something else but snoring.

"Just over a week, now, your Highness," Emala responded, stretching and yawning loudly.

"This is rather tedious, wouldn't you say?" Cassara asked, looking out of the carriage. Neither Carsyn nor Kaden were in sight. She guessed the extra horses were tethered to the back and the two were on the driver's seat, chatting or sleeping. She hoped at least one of them was paying attention, although she doubted it was necessary. Even the most untrained of horses could find their way on this straight road without a single fork.

"Another few days and we should be clear of Kosel,"

Emala said, grabbing the side of her bench as the carriage hit a bump.

"If the carriage lasts that long," she added, shifting in the cushioned seat. Cassara smiled at her.

"At least once we reach Rashim, the roads will be smoother," Cassara said.

"Yes, and faster," Emala said. Cassara nodded and looked out the window at the trees.

"I'm sure it's for the best," Emala mumbled again, as she had many times on their journey so far. She closed her eyes and was snoring within seconds. Cassara smiled. The only thing she looked forward to in Rashim was being out of this carriage. Although she was curious about seeing her future husband again, she couldn't help but feel apprehension towards him. If he had never proposed, she might still be home, instead of conveniently packaged and shipped off at the first opportunity.

She sighed and leaned back, closing her eyes. Who was she kidding? Bestian would have simply found some other royalty to marry her off to. At least now she knew the man she would be marrying.

"Know" him might be a bit of a strong statement, she thought, opening her eyes again as she felt the carriage lurch to a stop. The smell of burning firewood hung in the air around them and she quickly stuck her head out the window. They were by a small settlement, complete with an inn and what seemed to be several houses.

Kaden and Carsyn both climbed down from the carriage and Cassara shook Emala awake before jumping out. It had been so long since they had eaten anything fresh that Cassara's stomach lurched with excitement. Kaden and Carsyn were too old to hunt, and Emala was more likely to shoot them than an animal. And although Cassara was a fair shot, her entourage insisted it would not do for her to have bruises on her skin or scratches on her face from hunting in the forest.

"Why don't you three head over to that inn to get some rooms and something to eat?" Kaden pointed towards the old wooden shack. Cassara nodded eagerly, delicious-smelling smoke lazily escaping the chimney. "I'll see about putting up our horses."

Cassara knew that meant not only the horses had to be put up, but the carriage had to be placed in a secure location as well. The dowry was, after all, hidden in a false floor beneath the seats. Cassara was certain her brother-in-law wouldn't be amused if she sent word that the original dowry was lost and she needed another before the wedding could take place. Although the trouble it would cause Bestian might prove amusing, it would create more hassle than she wanted to go through.

Carsyn led the way towards the inn, several children running past them to see the horses. Kaden greeted them and introduced them to the horses. Cassara smiled and looked at the rest of her surroundings. She had expected, once the splendid stories of youth had fled from her mind, that Kosel would be inhabited by thieves and murderers, hiding from justice and their crimes in this secluded area.

Looking around her at the few faces, Cassara could

believe that theory no more than she could all the other fantastical legends. They were curt and nodded politely, and they seemed content, relaxed in a way she doubted individuals fleeing from the law would be. A few houses were sprinkled beyond the road, mixed in with the trees.

Cassara found it impossible to guess how many people might live in this settlement, but it had been the only one located right on the road, and she assumed it would be the only one they would see before exiting the woods in a few days.

It seemed that the truth of Kosel was not so enigmatic and magical as it was simple. The inhabitants sought peace and simplicity, a way to leave the troubles of the world behind. The scars on many faces spoke of battles fought, probably for causes not necessarily their own. More than likely, judging from their age, in the Western Wars.

"They just want peace," Cassara whispered. Emala nodded, her eyes wide and bewildered as she took in the details and people around her. Cassara realized for the first time that it was probably Emala's first journey outside of Edoline, and she had not been given much choice in the matter either. She flushed with shame and impulsively put her arm around Emala's shoulder, bringing the woman close to her. Emala turned to her, her look of surprise giving way to understanding as she slipped her arm around Cassara's waist and returned the hug.

"It's a beautiful sight, isn't it?" Carsyn said, looking

back for just an instant and grinning at the two girls, his eyes shining with something Cassara had never associated with him in her entire life. It was peace. She suddenly realized how little she actually knew of Kaden, Carsyn and Emala, even though she could easily call them her closest friends and confidants. She had taken too much for granted, including her maid's and guards' loyalties.

Crossing the threshold of the small inn, she wondered how different her life would now be, had she taken less for granted. And how different it would be for her family.

By the time they sat down at a small table, Cassara found that she had very little appetite after all.

A FLASH OF LIGHT.

Cassara concentrated, grasping the magic as it broke through the amulet, radiating outward from deep within, acknowledging her efforts by growing stronger and illuminating the walls of her small room in the inn.

Drawing a deep, gentle breath, careful not to let this simple action break her physical concentration, Cassara anticipated the next move. She exhaled, as slowly and purposefully as possible, willing her energies to ride her breath and fill the amulet.

The light grew again, pleasant warmth tingling from the shaped metal into her fingers. She drew herself up, trying her best to ignore the pain in her back from staring too intently at the amulet, willing the light to rise with her and become fire. White, pure fire. The light continued to grow and she grabbed at it with her mind. She urged the light on, focusing on the magic until it encompassed her world.

Something stepped in the way of the light for a moment. She expected it, as it had happened every time she had tried to use her magic lately. It still startled her and she forced herself not to look around and to keep focusing on the amulet.

I'm so close! she thought, feeling the sweat trickling from her hairline and tracing the contours of her face. She ignored the sensation. Her body no longer mattered. This was a battlefield of the mind.

May your thoughts be heavy, Cassara repeated as a mantra. Surely this was the key to magic. She simply had to find the door to unlock within her and unleash her powers.

Another shadow passed before her mind's eye, another break in the light. The image flashed again at her and for one second, she concentrated on the image instead of her magic. For one second only, but it was enough to lose the light.

The amulet became dark again.

"No," Cassara sobbed, her body and mind sucked dry from the effort of trying to master the magic that could save them all. And always failing.

Cassara let her exhausted body crumple on the floor, curling her legs against her stomach to ward off the chill that seemed to have grasped her body a week ago.

Everything seemed surreal. Her entire childhood, her home and most of her family were gone, and she had nothing left but her amulet's magic and an image that continued to haunt her and stop her from summoning her powers.

She brought the amulet to her cheek, knowing it would be cold, the metal either unable to hold the heat or the magic too weak to create real warmth. She let her tears run down on the cold metal, wishing she were home in bed, but wanting nothing less at the same time.

She knew what had broken her concentration in the light. What always broke her concentration. What tricks her mind played with her to continuously convince her the magic would never be hers.

It was not cries for help from her father, from her brother, or even from Klar, as she had originally suspected. Instead, it was an object, looming before her, its features outlined by crisp light.

It was what she had seen and, in a flash of light, had revealed to her that everything was over in Edoline. When she had known that it was not her magic that had failed her, but rather it was she who had failed them all.

It was the branches of the fallen weeping willow, dancing in the storm that had swept her world away.

"WILL you come help me get the carriage ready, Cassara?" Kaden asked softly once she was done her late breakfast.

Or lunch, as Emala kept saying, annoyed at how late the princess had awakened.

Cassara nodded and followed, knowing this unusual request was simply a ruse to get her alone.

Kaden led the way slowly, seemingly in no hurry to question his ward. She followed him, children running around them as they played, their laughter bouncing without effect off of her old guard, so deep was he in thought.

He was dressed simply. The sword on his back was a natural extension of him, more like an extra limb than a weapon. By the time they entered the barn in the woods where the carriage had been stowed, Cassara wondered what he would look like without a sword and without his ever-purposeful, although tired, stride. She wondered if it was even possible.

The inside of the barn was dark, humid and much cooler than the outside air. Kaden walked to the carriage and began removing the tarp that had been thrown over it. Cassara silently followed his lead, her simple brown dress dancing about her ankles as she stood on the tips of her toes to reach.

After removing the tarp, they immediately began folding it, Kaden not once making eye contact with Cassara.

The two grabbed the tarp and placed it in a small compartment under the carriage, yet another precaution against someone looking for the partition where the dowry was hidden.

The task finished, Cassara stood, waiting for a cue from her guardian on what to do next. Kaden took a moment longer to stand, but when he did, it was not with the usual weariness that had plagued him for the past few years, but rather with calculated precision. His eyes met Cassara's and held them as he spoke.

"Do you want to go to Rashim?" he asked softly, his eyes barely meeting hers as he glanced to see her reaction.

"What do you mean?" Cassara asked, her voice but a whisper, feeling like a child who might get caught doing something wrong. She jumped when a horse whinnied in the distance.

"Once we leave Kosel, it will be more difficult to vanish, that's all," Kaden said as he checked over the carriage one more time, unnecessarily.

"But you're under the king's orders to bring me there, Kaden," Cassara whispered, feeling more trapped than ever. She couldn't let her friends take the blame and pay the price for her running away, which they certainly would.

"I never swore loyalty to the man sitting on your father's throne," Kaden said, the harshness in this voice soothed only by his fatigue. "Cassara, I swore loyalty to your father, as did Klar, and many of the other guards, not because we're from Edoline, but because during the Western Wars, he saved us all."

"I didn't know my father had participated." Another story her father would now never be able to tell her.

Kaden shook his head and gave a short laugh. "He didn't, Cassara. And that's what saved us."

Cassara waited for him to continue. The lines in his face seemed to deepen as he spoke, shadows from another time still clutching his frail features.

"It was only twenty years ago, but there was a council, back then, of all the kingdoms in Graydon. Even Edoline was part of it," he said, a smile playing on his lips. "When the Western Wars began, the attacks were ordered before being brought to the council. When the attacks were finally discussed at council, almost everyone supported them, except for Edoline and a few of the southern countries. But your father was by far the strongest voice in the council. And when he had turned enough voices to his side, the troops were called back."

Kaden hesitated, opening his mouth and closing it before words escaped him. He looked to the side, his hand reaching for the carriage, as though he intended to do something further with it but, finding no purpose, they quickly fell back to his side.

He gave Cassara a weak smile, clearing his throat before continuing to speak. "Your father offered some of us a second chance. And so, we followed to Edoline, to where we thought we could find peace. And we did, for some time. But my loyalty was to Alexavier, and to him alone, Cassara. He believed every man and woman deserved to choose as far as they could, and he would want you to have that chance now."

He winked at her and his voice was strong again when

he spoke. "Otherwise, he'd have shipped you off to the first suitor."

Cassara gave him a slight smile, her arms feeling as though they had been unbound for the first time in ages. She still wished to know more of this strong political man that her father had once been. She suddenly understood why Edoline had been left alone, if it was being shunned by most nations for opposing a war. She didn't know why her father had opposed it, or why the remaining nations hadn't just attacked and conquered Edoline, but she would find out those details later. Of that, she was certain.

Right now, what mattered most to her, was the fact that she had been offered a choice again. It was at once liberating and frightening. Her goals were simple: to find Jayden, avenge her family, and find her way again. To do that, she needed to forge her own path, which would not lead her to Rashim. Should she marry Dayshon, she might become queen, and as queen, she could lead an army and make a difference. But that might take years to happen, as the prince's parents were both alive and healthy. Jayden, she was certain, didn't have that much time.

All of the small hopes that had burrowed into her heart over the last week without her knowing, hidden deeply beneath her grief, were coming into focus. She hoped Carsyn would retire and Emala would live happily.

She hoped to find Jayden, alive and well, and see him grow up to be one of the finest kings of Edoline.

And, in her most selfish thoughts, she hoped Kaden would come with her, no matter which path she chose, even if he could not defend her against the Eloms, even if he became slower and older by the day. And yet, at the same time, she wished he could soon retire comfortably. He could, had she but the courage to go to Rashim and marry Dayshon.

What Kaden didn't seem to understand, or perhaps understood all too well, was that the choice he was asking her to make wasn't only for her. It would affect all of them as well.

She swallowed hard as she remembered her sister's impassioned plea to find their missing brother. He had to be alive. He had to be.

"I'll choose, and then I'll never look back," she told him, repeating the same words he had told her what felt like a lifetime ago. Whereas the choices had seemed impossible then and unreachable but a few hours ago, now they tore at her and she found she could not choose. Either way, someone would suffer for her choice. Jayden might die if she chose to continue to Rashim, but her small party might suffer Bestian's anger now, if she chose to leave.

"We still have a few days before we exit Kosel," Kaden whispered. "Just promise me one thing, Cassara. When you go, tell me so that I can follow."

Cassara swallowed her tears, wishing she had the strength to refuse him his request.

Instead she nodded, and he walked out of the barn into the light.

Cassara stayed in the darkness a moment longer

before following, thinking on the fact that he had said *when you go,* and not *if you go.* She wondered if he was telling her it was all right to choose to go, and leave them all to live a life of exile, never to be welcomed back to their beloved Edoline.

Unless she could find Jayden, see him safely to his throne and win them all a hero's return. She clutched her amulet and, in the face of choice and hope, felt more helpless than ever before.

"Some people say there are demons out there," Emala urgently whispered to Cassara as they packed her few belongings. Emala had been ready to leave since the sun had risen, the sight of civilization in Kosel making her nervous. This was the first time in their journey that they had been in a village filled with strangers, and Emala imagined thieves and cutthroats behind every door.

Not that Cassara could really place blame on her for that. Even in the daylight, this place looked like it could hide Eloms.

"What if they're the same ones that attacked Edoline?" Emala pressed on when Cassara failed to answer. "What if...what if they're going to destroy this place next?"

Cassara dropped her bag on the bed and grabbed Emala's hands. "We're going to be fine, Emala." Cassara smiled reassuringly at her maid. "Kaden and Carsyn are with us, and we have each other to rely on. Besides," she added with a crooked smile, "do you really think that we'd be so unlucky as to be in two places attacked by those things?"

Emala seemed little reassured or amused by Cassara's words, and relaxed only when Cassara hooked her arm with hers as they exited the inn.

Cassara wanted to ask Emala for more details of what she had heard, but she didn't want to alarm her with her persistence. If there were Eloms in the area, she wondered if she could force her magic to work, like on the first night she had encountered them. If only she could be certain it would work, she could stand a chance at finding her brother.

Jayden...

One look at Kaden halted any thought of escaping into the forest to find Eloms. He too had heard the rumors and did not intend to let his ward run after them.

Cassara obediently stepped into the carriage with Emala. A few children waved goodbye to them as they left, calling Emala by name. She smiled at them, shouting a few jokes that only Emala and the children seemed to understand.

"You seem to know them well," Cassara said, smiling at Emala, who shrugged.

"I had a lot of time to waste this morning," she replied, a touch of accusation in her voice.

Cassara ignored it. "I'm glad you made friends," she said instead.

"I love children," Emala whispered, longing in her eyes

as they exited the small village and the laughter of the children was lost.

"Why did you never have any?" Cassara asked softly. Emala gave a short, dry laugh, taking Cassara by surprise.

Seeing the look on Cassara's face, Emala grew red and apologized, but Cassara stopped her by lifting a hand.

"Emala," she said gently. "I'd like to think we're friends, and that you can tell me anything."

Emala smiled at the words. "I still think of you as a little girl, Cassara, even though I wasn't much older than you when I became your maid. You were just eight then, just a wisp of a girl. I guess you grew up without my noticing."

"Even though I'm about to be wed?" Cassara asked with a raised eyebrow.

Emala gave a hearty laugh. "Even though." She sat quietly and did not offer any more information. But Cassara wanted to know everything, a thirst for knowledge as it seemed she would soon be leaving the well.

"Tell me about the children," she softly pressed, not caring if Emala spoke of her past or of the children from this morning. She simply wanted to hear the comforting voice so as not to be left alone with her dark thoughts.

Emala looked out the window. When she finally spoke, her voice seemed to have aged, yet for the first time ever Cassara saw the young lady, barely her own age, Emala had once been. "There was a boy, once, whom I grew up with in Edoline. He was a farmer of course, and I loved him. His eyes were blue, his hair forever tousled, and his smile melted my heart every time he looked at me."

Her face softened as the memories returned, flooding her with images from her past. "I was lucky, really, since I married for love, when I was even younger than you, and I still think you're too young." The last words were spoken in jest. Cassara smiled but did not speak for fear of breaking the tale.

"It was years before I became pregnant. Jirome and I kept hoping, since we both wanted a large family." Her face became softer. "Finally, like a miracle from Lady Fate herself, I became pregnant. Nine months later I went into labor and Jirome went out to get the healer." She paused, the light draining as quickly from her face as it had appeared. "We think he must have decided to take a shortcut through the woods, because he was found there later. Wolves."

Cassara didn't expect Emala to continue. Her hands and tongue felt numb. She wished she had some wisdom to share.

She was surprised when Emala spoke again, in the same slow rhythm, as though she had been waiting for a long time to tell this story.

"The healer didn't make it on time. I lost the child and will never have another. They said it was a miracle I had even lived. I don't know, Cassara. Sometimes I wonder about it all, though I try not to. When I could finally walk again, I just strolled outside for a few moments and a horse passed by, and there you were, with your mother.

She said she had heard what had happened, and since I could not keep the farm by myself, wondered if I would be willing to keep her daughter company."

Cassara's mouth dropped. She had completely forgotten that day, until now. It had seemed to her that Emala had always been present in their lives.

"I asked her why me, and she answered that she would soon be leaving for a journey and she had heard good things about me. I still don't know from who," Emala said. "But I went. And a week later, your mother, may she find her way, lay dead in the Courtyard of Travelers."

Emala stopped speaking, putting her tale to rest, as though she feared she might have said too much.

"Do you ever regret choosing to come?" Cassara asked softly, looking at Emala. The features on her face were still young and yet so old, now telling stories she had never heard before.

Emala stood quickly and slid onto the bench beside Cassara, placing her arm around the princess, who let her head fall on her maid's shoulder. As she had so long ago, when her mother had died and only Altessa and Emala could comfort her.

"Never, Cassara. I've never regretted it, and I never will, as long as I live."

Even if it means leaving Edoline and the graves of your husband and child? Cassara wanted to ask, but she let it rest, finding comfort in the warmth of the woman.

It was then that the carriage came to an abrupt halt.

8

Bestian paced the floor of the small throne room, wondering how Alexavier had ever accomplished anything in such cramped quarters. Granted, the demands of the populace of Edoline were not overwhelming, the monarchy's main role being to facilitate trade agreements and resolve minor land feuds, but Bestian decided that after the work was finished on the second floor, the throne room would be enlarged.

He felt certain they could easily give up a few other rooms for the throne room, since Edoline was to become a province of Laror. Let the Southern Coalition stop its growth afterwards, and let him and his soon-to-be expanded kingdom show them that the combined forces of Edoline and Laror were not to be easily intimidated. Unlike the current rulers of Laror, who were old and weak.

Bestian clapped his hands together, the noise echoing off the old stone walls. Maybe he would even make Edoline the seat of his power, as a final insult to the old rulers of Laror. They had, after all, been about to shamelessly sell out the country and his family's lands to the Southern Coalition. Rashim didn't even seem to care about the loss of the province, seeing it as more trouble than it was worth.

Someone cleared their throat to gain his attention, and Bestian turned to the guard, annoyed his plans were being interrupted.

"What?" he demanded, realizing his anger and fury were unjustifiable, but unable to stop himself.

"A woman is here to see you, your Majesty," the guard said, showing no strain in his voice. They were well trained, Delora's troops, but he had to be wise and remember that they were her troops, and not his own.

Delora. Bestian's anger receded a bit, replaced by fear and relief. It had been a week since Delora's visit and so this must be her "friend," come to claim the amulet.

"Send her in, and ask my wife to join us," Bestian said, sitting down on the small throne in an effort to stop his pacing and appear in control. He was pleased the messenger had finally come. Bestian did not like feeling under someone else's control, and he didn't like knowing his wife wore a dangerous item around her neck.

Especially since she now bore their first child.

The guard quickly returned, and Bestian suspected the

guest had not been made to wait in the courtyard as protocol demanded. He wished he could wipe his hands to remove the sweat from his palms. He felt his control vanish and fought to keep his temper down. Why couldn't he just stay calm? He used to be able to, before meeting that cursed Delora.

The woman entered. Bestian was careful to hide his surprise. She wore the traditional simple robes of the Circle. She was young, her blond hair reminiscent of Cassara's, but her dark eyes and cold features defied any other comparison. A threat lingered in her casual stance and Bestian took it seriously.

He hesitated, wondering if this woman was working with Delora, wondering just how important this amulet was.

It's just a piece of jewelry, he tried to convince himself.

"I believe you have something for me, from a mutual friend," the woman said without introduction, her voice as soft as a lute.

Bestian managed a smile, pleased that his voice did not show his fear. "My wife brings it momentarily," he answered, wishing he did not have to involve Altessa, but he had been warned by the Lady Delora not to remove the amulet from his wife.

He hoped Altessa would understand. It was for their future. The Southern Coalition could destroy everything they believed in and he needed to ensure a safe place for his family to grow up.

Altessa walked in and Bestian sat straighter, his breath still taken away every time he saw her, stately, beautiful, and meant to wear a crown. Her chiseled features, which some people might call harsh, reminded him of the strength and eternity of the mountains, and her eyes, as blue as her sister's, were bottomless pools he could lose himself in to the end of eternity.

She wasn't happy with recent events, especially after losing her family so suddenly. He knew she was angry with him for giving her sister away without her approval, but still her eyes softened at the admiration she must have seen in him. She loved him, he knew, and once this was over, he would love her as a husband should.

No more secrets, no more lies.

The woman from the Circle was observing them closely when he turned to face her.

"Altessa," Bestian said softly to his wife, while still keeping a regal air. "This woman from the Circle says she would like to see your amulet. Would you be so kind as to accommodate our guest?"

Please cooperate, Altessa! Surely she too saw the thinly veiled threat in the woman's eyes?

Altessa looked the woman over closely, apparently not intimidated by her.

"I'm afraid I can't do that," she said, her voice proud and steady.

Bestian felt whatever little control he had slip from his hands. Before he could find the saliva with which to speak, the woman spoke, the lute-like quality of her voice now chilling his bones.

"Why not?" She took a step towards Altessa. Bestian clutched the arms of his throne.

Altessa did not look down or flinch. Bestian could only tell she was afraid by her right hand, which had risen to cover her belly, and their unborn child.

"Because I gave it away," she said matter-of-factly, as though discussing the weather. The woman did not react with the anger Delora would have wielded. Instead, she smiled, and she too replied casually.

"To your sister, no doubt. It doesn't matter. Delora will wait for her in Rashim. Meanwhile, I believe I could use a little sport by seeing if I can catch your sister before she reaches her prince."

She spoke so casually that it took Bestian a moment to realize the impact of her words. Cassara was heading into a trap, and might not even be given the chance to reach it. But he didn't care, as long as he and Altessa were not involved. As long as they were left alone, by Delora, by the Circle, by the Southern Coalition...alone, with only Edoline's farmers to worry about.

"You monster!" Altessa screamed, grabbing the woman's arm as the Circle witch strolled past her to leave. The woman turned quickly and slapped Altessa, throwing her across the room onto the floor, still clinging to a ripped piece of the woman's robe.

The woman examined the tear in her robe's sleeve. She then frowned at Altessa. Without saying a word, she raised her arm. Bestian had seen this gesture before, on the first night he had met Delora and made to see her point of view.

He barely noticed Altessa rising to face the blow standing, so quickly did he move.

"No!" he screamed, seconds before the sound was lost in the inferno that engulfed him, and no more sound escaped him. With his last moments of sight, he saw Altessa running towards him, screaming what he thought was his name, but he could not hear her words through his burnt, decayed ears.

Then the pain was gone and he heard her clearly, her voice like a song carrying him to the Afterfate.

"Why were you at the manor the day of the attack?" Cassara heard Carsyn ask, his voice clear and steady. She was still in the carriage, Kaden having sternly warned them to stay there. But when Carsyn spoke those words, she disentangled herself from Emala's arms and leapt out of the carriage. She heard Emala speak words she never thought she would hear her maid say, even more surprised to hear her scramble after her.

Kaden was immediately at her side. Cassara ignored him, focused on the person that had stopped their carriage.

"Avarielle," Cassara said, feeling some relief, although not quite certain why.

The warrior simply smiled at her, her arms held loosely by her sides. Carsyn was standing before her with his sword raised. His stance spoke of experience and left little doubt that he would move as quickly as any other swordsman, despite his age.

Nobody spoke for a moment, and Cassara stopped approaching Avarielle just behind Carsyn's protective sword. Not that she didn't trust the warrior woman, but rather she feared Carsyn's reaction were she to move.

Avarielle was the first one to speak, shifting her feet, her piercing eyes focused on Cassara.

"I'm sorry," she whispered at first, then repeated it more loudly. "I'm sorry. I should have known there was another exit, but I didn't. And I couldn't find them. I looked, but they just...vanished."

She relaxed her shoulders, as though she had just freed herself from a heavy burden. Carsyn's stance did not change.

"You looked for them?" Cassara asked softly.

Avarielle shrugged. "They got away, and that upsets me." She softened a bit. "Besides, they never did find your little brother, did they?"

The last words cut through Cassara and all she could manage to do was shake her head.

"What do you know of this, Westlander?" Carsyn asked, his voice a soft growl. Cassara was surprised to hear this tone from her lazy and jovial guard, and was even more surprised to see Kaden hanging back, letting Carsyn handle the main line of defense, so to speak. It was not like Kaden to trust another, even Carsyn, with her defense.

Avarielle focused on Carsyn for the first time, a mischievous grin spreading on her lips. "More than you, apparently."

Carsyn took another step forward, holding his sword higher. Having seen the speed at which Avarielle could draw her sword, she had no doubt that Carsyn did not stand a chance. She stepped between them, which elicited a deeper growl from Carsyn's throat.

"Calm down, Carsyn. She's a friend, and I don't appreciate you brandishing a weapon in her face." She spoke calmly and with authority, but still the words did not pierce as much as she would have liked, and Carsyn only relented by lowering his blade. He did not sheathe it.

Cassara shot Kaden a quick look. He met it impassively, offering no advice, no hint of an idea. She sighed.

"You fought in the Western Wars?" Cassara asked Carsyn softly, his face reflecting old pain and anger. She wondered what had happened then, what had made so many men she respected and loved seek sanctuary in the forgotten lands of her ancestors.

He nodded.

"Carsyn, I appreciate that you must have seen horrors there, but you have to understand that it was over twenty years ago, and Avarielle was too young to have fought, if she was even born." She felt silly lecturing him, knowing he was painfully more aware of these details than she was.

Still, it seemed to help, and he nodded gruffly to Avarielle, who returned the gesture.

Carsyn gave a guarded grin. "She's right, you're too young. If that even matters," he added as an afterthought. Still, his sword remained unsheathed.

"I was born during the war, actually," Avarielle said. "Right before my mother was burned to death by an eastern raiding party," she added as an afterthought.

Cassara felt the blood drain from her face. Were they actually going to fight over a war that had taken place over twenty years ago?

"But that's in the past too, right?" she asked, raising an eyebrow as she eyed Carsyn's sword.

Carsyn looked down at his blade, his hand shaking a bit, the onslaught of memories that had grabbed him at the sight of the red-haired, piercing-eyed woman finally leaving him.

"It is," Carsyn whispered, his words hanging heavy in the air with unspoken memories. Cassara could only imagine what her guard had been through, what horrors he had witnessed and friends he had lost. She wondered if that was where he had met Klar and Kaden.

He sheathed his sword slowly, his age showing once more in his slow, deliberate movements. She placed a hand on his arm before quickly removing it.

"I take it you didn't come here just to apologize?" Cassara asked, turning to Avarielle.

The warrior gave a short laugh. "You are pretty cunning for a sheltered princess!" she exclaimed. Cassara was unsure whether it was meant to be a compliment or an insult, but she chose to believe the former.

"I think I have an idea of how the Eloms vanished," Avarielle said, every aspect of her stance changing. Gone was the jest in her eyes, the bend of her knee, the relaxed arms. Everyone around her, even Emala, seemed to pick up on the warrior's serious tone and they too straightened slightly, as if to be able to bear the new load they were about to be given.

Cassara wasn't sure whether to ask how they had vanished or why there was even the need to debate this, but she was spared the indecision when Avarielle continued to speak.

"At first I just didn't understand," she began, her voice picking up speed. "There weren't any tracks leading away from the manor, and they certainly hadn't gone back through the nest, or we would have seen them." Carsyn swore softly and Emala drew in a breath. So now they knew where Cassara had been on the night of the attack. Kaden did not react and Cassara wondered if he had already figured it out.

"It just didn't make sense," Avarielle continued, pacing as she spoke, oblivious to the reactions she had just elicited. "Eloms don't just vanish into thin air. Well, then again, they don't attack in an organized fashion, usually." Avarielle grinned, as though she had made a joke, but quickly thought better of it and continued.

"So I figured it was actually quite a simple explanation. Something we ourselves had witnessed that very night,

Cassara," Avarielle ended gravely, looking at Cassara, waiting for her to jump to the conclusion she had.

Cassara shook her head, feeling the fatigue and fear from that night invade her again, her mind and limbs weighed down by the memories.

"Teleportation, Cassara!" Avarielle exclaimed, exasperated.

Cassara shook her head. "Teleportation? But that would mean the Circle was involved. Why would the Circle attack my family?"

Gravity tugged at Avarielle's words. "The Circle, or someone from the Circle."

Cassara's eyes shot up, meeting Avarielle's gaze, her mind following the warrior's stream of thought this time.

"Shirina?" she whispered, half-question, half-statement. Some of it made some sense. The sorceress had been there that day, scouting the area. And she had admitted to being aware of the second exit to the nest.

But still...Shirina had helped them, and she hadn't attacked them. And Cassara had to admit to herself that she didn't want Shirina to be involved in her family's death. She didn't know if it was because she actually liked the woman, or because she couldn't live with the knowledge of having been so close to her family's murderer and yet not stopped her.

"She helped us," Cassara said, her voice seeming small and insignificant.

Avarielle shook her head. "Barely. And she admitted she knew that there was a second entrance. What if she was just a diversion, to keep us away? I'm sure she wanted something from you, Cassara, and I wouldn't be surprised if it had something to do with your magic." Seeing the anguish on Cassara's face, Avarielle softened a bit. "Well, maybe you're right. Maybe she was just facilitating something or someone. We'll probably never know now, anyway."

Avarielle shrugged and decided to drop the subject.

"I thought you should know." She looked at Cassara's small entourage. "I don't think this is over yet. I think they wanted something, and I'm not convinced they have it. Just be careful."

She hesitated for a moment, taking one quick look at Carsyn. Then she turned around and vanished into the woods.

"Wait!" Cassara called after her. The soft sigh of the wind in the trees around her was all that she received as an answer.

Wait, I want to come with you, to look for Jayden. But her mind failed to convince her feet, which remained firmly rooted in place.

"It's better to be rid of her, anyways," Carsyn said gruffly as he began climbing the carriage. "She looked and sounded like trouble. Crazy, too."

Kaden half-nodded, his attentions focused on where the warrior had vanished, before climbing beside Carsyn. "Get in, Cassara, Emala. We'd best get out of these woods." The last words lay heavily on Cassara. There was little time left to make her decision and make it easier for her entourage to vanish in Kosel.

The two climbed aboard. Cassara looked out the window, hoping to spot the warrior.

"She did sound crazy, didn't she? What could they possibly want with Edoline? And with us?" She gave a short laugh.

Still, they made quicker time on that day than on any other day, and when they set up camp that night, both Kaden and Carsyn stood watch.

TWO DAYS after encountering Avarielle they set camp for the last time in Kosel. The next half day would see them through the forested barrier. No one spoke of Eloms or of the mention of Cassara's magic.

At times she doubted they wanted to know and at other times she imagined that perhaps they knew more than she believed. Kaden's silence on the recently raised issues proved to be most perturbing to her, since he had never struck her as someone to blindly accept anything. Even her father's orders had sometimes warranted some discussion.

She grimaced as a splinter jabbed her finger while she stacked the wood for the fire. It would be another long night. The closer they came to leaving the forest, the more relaxed they became, all but Kaden, who had kept a closer eye on his ward ever since she had called after Avarielle.

There was still half a day after tonight, half a day for her to decide whether she would pursue the Eloms or simply accept her fate and continue towards Rashim.

Half a day to choose the rest of her life as well as the fates of Emala, Carsyn, Kaden and Jayden. Either way, someone would suffer, and there seemed to be no escaping that. She idly wondered if Bestian had sent troops to look for Jayden, but she doubted it.

Cassara hit the flint hard and the flames leapt to life, warding against the rising darkness of the evening. Spring was at an end, and the longer days of summer were proving to be a blessing and a curse for this journey. They were making faster time but, often, it seemed too fast for Cassara to make the decision she needed to make. She wished everything would stop and she would have a few days to mull over her choices.

"I've never had to choose anything in my life," she whispered, her hands reaching out to enjoy the fire's heat.

"What's that?" Emala asked as she sat by Cassara, holding a few supplies to make their supper. It seemed tonight would be stew, and Cassara grabbed a few carrots and began cutting.

"Nothing, Emala," Cassara said, smiling as the woman grunted. In the past week, if nothing else good had come of this, she had become closer to her three companions than she had ever been. And although her indecision was tearing her apart, it was a comfort to know that she hesitated to leave because her loyalty and friendship to them was just as strong as theirs was to her.

Emala, who had been chopping onions and potatoes with vigor, interrupted her work for a moment and announced bluntly: "I didn't pack the blue dress."

So sudden was the confession that Cassara simply stared at her.

Emala's face flushed from more than just the fire's heat. "I thought we could buy some fabric, and I could make you a better one," she said. "But now I don't know what you'll wear to go to court on the first day, so I think we should stop in the next town and use just a bit of money for some fabric."

Carsyn, who had just joined them, grunted from where he sat, poking the fire with a stick and sending embers scattering towards the celestial canopy, where stars were just beginning to appear.

"Oh, you old grump, you've just forgotten how to appreciate a beautiful woman in a beautiful dress," Emala shot back at him, the laughter in her eyes defying the harshness of her words.

"I have not," Carsyn replied, drawing himself up. "I've just seen your sewing skills, that's all!"

"As long as I can breathe in it," Cassara said, her hands coming together in dreamy supplication, "I will call it the most beautiful dress in the world!"

And so the evening began, their discomfort quickly forgotten as jests were thrown back and forth, the fire resupplied three times before talk of sleep even infiltrated the conversation. Cassara doubted Kaden had mentioned her choice to the others, but it seemed that they too were restless, and could feel something was not quite right. Even Kaden joined the three after a while, although he often cast wary glances at the surrounding woods.

"We can take turns with the watch," Kaden said as bedding was pulled out. Although Cassara and Emala could sleep in the carriage, they would be cramped and uncomfortable, and chose to sleep under the stars with the guards. Besides, they already spent enough time in there.

"I can take a watch too," Cassara said, looking towards Kaden, hoping her look reflected what she felt. She did not intend to leave without telling him, but on this night, she needed some time to think things over.

Kaden hesitated for a moment before nodding.

"I'll take the first one," Cassara said, standing from where she had been placing her bedding.

"Fine by me, let the young ones handle this late night folly," Carsyn mumbled as he cocooned himself in his blankets. He was snoring within seconds.

"They don't make guards the way they used too," Emala said, looking inquisitively from Cassara to Kaden before lying down as well.

"The past few nights have been long for you and Carsyn," Cassara argued. "And besides, I can always sleep in the carriage during the day."

Seeing Kaden's hesitation, Cassara placed her hand on his shoulder and held his eyes with hers. "Trust me, Kaden."

Kaden smiled briefly at that, bowing slightly before

heading to his own bedding, giving Carsyn a small kick for good measure.

Cassara smiled at the odd show of camaraderie before sitting by the fire, paying as much attention as she could to the sounds of the forest around her, but only able to hear her own indecision.

Cassara woke up with a start, realizing she had fallen asleep on her watch. She was leaning against a tree, and from what she could see of the stars, she guessed she had only slept for half an hour. Enough time for the fire to die down. Only smoldering embers remained in the darkness before her.

She squinted in the half light, her eyes not hampered so much by the darkness surrounding her as by her own fatigue. She wanted to stretch, but dared not move, haunted by childhood fears of winged monsters lurking outside her window, ready to strike when they spied one movement.

Or more recent and real monsters, she thought as she forced herself to look around cautiously. The safety of her friends was a responsibility she had claimed, and the last thing she wanted was to let them down. Slowly she moved her head, her neck stiff from sleeping while sitting against a tree.

She had barely stirred when movement caught her peripheral vision. She jumped up, jolted by fear, when she realized it was only Kaden, carrying more wood for the fire.

"Were you one of my guards," Kaden said, placing the wood within the containing rocks, "you would be out of my service by now."

Cassara felt the wild, frightened energies that had grasped her seconds earlier dissipate, and she realized that she was clutching her amulet with her right hand, instead of her dagger. If Kaden noticed, he didn't say anything.

She managed a smile. "If that were true, Carsyn would have been gone a long time ago." Kaden laughed gruffly at that, the sound comforting in the cold night. He leaned down to blow on the embers and coax them to life, but then seemed to think better of it. Instead, he sat beside Cassara on the ground.

"You can light the fire," he whispered. Cassara wanted to joke that of course she could light the fire using flint, but his set features were deadly serious.

Show me what you can do, the words lay heavy and unspoken in the air. Cassara looked down for a moment, slowly reaching up and pulling the amulet free. Without looking at Kaden, she moved forward to place herself before the wood on her knees, amulet in the palm of her hand. Still coursing with adrenaline, Cassara's hand shook, and so she put her left hand underneath it to steady it, wondering if Kaden would see her posture as one of imploration or of invocation.

She cleared her mind. This time, instead of repeating the Circle's mantra, she simply focused on the lack of fire before her. She closed her eyes and took a deep breath, willing her energies to fill the amulet. She could feel its soft warmth warding the cold from her fingers and face, and knew that it was glowing before she had even opened her eyes.

Seeing the glow, her heart accelerated. She wondered when it would be disrupted by visions of branches in the wind. She took some deeper breaths, concentrating instead on Kaden, who was still very much alive and healthy, sitting behind her. She clung to thoughts of her childhood with him, as he taught her self-defense in the day and told her silly stories at night just to make her laugh. She thought of his kindness, his laughter, and drew strength from those as she called forth the magic to rise beyond the confines of the amulet.

White fires broke free, and she urged them towards the logs, some of the flames hitting the ground around it instead. The wood was bathed with the white fire, although Cassara found it difficult maintaining it on one section for longer than a few seconds, and she felt that her fire wasn't nearly as warm as it should be.

It seemed different than the fire on the first night she had discovered her magic. She forced her mind to conjure up warmth, uncertain how to proceed. She clung to Kaden's laughter, but it was suddenly broken as visions of his older self haunted her instead. How he couldn't follow her in her adventures as he used to. How his laughter was less frequent now. And how he didn't tell her stories anymore, choosing solitude instead.

Ethereal, she thought. He was ethereal, and slowly vanishing, like her family had been, like she was, like Edoline was. As ethereal as the cold fire she was casting on the wood before her. In the moment it took to realize it existed, it could be gone just as quickly.

Branches swept her vision and she let out a cry of frustration as she felt the magic dissipate in their wake. The wood was as cold and dark as it had been before she began. Slowly, her hands came to rest on her lap, the amulet loosely clutched within them. She lowered her head, not wanting to turn around and face Kaden, not wanting to see the scars time had so plainly planted on his face, not wanting him to see the tears that thought had put on her own.

She forced a deep breath into her lungs, fatigue rushing through her body as she held back the panic that had gripped her heart. Did she really believe that her world, even the people she loved, were nothing more than smoke and shadows? That they were simply born to become casualties of time and consequence?

"You think too much," Kaden's voice shattered the stillness.

"What?" Cassara asked, turning around to face him.

"What?" Kaden said, gently mimicking her as he shook

his head. "You've been around Carsyn and Emala too much lately."

"I beg your pardon, then."

"I said you *think* too much," Kaden said, a slight grin on his face, and Cassara tried to break free of visions of younger days.

"I had heard you," Cassara said, biting every word, her fatigue dissipating. "What I would like to know, Lieutenant, is what exactly you mean, and how you might have come about that knowledge."

"Of course, Your Highness," he bowed his head. Cassara smiled, feeling the heaviness of the air dissipate as easily as her fatigue.

"What I mean is simply that, Cassara," Kaden said, his voice regaining composure. "You think too much of the magic, on how to make it grow, on how it should react and, inevitably, you become introspective and, even more inevitably, you become haunted by your own thoughts, feeding your energies to those instead of to the magic you're trying to create." He took a deep, dramatic breath before continuing. "In other words, it's easier to dwell on the past than it is to create, my dear. For what you're trying to do, you need to follow your gut, your emotions, to urge the magic in the right direction. Overthinking will simply paralyze you."

He paused, looking at the cold wood as though pondering something. Cassara wanted to ask how he knew this, but before the words escaped her mouth, he was moving, coming to sit beside her on the ground. He faced the logs instead of her.

"The Circle would have you believe that deep thoughts and control allow you to summon magic, and they're right, to a certain degree," Kaden said, his voice low and hypnotic, his gaze unwavering from the logs. "But the true strength of magic comes from emotions. Just like Graydon used his grief to block off the world of Elihor after they had betrayed his love. Great actions come from noble thoughts, yes, but true greatness and power come from deep and true emotions, unclouded by doubt or shame."

He paused, his eyes squinting for a moment. Green flames erupted from within the logs, before being replaced by less vibrant and calmer flames. She stared at them, open-mouthed, unable to turn away from the fire as she spoke.

"You did that?" she whispered, turning her head only enough to see him nod, his features drawn in pain by the fire's glow. She waited for his pain to subside before questioning him.

"Why did you never tell me you could use magic?"

He turned to her then and took a deep breath as if to focus. "For similar reasons you didn't tell me, Cassara. One, it's not normal for anyone outside of the Circle to practice any type of magic, and two, for that same reason, magic is looked upon with suspicion and fear, much like we all look at the Circle. It isn't something to discuss."

He paused. Cassara did not interrupt, waiting for him

to give her more information. But instead of offering her more, he asked a question, with a dangerous edge she had never heard in his voice before. "Do you think that Westlander was right, Cassara? Do you believe the Circle had something to do with the fall of your father?"

Cassara shook her head. "I don't know, Kaden. I have a hard time believing Shirina would betray us." She turned back towards the fire. "But, then again, it seems I know and understand very little of the world and the people I saw every day, much less of those I only met once."

The last was spoken with more reproach than she had intended. It had been Kaden's right not to mention the magic. Was she angry at him for keeping it a secret? Or was she simply angry at herself for having done the same thing?

Kaden sighed and chuckled a bit before speaking again. "You've more of your father than we like to speak of," he said softly. "How much do you want to know, Cassara?"

"I want to know enough," she said, unsure how else to word it. Kaden looked pensive for a moment before he spoke again.

"Green fire, the magic I use, is illegal magic, if you will. It was created by the Circle over twenty years ago, by putting a seed of magic in individuals who didn't have innate magical skills." Cassara looked at him, wondering what had been done to him, but Kaden smiled at her, a sad, tired smile. "It was out of choice, Cassara. I was over forty, had been a soldier all my life and it seemed I would never amount to anything. I had given up everything for my career, including the chance of having a family, and I was beginning to regret it.

"When I was approached by this initiative, I accepted quickly. Finally, I would make a difference." He paused, looking back towards the sleeping figures of Carsyn and Emala.

"I wasn't the only one. We were told that the Westlanders were planning to bring down the Wall and let loose demons upon the world. We were told that with our combined experience and magic, we could surely stop them before it was too late, while the Circle bought us a distraction with troops from the East."

Cassara's breath caught in her throat. A distraction? The war that had killed thousands on both sides of the border had been merely a distraction? Kaden continued, apparently unaware of her distress.

"Once the war was over, the Circle forbade us from ever using our magic again, threatening our families and futures if we did so. None of us were young, and we only wanted peace by then, so we accepted. But few of us were welcomed back into our old lives, since it was suspected that we had joined the Circle and had been tossed aside by them. A harvest had taken place not too long before, and no one wanted anything associated with the Circle near them."

He poked the fire with a stick, embers floating into the sky. "Only one man gave us a second chance, and that was your father, Cassara. The same man who had stopped the war, and the same one who made us promise never to use our magic again, and never to speak of our connection with the Circle."

He stopped intruding on the fire and turned to face Cassara. "I still don't know why your father did it, Cassara. But I do know that we gave him our word, and that most of my comrades kept that word until their death." He shrugged, as though to shed dark thoughts from his mind. "I thought you should know. That you deserved to know. Why Edoline was so withdrawn from the world."

His eyes flickered after speaking, wondering if he had said too much. It did not take long for Cassara to understand what he had implied.

"Was the Circle responsible for my mother's death?" she whispered, feeling cold despite the fire.

"I don't know, Cassara. But I do know that your father grew more frightened after that day, as if at any time the lives of all those he loved could be stolen from him. Instead of dismissing us, the cause of the Circle's ire with Edoline, he simply withdrew from those he loved."

His words seemed to come with more difficulty now. "Had we been certain it was the Circle, I truly believe we would have left Edoline, in gratitude to your father. But we were never certain, and we remained to protect the family, just in case. We had promised the king we would never use our magic but, while waiting, we simply grew older, until all that might have saved the king was the very magic he had forbidden us from using."

Cassara looked into the fire, the traveler's song playing softly in her mind, a tune she could not stop, as though it was all that remained of her childhood. Even Kaden seemed far away now and she felt trapped in a darkness she could not understand or break.

"If this was the Circle's doing...if we had not waited to grow old, if we had not waited until our magic was slowed by age and too difficult to wield in battle, we might have been able to protect him, and the young prince," he whispered, years of regret clinging to each word.

"What would you have done, Kaden?" she whispered as she gently turned him to face her. "Would you have destroyed the entire Circle, just in case they were responsible and planning more attacks?"

Kaden smiled weakly and nodded. "Just like you would destroy all of the Eloms in the world, by yourself if necessary."

She wanted to say more, but found she couldn't. Still, as they watched the fire grow smaller and the night wore on in silence, she felt like she had gained some peace.

The fate of her family had not rested solely on her, and she did not carry the grief and pain alone. Circumstances, time and decisions kept them apart, but the results united them.

Still, she felt it was easier for her to accept the consequences of her actions, than it was for Kaden to accept the consequences of his inaction.

"It wouldn't have made a difference," she whispered as much to herself as to him. But in the shadows of twelve deaths and on a journey of exile, she doubted she convinced either.

WHATEVER CHOICE CASSARA was contemplating by the fire as dawn slowly streaked the sky was ripped away from her as she caught a strange, pungent smell on the wind.

Carsyn, who had been awake for the past two hours, theatrically yawning and stretching every five minutes, raised his head in mild interest, but did not reach for his sword. Emala and Kaden still slept, the maid not having stirred once in the night except to grumble at Carsyn to be quiet and let those that still had hope get their beauty sleep.

Cassara, on the other hand, was on her feet before the smell had fully registered, reaching for her dagger before thinking better of it and pulling her amulet free. Carsyn, surprised by his princess' movements, quickly followed her lead, pulling his short sword free.

He walked to Kaden's side and kicked him awake. Kaden woke up and jumped to his feet, sword drawn. Carsyn next headed to Emala, her grumbling ending the second she saw the two guards' swords out. She turned as pale as a sheet and followed Carsyn's whispered instructions to hide in the carriage, glancing back at Cassara with a look of supplication.

The smell became stronger.

"Are those the same demons?" Kaden whispered, to

which Cassara only nodded, not trusting her voice. The two guards flanked her and Cassara willed the amulet to life. It flared with light.

Don't overthink, Cassara repeated to herself, wondering if Kaden, and presumably Carsyn, would use their forbidden magic to save her and themselves. After seeing the look of pain on Kaden's drawn features following his use of magic last night, she doubted he ever would again. She wondered if he could even summon his green fires quickly enough to be effective in battle.

She tightened her fist around the glowing amulet as the trees of Kosel seemed to give a groan of pain in the cool wind.

Without further warning, two dark creatures broke free from the surrounding trees and attacked, their long claws slashing down on Carsyn's arm before any of them had the chance to react. The old guard went down with a scream of pain, but through some strength Cassara did not know he possessed, he maintained his grip on his sword and hacked at the nearest creature's legs. He didn't inflict much damage, but he did succeed in making it retreat.

The second creature targeted Cassara and half-ran, half-leapt towards her. She was too distracted by Carsyn's fall to notice. Kaden's speed saved her. He threw himself before her, absorbing the blow with his sword, only to have the claws slide down his blade and gash him, bright blood streaking down his face as he fell.

"Kaden!" she screamed, her fear replaced by anger in

an instant. She felt the amulet come to life, and grabbed at its magic, throwing it in the face of the creature looming over the fallen Kaden. White fires burst all around it and a guttural sound escaped its throat as it backed away and fell, as dead as the fires that had consumed it. Cassara fell to her knees, tired and stunned. She had done it! She had killed it using her magic!

Kaden struggled to stand. Cassara wanted to help him, but the second creature was coming back. Carsyn, on his knees with his left arm dangling uselessly by his side, raised his sword to brace for the attack he would not be able to stop.

Cassara took a step towards him, clinging to her anger, trying to find any strength left in her to repel the creature, yet all of her energy had been spent in her first burst of magic.

"Carsyn!" she screamed, pulling her dagger free, not sure what she could do but certain she would try. She ran towards him, but she was too slow.

Carsyn's blade reflected the first rays of the sun when a battle cry broke through the forest and white flames consumed the creature.

The creature fell to reveal Avarielle standing behind it, her blade, cleansed by its own fires, quickly sheathed again. Carsyn, bleeding profusely from his arm now, managed to grin up at Avarielle before falling over. Avarielle caught him before he hit the ground. Without a word, she began bandaging his wound. Cassara turned to tend to Kaden, but Emala had already exited the carriage and was gently speaking to the old guard.

In a rare moment of clarity, Cassara saw the choice before her as it had stood since she was a child. To stay or to leave. Even while escaping to the village, she had pondered the same choice. And she had always chosen to stay. But now, by Carsyn's bloodied arm and Kaden's deeply cut cheek, armed with a magic she was certain could make a difference, Cassara knew that whatever she chose, she would never be the only one to pay. If she left, they might be accused of kidnapping or killing her. But if she stayed, it seemed the dark creatures would continue to hunt her, and their hunt would likely end in one, if not all of their deaths.

She looked down at the amulet, her mind clear, her decision made.

With a single wish, the amulet's magic flared to life, warm against her palm. It was hers to make a difference with. Not to simply be hunted for it, but to hunt with it.

It was time to stop being a princess, and start being the queen she might never become.

It was time to take control of her destiny.

IT WAS NEARING noon when Cassara finished packing the few belongings she would be bringing with her. She could hear Carsyn, Emala and Avarielle laughing from the fire, and was not surprised when Kaden joined her on the other side of the carriage. The wound on his face was red and angry, but Emala would take good care of it, and the infection would subside.

"Kaden," she began, unsure how to approach the subject. She loved him so much she never wanted to part from him, but that same love forbade her from even considering his joining her on this quest.

Kaden didn't give her the time to voice her thoughts. "The three of us will be back at the last settlement we crossed, in one of the hidden houses," he said. "Call for us when you need us."

Cassara smiled up at him, swallowing back the tears. "I will," she whispered, and hugged him. He smiled at her, a hint of sadness sparkling in his eyes, before grabbing her bag and bringing it back to camp. The three stood up from around the campfire when she joined them.

"What a waste," Emala whispered, shaking her head back and forth. "What a sad waste of a beautiful princess."

Cassara embraced her, to be rewarded by a bone-crushing hug. "I expect that dress to be ready for me when I come back," Cassara said as they broke free from each other. Emala grinned and nodded. "And not too tight, please!"

"Corset back it is," Emala said. Cassara forced a small smile to cross her lips, for Emala's sake. Making a dress, as simple as it was, would give her purpose. Until she could find another.

"Be careful, old man," Cassara said teasingly to Carsyn as he came towards her, his arm wrapped closely to his body. "Kaden thinks we'll slow you down too much. Speak for yourself, I told him." He paused and swallowed hard. She placed a hand on his good shoulder and squeezed it.

To Kaden she said nothing, all of their farewells already made.

She turned to all three and pointed at the carriage. "The dowry is yours," Cassara said, and raised her hand to stop their arguments. "You'll need the money to live, and to live well."

"Besides," she added softly, smiling at Kaden and Carsyn. "Until I call for your services again, consider these your retirement funds, and enjoy them. You've both earned it."

Carsyn's face broke into a wide grin and Kaden shook his head.

"We should go," Avarielle said from behind Cassara, the warrior looking impatient to get moving. Cassara nodded and picked up her bag.

She turned to follow Avarielle, feeling that all had been said and done.

"Westlander," Kaden called after them. Avarielle turned, eyebrow raised questioningly.

"What is your name?" he asked softly.

She hesitated for a second before answering with pride. "Avarielle Grayloft."

Kaden nodded, as though not surprised to hear her last name. Cassara wondered what significance this name held for him.

"Does your family's oath still stand?" he asked, squinting his eyes slightly.

"It does."

Kaden nodded and then winked at Cassara when he saw her confused look.

"Let's go," Avarielle said, turning away from the three. Cassara stood still a moment longer, but with nothing left to say, she turned around and followed Avarielle into the forest, the last noise from her beloved Edoline she was to hear for a long time being Emala's lament on the waste of a princess.

10

Altessa Edoline Bestian sat on a cold bench in the Courtyard of Stars, embroidering a bathrobe for her husband, the summer's promise of heat so far being a false one. Pricking her finger again for lack of attention, she bit back a small cry and continued drawing the needle through the wool, grateful that the dark purple fabric would hide the traces her blood would otherwise have left.

She scolded herself for not paying enough attention, her usually steady hands trembling and difficult to control, resulting in disheveled needlework her concentration was too weak to fix.

Tears welled in her eyes. She would not cry, not now, not with the guards just outside the courtyard. Her husband still lay in bed, alive by a strength even she had not known he possessed. His skin was burned almost beyond recognition, his features, which she had once found handsome, vanished under ravaged skin, ointments and bandages. His breathing only grew shallower as the days progressed and Altessa suspected that he would wear the robe she was currently embroidering not to his chambers but to his burial.

It had been a week since the attack, and today was the first day that she had been allowed by Bestian's guards to exit the manor. She had spent one week trapped with her dying husband, the only sound in the room being his shallow, broken breathing, which even her singing could not disguise. Never before had she felt such despair and loss of control, and she hoped it would end soon, one way or the other.

She looked around the courtyard, the fountain of the broken horse now gone. She found that she missed the constant gurgling. In some strange way, that sound had meant to her that her parents would love each other always. One night, a month after Alayna had died, a month after Altessa believed her father would forever remain locked in his study unable to grieve, King Alexavier had brutally battered the horse statue, pouring all of his grief into destroying it.

It had proved to Altessa that love lived beyond life, a fact that was always reinforced by the creaking steps to her father's chambers, and by the peace he had found after that night. Even if the sight of Cassara's long blond hair was too much for him to bear at times.

Still, she thought as she breathed in the cool air, *I wonder if I will feel that way about Anesh Bestian once he is gone.* The thought did not sting her as it once would have, but she did prick her finger again. She lowered the embroidery and laid it on her lap.

"My Lady," she heard someone say, surprised by the kindness of the voice. The guards that Bestian had brought from Laror were not the most respectful, and she had always suspected they weren't really under her husband's command, a fear that had been confirmed last week.

She looked up and saw the guard that had been introduced to her by Cassara, Gragor. He was the youngest and newest of the guards of Edoline, one of the few to have survived the night of the attack, even though the wounds on his face looked like they would never heal.

Altessa smiled up at him, remaining seated so as to not draw any further attention to herself from Anesh's guards.

"I heard you needed some supplies from town for your embroidery," he said, his voice smooth, only his eyes betraying his nerves as he cast a wary glance towards the guards posted just outside the entrance.

She smiled reassuringly at him. "Yes, Gragor, thank you for running this errand. I realize this is hardly a part of your duties."

Gragor bowed slightly. "Without a maid to tend to you, and your husband having taken...ill, my Lady, it is my pleasure to assist you in any way I can." His voice was steady.

"Thank you. I need some more thread please, and red

dye, as well. I wrote it down on this list for your convenience, Gragor."

"Thank you, my Lady." He bowed deeply. When he stood, he allowed his eyes to meet hers for only a moment before taking the piece of paper and placing it securely inside his coat.

"I will return by nightfall," he replied softly. She nodded, knowing the guards would hear and his words would reinforce the rumors traveling through the corridors of the manor that she and Gragor were having an affair.

She did not care. She watched him go, the last loyal guard she had found in Edoline, the only survivor who had stayed after the attack, and who had taken the chance to tell her that his loyalties remained with Edoline, not Laror.

She heard his horse whinny and the hooves wildly beating towards town, to be lost in the sound of the surf. He had not been challenged and would not be, since it was not the first errand he had run for his queen. Despite the guards' merciless teasing, Gragor had never once faltered in his loyalty, and she knew that he would succeed today, as well.

Only when he did not return at nightfall would they grow suspicious, but Altessa's tears would make them believe he had simply left a demanding lover, and they would be glad to be rid of the one amongst them that did not bow to the same flag. They would never suspect that he was riding towards Massir, to save her little sister from a marriage she did not want, and maybe win help for the new queen of Edoline, held captive in her own kingdom as her husband breathed his last.

———

CASSARA CROUCHED IN THE SHADOWS, her bow, a weapon she had only rudimentary training with, clutched tightly against her breast. Her prey was in sight. A rabbit, one of the last remaining in the area, twitched its ears only a few trees away from her.

Breathe, aim, shoot, she repeated in her mind as she extended the bow and pulled back with her right hand, arrow nocked and secured with her fingers. She stood, her legs complaining at the movement after having crouched for so long. She ignored them, forcing her knees to follow the movements of her weapon.

Gazing down the shaft of the arrow, she let it loose. Before it could reach its target, a cracking branch sent the animal scurrying for safety, her arrow piercing the land right where the rabbit had been instants earlier.

"Nice shot, Cassara!" Avarielle walked out from the woods behind Cassara, clapping her hands.

"Why did you let it get away?" Cassara said, not bothering to hide her frustration. "We haven't eaten anything today. We need to eat to be ready before the Eloms come out tonight!"

She paused, out of breath and shaking from hunger and anger.

Avarielle grinned and gave Cassara an incredulous look. "Do you really think that scrawny thing would have been enough to feed us both?"

Cassara shook her head. "Maybe not, but it would have been better than nothing. And it's the only game we've spotted all day."

Avarielle shrugged and started walking, leaving Cassara with little choice but to follow. As far as Cassara could tell, the past three days had taken them almost out of Kosel, near the borders of Rashim and the Maple Mountains. She still had no idea where Avarielle was taking her. Most of the previous days having been spent on training with the bow and tracking, skills that had been touched on but largely neglected in her upbringing. Not that she had ever needed them before.

"It's a loopy situation, that's all," Avarielle called back to her, not once breaking her stride. Cassara followed silently, concentrating on matching the warrior's speed without tripping.

"Most of the game has fled, since Eloms lurk here," she continued without pausing for breath, although Cassara could barely catch hers. "But we need food to have the energy to kill these Eloms, right?"

Not expecting an answer, she continued, "So our only solution is finding decent food and maybe even a room for after our nightly escapade."

She didn't need to turn around for Cassara to imagine the curve of her lips.

"But...we don't have any money!" Cassara said between breaths.

"Because you had to give it all away," Avarielle said, stopping so abruptly that Cassara bumped into her. Avarielle ignored the impact and pointed ahead towards a thicket of pine trees.

Cassara opened her mouth to ask her what she was pointing at, when she noticed that there was a building up ahead. In fact, there were several of them, nestled in the pines, with paths created from their fallen needles.

"Hidden in plain view is sort of Kosel's slogan," Avarielle said, obviously pleased that Cassara had spotted the buildings without her help.

"I know an innkeeper here who'll barter work for food," she said, beginning to walk at a much more reasonable pace. Cassara followed, looking around at the buildings, a few souls wandering about. It struck her how pretty this place would be in full daylight, without the stretched shadows. In a few hours those same shadows would unite to form the night, and Eloms would come roaming.

"Why don't we warn these people?" Cassara asked as she reached Avarielle. The warrior merely shook her head.

"It'll send panic if not disbelief, and maybe a poor attempt at defense that'll only draw unwanted attention to them. Believe me, Cassara, it's better that we handle it."

Cassara nodded, wondering if she could handle the fight. Thankfully, she had proven skilled with the bow, but she was still too slow to draw for it to make a great difference.

"Hope you don't mind washing dishes," Avarielle grinned at Cassara as she stopped in front a tall, unmarked building.

"Wash dishes?" Cassara asked in disbelief. "Is that really the best trade you can do?"

Avarielle's eyebrow shot up in surprise. "Oh, you have a better idea?"

It was Cassara's turn to grin. "If nothing else, being a princess will teach you the art of negotiating." She looked sternly at Avarielle, adding in the same tone the warrior had often used on Cassara: "Watch and learn, Avarielle."

Avarielle shook her head, a smile nonetheless gracing her features as she followed Cassara into the dark inn.

***

CASSARA GENTLY RAN her finger down the flute, the dryness of the wood crying out for a much-needed oiling. She sat on a chair set on a table, the only place in the inn that elevated her above the patrons, which were thankfully out in great numbers.

Avarielle sat in a corner at the bar, looking at Cassara with curiosity, an odd contrast in the dark room. Candles flickered as the innkeeper lit more to ward off the darkness. Cassara smiled at him gratefully when he brought a few candles to the table at her feet.

Without introduction, taking a deep breath, Cassara

launched into a playful tune a villager of Edoline had taught her when she was barely fourteen and already escaping the confines of the manor.

The residents of the unnamed village of Kosel picked up the tune quickly. A couple of the men even began to sing. Cassara had never heard the lyrics of this song before, and she would have never guessed them to be so lurid and downright vile. She blushed as she played, but was still pleased that the patrons seemed to be enjoying the song. Most of all Avarielle, who was laughing at the bar.

Victory occurred when the first patron tossed a coin on the table. A single bronze coin, but it was only the beginning. She picked up the tempo, to the singers' delight, and soon many more coins followed.

The song ended to clapping, cheering and lewd calls, and Cassara began gathering her earnings. Not enough for a meal and a room, but a few more songs would remedy that.

"Okay, I'm convinced," Avarielle said as she approached, grinning at the sight of Cassara's earnings. "First you manage to convince the innkeeper to let you play, then you convince the patrons to give you money! This should get us a meal in no time!"

Cassara pocketed the coins and, still on the table, stood up and stared down at her companion. "You mean this will buy *me* a meal in no time."

Avarielle's mouth opened and closed a few times,

much to Cassara's satisfaction, before the warrior broke out in laughter, a bit to her disappointment.

"I suppose that's revenge for making you lose that rabbit! Well, pick up the tempo, princess, and see how I'll help you gain *our* wages."

Cassara raised an eyebrow as she sat back down. "Oh? Any requests to help you fulfill such a bold claim?"

"Anything you'd like," Avarielle challenged.

Cassara grinned before bringing her flute to her lips and letting the melody break free, complex and vigorous, much to the delight of the crowd.

Avarielle walked to the side of the table, slowly removing her coat, her weapons and boots. Cassara felt a slight moment of panic, tripping on a note, wondering if Avarielle believed the lurid tones of the previous song were a natural part of her repertoire.

The warrior paused, standing by the table, her head cocked sideways as she listened intently, and her drumming fingers creating tremors more disturbing for Cassara than the entire crowd's combined movements. What exactly was she planning to do?

Cassara finished the first refrain and engaged the second stanza when Avarielle went into action, her body moving with every rhythm, adding a nuance entirely her own yet perfectly matched to Cassara's style.

The appearance of a skilled dancer only brought more cheers, to the point where Cassara wondered if they could even hear the music. She picked up the pace, throwing in extra harmonies to see how well Avarielle's feet kept up, and was amazed and pleased to see the warrior gracefully meet her challenge.

The song's end drew near and Avarielle's steps grew lighter, as though she might fly away with any of the rising notes. Cassara ended the song, for fear she might lose her companion to the ecstasy of the music. Although Avarielle ended at the same time, her body seemed to have difficulty letting go of the rhythm.

"Not bad," Cassara said when Avarielle grinned up at her, only to be rewarded by a nasty look.

Patrons brought the coins afterwards, having been too enthralled by the performance to think of it before. Once the coins were collected and they were assured of enough money for their stay, Avarielle looked questioningly at Cassara.

"They say three's a lucky number in the West."

Cassara smiled at Avarielle, feeling a bit drunk on the success of the evening, and climbed back on the table as patrons cheered, convincing her once and for all that Kosel was in dire need of more entertainment.

She played a softer tune this time, to calm the villagers' spirits and prepare them for a quieter evening. Avarielle followed the melody without pause, arms arching up when the notes elevated, to then lower at their mournful end.

Watching her carefully, Cassara realized that Avarielle's movements were very similar to her fighting style. Only a tiny delay existed before Avarielle followed a note struck by Cassara, just as there would be in her reaction to an enemy's attack. Her arms, legs, head…her entire body parried the notes as it would the enemy as soon as she understood its intentions, which took so little time they seemed to be in perfect unison.

As she ended the song and she took a bow beside Avarielle, she realized how little she knew about the warrior. Avarielle was dangerous, and the quick, unhesitant movements of her dance were further proof of it. But Kaden had trusted her. Otherwise, he would have never let Cassara leave with her.

All because of a name and an oath. Every time Cassara had asked her about the oath, Avarielle had shrugged the question off and embarked on another training exercise, which usually involved some degree of pain. She wished she was skilled enough to succeed alone and wasn't in need of Avarielle's skills to find Eloms and Jayden.

"I need to know about this oath, tonight," Cassara said after the innkeeper served them their food and thanked them for the entertainment.

"Still on that?" Avarielle asked casually, not even looking up from her plate as she speared what might be meat with her knife.

"Wouldn't you be?"

"I suppose I would be." Avarielle stared into the flickering candle on their table as she spoke. "How much do you know of your family's history?"

"The Edolines were rich landowners when the kingdom of Graydon dissolved into civil war over 650 years ago," Cassara recited as her old teacher so often had, drilling into his young pupil the facts of rule. "Almost two centuries later, when some order was restored and Rashim formed, Edoline was founded by a queen, and has been ruled by that name ever since."

"Before that," Avarielle urged, gesturing with her knife. "Before the civil war."

Cassara furrowed her brow. "I'm not certain that much is known."

Avarielle glanced at her before speaking. "We've kept more history in the West. When the thirty-first king of Graydon, also known as the Lost Lover, the Great Destroyer, the Fallen One, and so on, and so on...Anyways, during the Last Great War, he left his cousin in charge of his kingdom while he went to the Eastern Shores to meet in the last council of his reign. His cousin's last name, the only thing we still know of him, was Edoline."

Cassara looked up at Avarielle, stunned. That meant that in her blood flowed the blood of Graydon. The man who, out of grief for his beloved Elihor, had erected the Wall of Loss before taking his own life. The Wall had since kept the two worlds apart, worlds now known only by the names of the lovers: Graydon and Elihor.

"If you're going to keep that mouth of yours opened, at least put some food in it," Avarielle said. "Because the food isn't getting any better as it gets colder."

"On the first night we met," Cassara said, ignoring Avarielle's teasing, simply trying to make sense of what she was telling her. "You said, upon learning my name, that it made sense Eloms would attack me."

Not certain what exactly she was asking, Cassara stopped speaking, hoping Avarielle would give her an answer.

The warrior shrugged. "Just a guess, really. The word Elom was bastardized from *Elihor's demons*, so I thought maybe they'd sensed Graydon's blood in you and wanted to extract some vengeance on him for making that wall."

Avarielle took another hearty bite, as though the two companions were simply discussing the weather.

Cassara forced her voice to remain calm. "You mean those things come from Elihor? From the Land of Darkness?"

Much to Cassara's infuriation, Avarielle shrugged again. "Don't know," she mumbled in between bites as though she was losing interest in the conversation. Seeing the frustration on Cassara's face, Avarielle grinned. "But I know who does know."

Cassara's eyes widened. "The Circle."

Avarielle nodded. "That's where we're headed. To Ravenhold. Not through Lisal, since that might as well be Circle territory, but around the mountains through Rashim and Solir. Once there, I have ways of finding out what we need to know."

"What ways?' Cassara asked suspiciously.

"You'll find out when we get there," Avarielle simply answered.

"I want to know now," Cassara said, her anger seething to the surface. There was too much she still didn't know, and she very much disliked being at such a disadvantage.

"Avarielle," Cassara said, her voice gaining a dangerous edge as she fought to control her temper. "I have just walked away from everything in the hopes of making a difference and of saving my little brother," she swallowed hard. "And now you're telling me we're going to travel through Elom-infested territory towards probably the most dangerous place in all of Graydon, and I should simply trust that you can get the information we need once we're there? And get it from the strongest users of sorcery? That's ludicrous! You can't ask that much of me!"

Avarielle took a long, deep drink before answering, looking directly at Cassara, her unwavering eyes serious, for once. "How can I prove to you that you can trust me when I'm not even sure I can trust you yet?"

Cassara reeled back, the truth of it stinging. It seemed they were both in the same situation. One of them would simply have to make a compromise and take the first steps. Besides, what other choice did she have but to trust the warrior? Even if it meant going against the Circle. Avarielle had gotten her this far, hadn't she?

Cassara stood up, her plate barely touched, the chair scraping on the wood floor as she pushed it away with the back of her knees. A few patrons looked up in anticipation.

"Very well," she said formally. "To Ravenhold we head. In the meantime, you'll have to excuse me. I intend to get some sleep before we hunt the demons of Elihor tonight." She turned to go to her room and was surprised when Avarielle called out after her.

"Cassara!"

Cassara hesitated, but curiosity won over and she turned around.

"You never found out about the oath," Avarielle said as she leaned back against her chair, her plate quite clean.

Cassara simply stood and waited. Avarielle did not seem to notice her silence.

"Pretty story, really, but the short version of it is, all children of Grayloft who wield Graysword," she motioned towards her sword, leaning against the table in its scabbard, "are sworn to protect the children of Graydon, and therefore Edoline."

Avarielle started picking at Cassara's plate. Deciding she had enough to deal with for one day, Cassara turned around and headed upstairs towards her room, hoping sleep would restore some much-needed clarity and focus.

CASSARA WAS SO preoccupied by the information Avarielle had just given her that she did not immediately notice that she was not alone. The room was simple, with only a bed, a table and many shadows. While her fingers loosened the first clasp of her shirt, instinct made her turn towards the small table, and in the dark shadows beside it, she realized that a cloaked figure stood.

"Who are you?" Cassara asked, her hand reaching for the dagger she had already removed and placed on the bed. She hesitated to signal her amulet's existence.

"What's wrong, princess? Aren't you going to reach for your amulet?" the voice whispered, almost a hiss. The woman stepped out from the shadows, her face concealed by the dark hood of her cloak. Only the small section of white showing at the bottom of the cloak as she walked alerted Cassara that she was dealing with the Circle.

"Does the Circle have nothing better to do these days?" Cassara asked, hoping to sound casual, doubting she succeeded in fooling the intruder. Avarielle and Kaden's voices haunted her as she debated reaching for her amulet, frightened that the very act of raising her arm might elicit anger and magic.

"Hardly," the woman said. Cassara heard in that one word a slight, melodic and familiar lilt that alerted her of the intruder's identity. The words escaped from her before she could think better of them, meant to hurt the intruder but stinging Cassara just as badly, if not worse.

"I didn't think you'd ever have the nerve to show your face to me again, Shirina." She was satisfied to see the sorceress grow rigid. "Or will you even have the courage to show me your face, oh cloaked one?" Cassara's anger boiled now that she was faced with the most likely murderer of her family.

The sorceress reached up and lowered her hood, revealing the sculpted features and raven hair that had once saved her.

"I didn't kill your family, Cassara," Shirina whispered, with a hint of pain Cassara would have noticed were she not drowning in her own.

"You did nothing," Cassara said, her words escaping her like poison. "And even if you somehow convince me that you had nothing to do with the attack, I could never forgive you for failing to prevent it, Shirina."

Shirina shuffled her feet, a normal movement for anyone else, but one Cassara had never expected of an Elite of the Circle. She felt her anger losing its edge, leaving in its stead a deep scar that would never heal.

The sorceress stood passively, only her eyes betraying uncertainty. Cassara felt very tired at that moment, tired of sparring with Avarielle and now Shirina, tired of the theories, of the uncertainties, of the fear, the betrayals... her entire body began to crumble under the fatigue her mind had been struggling with for a week now. Even questioning Shirina on what she might know of her little brother seemed a great effort at the moment, for all that she wanted was to lie down and sleep a dreamless sleep. But this might be her only chance, and she didn't intend on letting it slip away.

She was debating how to broach the subject of Jayden when the door to her room flew open. Avarielle entered quickly, sword drawn.

"Come to finish the job?" she hissed at Shirina as she positioned herself between the sorceress and the princess.

Cassara was about to protest when soft laughter escaped Shirina. Avarielle's grip on her sword tightened. Her breath caught in her throat as she forced herself not to take a step back.

"You just don't change, do you, Grayloft?" the sorceress

said, the softness of the words sprinkled with a hint of sadness. Cassara placed a hand on Avarielle's arm, urging her to lower her sword.

"You're as crazy as she is if you think I'll lower my sword with her here," Avarielle said, never looking away from the sorceress. Then she added incredulously: "Especially after what she did to your family."

The words stung Cassara, but still her hand remained on the warrior's arm as she spoke. "I just think we might get more answers if we all lowered our weapons for an instant." She glanced at Shirina, wondering if there would be any warning of her attack.

"Why do you insist on trusting her after everything she's done to you?" Avarielle asked, her grip loosening on the pommel of her sword.

"Because I'm still not convinced she did it, and I'm more concerned over my little brother than I am with revenge."

She could feel the tension in Avarielle's muscles increase, but the warrior lowered her sword and sat slowly on the bed, her eyes focused on the sorceress. She placed her sword on her lap, refusing to sheathe it.

Fair enough, Cassara thought.

She looked pointedly at the sorceress, who met her gaze and nodded, sitting on the chair by the table, her hands kept in plain view on her lap. Cassara looked back towards the warrior, but Shirina's apparent truce did nothing to soothe Avarielle, who still looked as tense as a wolf eyeing its prey.

Cassara sighed and walked back to close the door in case someone should wander by. She was glad some type of truce had been reached, but the last time that had happened, Shirina had not been the most helpful of participants.

She turned back after closing the door. Avarielle was still staring intently at the sorceress while Shirina sat passively, unfazed.

This is going to be pleasant, she thought as she leaned against the door, choosing a neutral area between the two, hoping that Avarielle could still react quickly enough should Shirina actually choose to use her magic against her.

She's done nothing so far. The words held little comfort for her. She took a deep breath and forced her voice to remain steady.

"Where is my brother Jayden?" She paused. Seeing no reaction from Shirina, she decided to take a chance, her throat going dry as she spoke the words for the first time.

"And why did the Circle kill my mother?"

11

*S*hirina had promised herself that she would remain calm and that no matter what, she would get the information she had come for. She hadn't expected the princess to be happy to see her, given the circumstances of their last meeting, but she had certainly not expected the cool, confident reception she was now receiving.

When she had first met the blond-haired, blue-eyed princess of the small, meaningless kingdom of Edoline, Shirina had dismissed her offhand as a useless girl, whose magical potential would no doubt be wasted. The night in the nest had not changed that perception, simply adding foolishly brave to the list. But now, Shirina found herself respecting Cassara's confidence and, seeing her strategically leaning against the door, knew that her answer should be given carefully.

She was no longer playing with a simple girl princess,

but the beginnings of a queen. Unless she got herself killed, of course.

Shirina shrugged. "I don't know about that. Your mother died when I was merely a student, not an Elite. I have no way of gaining that knowledge." Cassara did not look away from her, coolly matching her gaze.

"She's lying," Avarielle said casually from the bed, and Shirina instantly felt her blood boil. That woman was the most useless, stubborn and proud trash she ever had the misfortune of meeting, and she fought back the urge to slam a wall of fire into her.

"See how she's clamping her hands in anger? She's not that friendly now, is she?" Avarielle said, a grin tugging at her lips, her eyes cold and as calculating as the princess'. Shirina cursed herself for letting her emotions show, forcing her hands and face to relax.

When Shirina had first planned to find the princess, she had not considered that the bothersome warrior woman might still be with her. She would have to give out more information than she wanted to in order to gain their trust.

"I don't know anything about your brother or your mother," Shirina said slowly, measuring the impact of her words on both women. "But I do know who does."

She waited, forcing herself to remain calm, wishing they would both just lose control and be their usual emotional selves. She found their silence troubling and felt like a young girl again, facing the Circle Elders for the first time, unable to predict the outcome of the situation.

She detested feeling out of control.

"Oh, all right," Cassara said, the impatience lacing her words a comfort to Shirina. "I'll ask. Who is it, Shirina?"

The warrior looked sharply at Shirina.

"Her name is Tangia. She was...is my mentor at the Circle." She wanted to hit herself for the slip, and from the victory flashing in Avarielle's eyes, she knew that it had not gone unnoticed.

The warrior said nothing, simply raising an eyebrow questioningly.

"She was thrown out of the Circle over a month ago." *While I was busy chasing you.* "And has been sent to Siabala's Rage."

She was satisfied to see terror flash in Cassara's eyes, though Avarielle remained strangely passive.

"Siabala's Rage?" Cassara whispered, shock in her voice. "The Circle sent one of their own Elders to Siabala?"

"What did she do to deserve that?" Avarielle asked casually, although the slight tone of pleasure in her voice angered Shirina.

"It's not what she did," Shirina said, biting off each word. "It's what she refused to do." She turned towards Cassara. "She was ordered to take back the amulet of the royal family of Edoline, but refused so strongly she was sent to Siabala's Rage, for reasons I do not understand."

Cassara's face grew pale, and Avarielle became more alert.

Morbidly enjoying their fear, Shirina continued.

"And now I have been ordered to finish what she would not begin." Although Shirina had predicted that the statement would not be well received, she had not expected the simple clutching of the sword and hardening of the jaw line that she saw before her.

"What's wrong, Avarielle?" Shirina said, feeling like a child teasing another and not caring. "Aren't you going to try to lop my head off before I can get at the little princess? She is under your protection, oh Grayloft, correct?"

She had hoped to elicit anger, but instead drew laughter from the warrior. Shirina felt her face grow hot.

"This is getting a bit childish for one of the Circle's Elite, isn't it?"

Cassara stepped forward before Shirina could throw back a reply. "Why would they want the amulet?" she asked, drawing their attention back towards the problem at hand.

Shirina shrugged, her anger dissipating as quickly as it had formed. "I might know if I could analyze it closely," she began, continuing as she saw the princess tense. "Something I realize you don't want me to do. But my best guess is that it has something to do with your ties to Graydon."

Cassara nodded. "I was thinking the same thing." Shirina was surprised to see that the princess was even aware of Edoline as Graydon's descendants, and wondered how much of the story she actually knew. Since she was trying to win some of the woman's trust, Shirina did not share the unpleasant details, although she would have enjoyed it, just to see Cassara's respect for Avarielle vanish.

A pleasure for another day.

"But what does this have to do with my brother?" Cassara pressed, more concerned with a possibly living relative than her dead mother. It was not a choice Shirina could fault her for, and found that she was beginning to enjoy the straightforward dealings of the princess. It was much more relaxing than Avarielle's constant taunts.

"I'm not sure," Shirina said honestly. "But the orders came from high within the Circle to capture the amulet, and I find the timing of the attack and the disappearance of Edoline's heir difficult to dismiss as sheer coincidence. Tangia, who refused the orders for reasons that are still unclear to me, must know more details about this, or at least she should be able to point us in the right direction."

Cassara looked at her pensively for a moment and Shirina did not delude herself into thinking the princess was taking her at face value. She knew Cassara was deciding whether or not to trust her.

"And so you want us to help your old mentor?" Cassara asked incredulously after a few moments.

Shirina allowed herself a slight laugh. "Hardly. Although you two have strong powers to contend with, I doubt we would even get past the guards of the gates of the West. But I think we could find answers at the Circle."

She paused, hesitating, before choosing to be honest. "The truth is, I can't arrive at Ravenhold without the amulet. I would be turned away. Or killed, in the worst case."

Avarielle scoffed at the last words, and Shirina ignored her. Before she could continue, Cassara cut in.

"So you want me to lend you my amulet, and I could stay near, in sight of Ravenhold even, and wait for you to return with the information we need and my amulet, even though you have absolutely no idea why they're seeking it."

Shirina nodded, a bit stunned. The princess had guessed most of the details of her plan, but now that she heard it, she knew that it was full of downfalls and nearly impossible to pull off. She felt ridiculous for even having approached them and wished she had simply taken the amulet when she had had the chance. With Avarielle in the room, she doubted she would get halfway through a spell recital before her head would be lopped clean off her body.

"This sounds as great as your plan," Cassara said sarcastically as she looked at Avarielle, who grinned up at her. "And yes, we were planning on going that way, in case you hadn't figured that out already," Cassara said coldly as she looked at Shirina, who felt as though she had been slapped. She had been so concentrated on convincing them of her plan that she hadn't even given thought to their own.

"It doesn't sound that great when it's said out loud," Shirina said about her plan, leaning back against the chair for the first time since sitting in it.

"Rather not," the princess said, her voice taking on its royal lilt.

"And then some," Avarielle scoffed.

"So what do we intend to do about it?" Shirina asked, annoyed. She was really regretting ever approaching these two.

"Well, I'm tired of this useless chit chat," Avarielle said, relaxing her stance a bit, although Shirina knew that she would spring into action instantly if threatened. "And Eloms will be out tonight, so why don't we just part ways and meet up again in the next world?"

Shirina stiffened, trying to think of an argument to stay with them. Otherwise, she could just leave and return later. The warrior would let down her guard sooner or later with Cassara, and she could take the amulet then. Shirina failed to convince herself, since the warrior had been escaping and fighting her off for months, now.

Cassara saved her the trouble of choosing a path herself by asking: "Why don't you come with us?"

Avarielle cursed.

"Eli, Cass! What are you thinking? The woman's dangerous, she works with an organization that might have killed your mother and father, and kidnapped your brother, not to mention the fact that she's just admitted that she wants, Eli, she *needs* to steal your amulet! She cheats, she lies, and she's incredibly annoying!"

Cassara took the onslaught quietly, until Avarielle exhausted her objections and sat glaring at the princess.

"We'll all go together," Cassara said coolly, "because I

believe that will give us the best chance of success in entering Ravenhold and finding Jayden." The princess paused, a silent plea on her face as she looked at Avarielle, who grunted, unconvinced.

"Look," Cassara said, exasperated, looking towards Shirina for help. "Shirina knows Ravenhold better than we do, and you know the Eloms better than anyone else. It's only logical for us to join efforts in solving our problems, which I have a feeling are all linked."

She continued to look at Shirina, and the sorceress decided to help her. After all, for reasons she did not fully understand herself, Cassara was helping her out, and she could use at least one ally right now.

"There's a secret entrance to Ravenhold," Shirina said slowly, wondering how many of the Circle's secrets she would be willing to betray to free Tangia.

Avarielle's head shot up and Cassara took a step towards her, her earlier caution apparently forgotten.

"Where?" Avarielle asked eagerly.

The answer felt like bitter poison as she spoke, knowing she was effectively destroying her life in the Circle if it was ever discovered that she had spoken to outsiders of this.

"In the Maple Mountains, near Solir. It was built as an escape route, but it can be used both ways."

"It's poorly guarded," she added, seeing the question in the warrior's eyes. Avarielle smiled a bit at the information.

"How do we know you're not leading us into a trap?" Cassara asked.

Shirina shrugged. "I guess you don't. You just trust me." Cassara was the first to break her eyes away.

"Not good enough," Avarielle whispered.

Shirina looked directly at Avarielle, not shying away from the warrior's distrusting gaze. "The Circle has just sent the woman who is responsible for my life to Siabala's Rage, without good cause, to make her suffer the worst life and die the worst death. I must admit that my loyalty to them, although not fully destroyed, is rather wavering at the moment. And, sadly enough," she added, with a crooked smile, "you're the safest allies I could think of approaching."

"With your warm personality, I'm surprised you don't have armies of friends," Avarielle mumbled. She paused a moment.

"We'll try this," Avarielle suddenly said, shrugging as Cassara looked at her. "If she lies, she'll be dead before we are. But we do things my way," she added threateningly.

Shirina nodded. She had little choice and still had to decide on the best way to proceed. She wondered if she would be given the opportunity to get the amulet. Yet that would not free Tangia.

She hoped that they could each gain the information they sought in Ravenhold and go their separate ways afterwards. As she followed the princess and the warrior out into the cold night to help them fight the nearby Eloms, she knew without a doubt that she would soon be more insane than Avarielle if she had to stay in their company for too long.

For having planned her entire life so carefully, Shirina felt helpless now that she was left without her set path, without the guidance she had counted on all of her life.

She hated the feeling of helplessness, which reminded her too much of her life before the Circle, a life she had hoped to forget.

FIRES FLARED from the amulet and Cassara let them free, sending the Elom reeling back as they struck its face. Beside her, Avarielle finished another with her blade, and Shirina was, as usual, nowhere to be seen.

"That's it," Avarielle said, cleaning black blood from her blade before sheathing it. Cassara nodded and put her amulet back around her neck and safely under her shirt.

"At the rate we're going, we're not going to reach the entrance to Ravenhold for another three weeks," Shirina said as she walked out of the woods.

"The rate might be faster if you helped out a little," Avarielle spat at her, although not with her usual passion. The warrior was drawn from a week's travel, endless arguments and frequent usage of magic. This fact did not escape Shirina's attention.

"You seem tired, Avarielle. Perhaps you'd like to rest a bit," she cooed at her, winning an angry scowl for her efforts. Cassara sighed and leaned against a tree, giving herself a moment to regain her breath, slightly dizzy from the magic that had coursed through her.

"I wouldn't mind a good night's sleep," Cassara said, hoping to diffuse the situation. Shirina and Avarielle argued about everything and seemed to enjoy it. Cassara had quickly learned it was best not to get involved.

"There's a town not far from here," Shirina said, pointing to the base of the mountains, which were looming close now. "But we'll need money to stay at the inn and, as far as I know, the last of our money was used in the last town to buy Avarielle a new dagger."

"If you did some fighting yourself," Avarielle said without a moment's hesitation, "you too might break a weapon or two, or better yet, a limb or two."

"An inn sounds nice," Cassara said, ignoring them. "As for money," she added, smiling mysteriously at Avarielle, "we have our ways."

Avarielle grinned at her and Shirina stared back and forth from one to the other, before shaking her head. "I'm not sure I want to know."

"Well, if you want to eat, you'll find out," Cassara said, before firmly adding: "And you'll find a way to participate." Shirina looked surprised and insulted, but Cassara continued before she could object. "Although Avarielle may like to make you believe what we do to win money is lewd," she blushed slightly as she remembered the song she had opened the first night with, "our methods are perfectly legal and couth. Besides, Shirina, you haven't done much to earn your keep so far, and if you don't, I believe I might prefer Avarielle's even shakier plan over yours."

Shirina's face darkened and Cassara knew that her unspoken threat of leaving her behind had not gone unheard. The sorceress seemed to struggle for a moment, weighing Avarielle's intentions. The warrior returned the sorceress' gaze with a look of warning.

There's more to their story than they're letting me know, Cassara thought, wondering if Avarielle was any more trustworthy than Shirina. All that she really knew of the two was that Shirina had been hunting Avarielle for months in an effort to acquire Graysword, on the Circle's orders, of course. But Shirina knew as little of those orders as she seemed to know of the orders to capture Cassara's amulet. She hoped that one day she could trust her new allies completely. She missed Kaden horribly.

"Fine. I'll follow and find a way to join in your little game," she added. Cassara almost told her they simply performed to win their keep, but she was currently finding it amusing not being the one kept in the dark for once. Avarielle did not seem to want to enlighten the sorceress any more than she did.

The inn was only a half hour's walk away, located inside a small barricaded village. They entered the quaint place gingerly, glad to find a place to rest. Cassara headed for the innkeeper immediately, explained the situation, and this time was set up on a small stage at the back of the inn.

"Used to be lots more traveling performers around

here before those monsters came a few months ago," the innkeeper mumbled to her as he finished dusting the stage. Cassara coughed and nodded, smiling weakly at him.

She took her seat on the side of the stage, leaving most of the room for Avarielle's dancing. Shirina stood aside, her arms across her chest, waiting to see what folly the two women were about to drag her into.

"Let's take it slow, tonight," Avarielle whispered as she came up on the stage. "I'm more tired than the first time we did this." Cassara nodded and shot a quick look at Shirina before bringing her flute to her lips and beginning a gentle and slow song about a peasant's daughter's dreams of glory. It wasn't her favorite, but the tame rhythm allowed Avarielle to show off her balance as she undertook impossibly slow movements.

The inn, almost empty at first, quickly filled up, and for the first time, Cassara was glad that the Eloms were beginning to appear earlier and earlier after the sunset, since it wasn't so late that the villagers would be asleep and caught unaware.

From their tired eyes and long faces, Cassara guessed that their lives had not been easy of late, living under the constant threat of attack by Eloms. The leaders of Solir had abandoned their people, including these villagers, when Eloms had attacked the capital about a month ago. Cassara couldn't help but increase the tempo a bit, in order to give the villagers something cheerful to listen too. Avarielle, now warmed up, did not seem to object, her muscles easily following the faster pace.

The villagers clapped when the song ended, their cheers bringing in more of their neighbors. Although money seemed to be rare, the innkeeper indicated that a few more good songs would win them three rooms and three warm meals. Cassara agreed to the offer, casting a look at Shirina before breaking into a cheerful ballad from Rashim about the beginning of summer.

About half way through the song, Cassara was surprised to feel someone standing beside her. She turned around to see Shirina, her arms still crossed, and thought she heard her mumble, "I can't believe I'm doing this."

Seconds later, Shirina broke out into song, apparently already familiar with the ballad, the words rolling from her tongue with ease.

Avarielle gave Shirina a surprised look as she danced, a grin breaking out on her face. For once, Cassara didn't think the warrior was mocking the sorceress.

The song concluded and Cassara quickly began the next one before Shirina could think better of her involvement. This time, she chose a light tune about Elihor and Graydon's love, another song from Rashim. She was pleased to hear Shirina's voice join the notes of her flute, clear and bright, never hitting a false note or missing a cue.

The villagers were more subdued for this one, but clapped just as loudly when the song ended. Cassara led her little band through two more songs, and then she let her flute rest, deciding she had pushed enough for the moment. The innkeeper was ecstatic, giving them the best table in the house before bringing them three warm meals.

"You sing beautifully," Cassara ventured as they began eating.

Shirina shrugged. "Music is one of the first arts mastered by the Circle. Knowing how to control the pitches and tones of our voices help us incant better later on." She cast a quizzical look at Cassara. "I understand why Avarielle can dance so well, considering her upbringing and sword fighting skills, but I'm not sure I understand why a princess plays such a cheap instrument."

Cassara looked down at her flute lying beside her plate, smiling at Shirina as she spoke of the fond memories. "My mother showed me how to carve when I was very little, and she helped me make this." She paused and looked back at the flute, speaking softly as she did so. "It was the last thing we made together."

Realizing the somber mood she was casting, she looked up and grimaced. "Apparently I enjoy splinters in my hands." Shirina didn't say anything, simply returning to her meal, and Cassara followed suit. She wished she could reach deeper into the sorceress' psyche, but she also knew that now was not the time, not with Avarielle listening closely to everything that was said. She momentarily wondered what Shirina had meant by Avarielle's upbringing, surprised when the question was answered seconds later as a dark-clad red-haired man approached their table.

Avarielle looked up, her eyes wide with surprise. The man kneeled beside her.

"My Lady, I've finally found you."

"TREVON!" Avarielle said, rising from her chair to give him a hug. The man, surprised but pleased, hugged her back.

"Join us, please," Avarielle said as she returned to her seat. Cassara stared at him as he took the fourth seat at their table. He must have been around forty, the visible scars on his face marking him as a seasoned warrior.

"What are you doing here?" Avarielle asked, concern flickering in her eyes as she leaned closer to him.

"We think a bigger breach occurred," Trevon said, leaning towards Avarielle.

"How much bigger?" Avarielle asked, "I thought the last one was contained!"

Trevon shook his head. "We don't know. We don't even know from where, but there have been other creatures stalking the West."

Avarielle hissed and leaned back against her chair.

"What do you mean, breach?" Cassara asked, leaning forward. Shirina looked on with interest.

Trevon turned to her, seemingly noticing her for the first time.

"These are my traveling companions," Avarielle said,

waving towards Cassara. "This is Cassara, from Edoline," she omitted the fact that Cassara was the princess, for which she was grateful. "And Shirina," she paused, as if she would say something more. Shirina tensed, but Avarielle let it drop. "You can trust them," she said after an instant's hesitation. Shirina stared openly at Avarielle, whose jaw line was firmly set.

Cassara was surprised that Avarielle had not revealed Shirina's origins, since the Westlander must hate the Circle as much as Avarielle did, but she was astounded by the fact that she had just called the sorceress trustworthy.

Trevon nodded and answered Cassara's question. "A few years ago, maybe five or so, Eloms started appearing in the West. At first, we didn't know what they were, and we just figured it was another Circle trick." Cassara resisted the urge to glance at Shirina.

"But it became clear quickly enough from the type of magic they wielded," Avarielle picked up. "That the creatures came from the Wall itself. From the Land of Darkness." Cassara nodded. This much she already knew from what Avarielle had told her.

"But now?" she asked, looking towards Trevon, who waited a moment to answer as the innkeeper brought him ale and food.

"Now there are other creatures," Trevon said softly. "Stronger ones. Dark things made of rocks that wield powerful fires." He paused, swallowing hard. "They took us by surprise, but so far, they seem to be staying near the Wall, as though dependent on it for life. But it's only a matter of time before they too start moving further east, just like the Eloms did, and I'm not sure our defenses will hold against them."

He stared hard into his cup. "We need you back, my Lady," he whispered, looking at Avarielle.

Before she could answer, Shirina spoke. "You can't go." Avarielle shot her a furious look.

"What right do you have to tell me that I can't go save my people?" Avarielle said, her voice rising with anger. A few of the patrons looked up in curiosity, whispers erupting in the room. Two Westlanders at a table was not a common sight to see on any day. Thankfully, the villagers were tired enough not to care, but if they heard them speaking of Eloms, they might get the energy to care.

Cassara grew concerned. "Keep it down," she warned them both, relieved that Shirina's voice was very low when she spoke again.

"Unless we find out why this is happening, taking for granted some force in the East is causing this." It seemed everyone would avoid mentioning the Circle for now. "We have to continue towards our original destination and find out what we need to know. Besides," she added before Avarielle could object, "we'd still be heading west, so you can just continue alone, afterwards."

Avarielle opened her mouth as if to speak, but clamped it shut, nodding instead.

"Where are you headed?" Trevon asked, looking from Avarielle to Shirina.

"To Ravenhold," Avarielle whispered. Cassara held her breath as she waited for Trevon's reaction.

It came first as a look that let them know he thought that they were all insane, and then as a quick, deep laugh.

"Always crazy ideas, Avarielle. Just like your father!" He laughed some more before taking a deep drink of ale. "Guess I might as well come with you!"

Avarielle shook her head. "Although I'm glad to see you after almost a year, Trevon, and I'd love to have you come with us, quite frankly, I have enough of these two annoying companions to deal with, without having you tagging along as well."

Trevon grinned at Avarielle, but his eyes screamed in protest.

"Go back to the West," Avarielle said, stopping his objection before he could even form it. "And make sure everyone is safe. Bring them as far east as you safely can. I should reach the West no later than a month after you."

Trevon reluctantly nodded, the command in Avarielle's voice too strong to ignore. "I'll do this," Trevon said. "As long as you promise me that you'll come back alive. And soon. I don't want to have to bury another Grayloft in my lifetime, Avarielle."

Avarielle nodded and offered him a weak grin to try to break the tension.

"It was good seeing you again, Lady Avarielle," Trevon said softly as he rose. "Now if you ladies will excuse me, I've learned early on that it's safer for a Westlander to travel at night, even if that is when Eloms lurk."

Avarielle stood and hugged the man goodbye. "Thanks for coming to find me."

He nodded and grinned at her. "It was a fun chase, too! I thought I'd never find you until that innkeeper at Kosel told me of a dancing wonder matching your description. Didn't believe him until I saw you tonight, except I hadn't heard of the beautiful singer," he said, smiling at Shirina. Cassara could swear the sorceress blushed a little.

His grin widened. "Guess Eliya's dance lessons and my sword lessons have been useful out here!"

Avarielle laughed gently at him. "Of course they were. Now get going, or you won't reach the West before the summer's end!"

"Even I'm not that slow!" He gave Avarielle a small, barely perceptible bow, but filled with respect nonetheless.

"Until we meet again, may your paths be clear," Trevon said, hesitating a moment before turning around.

"May yours be safe, Trevon," Avarielle called after him, but he didn't turn around. Without hesitation he pushed through the door and was gone. Avarielle sat back down and started picking at her supper.

"Lady Avarielle?" Cassara asked, breaking through her friend's silence. Avarielle looked up, but it was Shirina who answered for her.

"The western provinces can't become a unified power, because Rashim and the entire East would be concerned and it might be cause for attack. But an unofficial ruler is not something they would necessarily object to, especially if that ruler was gone for most of the time."

Avarielle didn't object to Shirina's analysis as she continued eating in silence. *Unofficial ruler of the West.* A huge piece of land bordering the Wall, a land torn by war less than twenty years ago, and now under attack by ferocious dark creatures. And her people trapped there, unwelcome in Rashim or its neighboring countries, which still believed that the Westlanders kept most of the precious mines of Graydon for themselves. Seeing Trevon and Avarielle's concern over the failing Wall, she doubted that was true.

All of the cards seemed to have been stacked against the West, and Cassara felt like she still understood so little of the situation. With Avarielle brooding in darkness and Shirina rising to go to bed, Cassara knew she would get nothing from either that night and would simply have to wait patiently for the right moment to question them.

She wondered how Avarielle could continue to eat, knowing that her people were in danger of extermination.

12

"You never told us who Trevon was," Cassara ventured the next morning as the three women walked away from the village with some extra supplies in hand.

"He was the youngest leader of one of our armies during the Western War," Avarielle said. "He taught me how to fight, and he's been one of my most loyal since my father and brothers died five years ago."

"I thought your family was killed when you were just a baby?" Cassara asked, surprised. Shirina walked ahead, apparently uninterested in the conversation.

Avarielle shook her head. "My mother was killed then. The war ended after that and my father and two brothers were spared. They were killed later though."

"How?" Cassara asked softly.

"The youngest of my brothers and my father were both killed in the first wave of Eloms. My oldest brother, he was eighteen at the time, was killed by humans, trying to gain Graysword for their own protection."

Cassara walked silently by Avarielle, not sure what to say. Having grown up in a small quiet kingdom where a murder had never been committed in her lifetime made it difficult for her to even grasp the concept of how one human could kill another.

"How could they do that?" Cassara asked, shaking her head. The trail they were on began inching upwards. Their slow trek up the forested Maple Mountains was underway.

"They were desperate," Avarielle said as she looked at her surroundings, the trees already lush, maple keys twirling down all around them every time the wind rattled the leaves.

"The Eloms were spreading then, and my father, their leader, was gone. My older brother was more of a hot head than I'll ever be." She glanced at Shirina to make sure she wouldn't take the opportunity to comment before continuing. "And he wasn't trusted by the people. They thought he would get himself killed and the West would lose Graysword, their only defense."

"What they didn't realize was that Graysword only responds to those of Grayloft blood. So it was useless to them when they went to use it, and they were all slaughtered too." She shrugged. "I took the sword back and no one else ever came for it. Of course, if they kill me, they're out of luck."

"What do you mean?"

"I mean, as far as I know, I'm the last Grayloft. No Grayloft, no magic."

"But you left the West," Cassara said, glancing sideways at Avarielle, whose red hair reflected the sunlight. The day would be warm.

"I couldn't find the answers I needed in the West," Avarielle said, reaching out to catch a leaf. "None of our lore told us what could have caused this, and I thought maybe I could find some answers in the East. If nothing else, I could maybe see if the Eloms' attacks followed a pattern, if they were heading somewhere."

"Did you ever figure one out?"

Avarielle shook her head. "I followed them over the last year, and came to the conclusion that they're like wild animals, interested only in survival. Until I came to Edoline, following them to the other corner of the world, and then, well, you saw. They were different somehow."

Cassara nodded, remembering the difference between her first two encounters with the Eloms. How had they evolved from mere wild animals to calculating royal assassins in the span of one night? She felt a chill despite the warmth of the day.

"Did you ever figure out exactly where the Eloms came from?" Cassara asked, the forest around her feeling more threatening now that the specter of the Eloms had been raised.

Avarielle shook her head, furrowing her brow. "I'm not sure, but we can guess. It's somewhere west, I mean really west, close to the Wall. So we figured it was a breach. But no one lives that far out for fear of the Wall, and by the time we thought it would be wise to check it out, it was too infested for us to get remotely close."

She paused and then spoke more slowly. "The Eloms seem to get their strength from the Wall, so we don't understand why some started to stray from it. It's all just guessing, really, and my time here hasn't helped much, especially since I was being hunted myself." She gave Shirina a look that could pierce the strongest armor.

"Circle orders," Shirina said, turning only momentarily to look at Avarielle. "I was told we were to get Graysword before the last Grayloft got herself killed, and to ensure that she remained alive, as well. Of course, that proved to be difficult."

Avarielle grinned a bit at that. Seeing Cassara's confused look, Avarielle explained. "She had to save my life once, and then she lost a bit of her edge, since I was certain she couldn't kill me. It made things more fun after that."

"More fun?" Shirina turned around and looked angrily at the warrior. "Because of you, Tangia is locked in Siabala, probably beyond help by now! If I'd have been there, if I could have helped her!"

"You'd probably be dead and you know it," Avarielle said, cutting her off. Cassara stared at the face off, taken aback by the sorceress' loss of control. Tangia must have been very special to Shirina. "Besides, you didn't have to keep following me. Graysword stays with me, where it's useful." The last was spoken with a barely-veiled threat, and Cassara cringed at the thought of what might come of it.

"Just remember," Shirina said softly, "I've already trod far enough from the Circle that I may never be able to freely walk the halls of Ravenhold again. And when that happens, all of my oaths, my missions and my prohibitions will be gone. Including the orders that are stopping me from killing you."

Cassara's breath caught in her throat, waiting for Avarielle to down the sorceress in one blow. Instead, Avarielle shrugged at Shirina.

"Maybe then you'll just turn out to be more pleasant."

Saying nothing, Shirina turned around and continued walking. Avarielle grinned at Cassara and followed. Cassara shook her head as she, too, followed, wondering how long it would take before one or both of them lost it completely.

THE FOREST STOOD STILL as Cassara hid between two trees, willing her ragged breathing to slow. Her ears ached for noise besides her own, but nothing reached her, the stillness unbroken by even the sound of an insect.

Her eyes could barely see anything in the darkness, and the smell of burning leaves clung to her.

The amulet clasped tightly in her hand throbbed with unleashed magic, held prisoner by Cassara's will and fear. Without a target, it was impossible for her to use it.

She wished she could call out to her companions but didn't dare make a noise, and she wasn't even sure that they still lived.

A moment earlier, while fighting a group of Eloms, Shirina had shouted a warning and pushed Cassara to the side as a wall of fire plummeted into them. The fire was so hot Cassara felt it searing her skin even from where she stood, a few feet from its edge. Then the fire had retreated, leaving a few trees still burning, but the wet ground and leaves prohibited the fire from getting far. Or so Cassara assumed.

Moments after the fire, before she could regain some sense of orientation, Eloms had swarmed the forest. Cassara saw them walk by from where she crouched. They weren't the usual wild Eloms, but rather the dark, cunning Eloms that had killed her family.

She had run as far as she could and now felt trapped, not knowing where the Eloms, her friends, or the source of the fire were.

She took a deep breath, her ears prickling as they picked up a sound. She strained them, trying to identify the noise, holding her breath so it wouldn't interfere.

Sobbing. She could hear someone sobbing, somewhere off to her right. Could a child be lost all the way up here? As far as she knew, there were no villages in the area. But could someone have been trying to escape the Eloms' movements, thinking it would be safer up the mountains?

Well, I can't just stay between these trees all night, she thought, knowing that sooner or later she would be discovered. She clutched her amulet so tightly she felt its crescent cut her skin. She took a deep breath, forcing her numb feet to move quietly on the forest floor as she headed towards the noise.

It seemed hopelessly far, and each time she thought she was nearing it, the sobbing seemed to move further away. Every small, barely perceptible noise her feet made seemed like thunderclaps in the quiet night, and although she moved slowly and carefully, her breath still came ragged and heavy.

Finally the trees broke onto a small clearing, only about ten feet wide. From where she crouched in the line of trees, Cassara could see the child huddled, wearing what looked like a simple nightgown. The child covered its face with its arms, small shoulders rising with every frightened sob.

She moved to go to the child, but before she left the shelter of the trees, an Elom broke into the clearing. The child raised its face, two familiar frightened eyes piercing the darkness before his scream.

"Jayden!" Cassara screamed, recognizing her little brother immediately, forgetting her own fears as the Elom plunged towards him. She broke free of the forest, tangled branches cutting her skin and pulling at her hair. Jayden did not notice her, his wide eyes seeing nothing but the Elom.

Cassara screamed and ran in front of her brother, unleashing her magic and fury. Fires erupted, swallowing the Elom in its wake along with part of the forest, the smell of burning flesh and wood stinging the air as she willed the fires to end. Black marks and withered leaves scarred the trees, but Cassara didn't care. She turned towards Jayden.

He was scared and hadn't noticed her yet, but he seemed fine, and Cassara fell to her knees beside him, hugging him fiercely.

"Jayden, I'm so glad you're safe!" she gasped as she cried. In her ecstasy, it took her a few moments to realize that Jayden wasn't reacting to her hug. Concerned, she broke from him to look him over, but found that he was gone, a blond-haired woman in his place.

Cassara jerked back and fell to the ground. The woman smiled broadly, frightening her more.

"Jayden?" she croaked, confused, her earlier relief turning to nausea.

"I'm sure he misses you too!" the woman said in a sickly-sweet tone, towering over Cassara. Cassara struggled to get up, but strong arms reached out and grabbed her own arms and legs like vices. She struggled to break free, but her bonds only became tighter.

What was holding her?

She screamed in terror as she realized Eloms were all over her, pinning her to the forest floor. She reached for the amulet, but her entire body went numb as she realized that in her earlier relief, she had dropped it to hug Jayden.

"Looking for this?" the blond woman said as she perched over Cassara, the amulet dangling from her hand.

A smile colder than the frozen sea defaced her, the chill of it grabbing hold of Cassara's bones.

"Where is Jayden?" she asked weakly, struggling to contain her nausea.

The woman shook her head, the blond hair caught by the passing moonlight. Cassara's head pounded as elation vanished into fear, the smell of the Eloms more than she could bear. Her stomach lurched and she fought to keep control, cold sweat breaking out all over her body.

She turned her head and retched on the ground, wishing she could free her hand to wipe her mouth.

"Oh dear, it isn't your family's lucky time, now, is it?" the woman said, her white robe suddenly clear, and all that Cassara could see was the emblem of the Circle, emblazoned above her heart.

"I need a favor from you," the woman said, kneeling beside Cassara, as she struggled weakly against her captors. The creatures came slightly closer with their mistress, dark eyes darting with intelligence, deformed features twisting into what looked like smiles. She fought not to retch again. "There's still one item I seek here, and I need your help to get it."

"I'll never help you," Cassara rasped, wishing she could spit in her face. "Tell me where my brother is!"

"Oh, I think you will." The woman from the Circle looked down, satisfaction flashing in her eyes. Cassara's stomach turned, but she forced herself to meet the gaze, ignoring the Eloms' cold clammy skin against her arms and legs.

"You see, what I need from you is quite simple." She flashed her wicked grin once again.

"All I need from you are your screams."

Avarielle was desperately trying to fend off five Eloms when the screams began. They were so deep and guttural that it took a few screams for the warrior to recognize the usually soft voice of the princess.

"Elihor's blood!" Avarielle swore, bringing her sword down on an Elom and taking another one out on the upstroke. Three more appeared and Avarielle was surrounded, barely keeping her footing on the damp forest floor. She blocked out the screams, concentrating instead on not getting impaled by the creatures.

Claws came down and very nearly struck her in the head in what would have surely been a fatal blow. She grasped the hilt of her sword, forcing herself not to call on the magic unless absolutely necessary. These beasts could be felled with a normal blade, and with all the magic she had used of late, she was already drained by the combat.

She swept sideways, attempting to bring down two Eloms, but even with her sharp blade, she lacked the strength to spear them both through.

Cassara screamed again. The cries grew weaker, as though she was breathing her last.

"Enough of this!" Avarielle bared her teeth and struck again, calling on her magic, taking three Eloms out with ease. But more appeared to take their place, and Avarielle's sword became heavier and more unwieldy by the second.

And she couldn't hear the screams anymore.

Hang on, Cassara.

She gathered her magic and, estimating the point of origin of the screams, slashed a path through the Eloms, thinking of nothing but her goal, letting her tired limbs be guided by honed instincts.

The hope that she might not be too late gave her strength.

CASSARA GRASPED AT CONSCIOUSNESS, her body numb from the pain and her mind incapable of any thought beyond *stay awake.*

She was lying on the ground. She thought she might be on her side, but it was hard for her to see, her vision as foggy as her mind. Everything moved as if she were in a dream. She knew the Eloms no longer held her and a sickly gray light washed the darkness of the forest away.

A stinging, awkward sensation on her left side led her to believe that her left arm was tucked underneath her, but she couldn't even fathom how to move her head to check, much less how to make her body obey her.

Her stomach lurched and she let the waves of nausea flood her system, too tired to fight them. The nausea passed, but left her feeling shaky. Her limbs were regaining some sensation, but turned frigid in its wake. She wanted to see the woman from the Circle, but she couldn't focus her eyes. Every time she tried, the world tilted below her and the nausea struck again. She closed her eyes, fighting back tears of frustration.

"Oh dear," the woman said. Boots, almost fully covered by robes, halted in front of Cassara's face.

"I have a secret to share with you." The woman from the Circle crouched down and Cassara could almost see her face, the long blond hair and chin now in view.

The woman whispered to Cassara, as if they were two girls sharing a secret about a crush. "I'm not supposed to kill you," she said. Cassara half-expected to hear a young girl's giggle. "But I will, if I have to. I can't kill the other, but you, you're, oh, how shall I say...ah yes, expendable."

Her robes shuffled and Cassara felt the woman's cold touch move back some hair that had strayed from her braid onto her face. She tried to jerk her head back and actually managed to raise her head a bit, but then nausea slammed into her. She let her head fall back to the ground.

"You're not going to like the rest of this, but your friend is a bit slow and I'd like her to come here now," the woman said. Cassara forced her eyes to open, and watched the woman rise. She wanted to ask a thousand questions, but she could not manage to make a sound. She imagined the wicked grin on the woman's face and flexed the fingers on her right hand.

*If I could just move my limbs...*Cassara wasn't sure what

she would do, but she had to try to stop her. Better to die trying than to just die. *Just a little bit more...*

With blood flowing freely again her limbs regained more and more sensation, and pain throbbed through each muscle. Cassara knew it was only a matter of seconds before the pain would intensify with magic.

"Enough of this suspense, princess," the woman said in a haughty tone, "wouldn't you agree?"

"I hope Siabala picks your bones," Cassara mumbled.

"Jesimae." The voice broke through the forest like cold steel. Cassara knew without seeing her that the speaker was Shirina. She didn't know whether or not to rejoice.

Had she come to save her or had she come to help the Circle? The sorceress' loyalties were still not clear to her. She moved her fingers uselessly by her side, wishing her body remembered how to move her entire arm so she could at least push herself up.

"Shirina," the woman named Jesimae said, turning around to face her. Cassara moved her head slowly so that she could see Shirina's face, hoping the all-too-often passive features would reveal her current loyalties. She shifted her neck, straining from the effort, the fresh air she breathed in while moving away from the ground soothing her stomach. She could feel the grass that had been plastered into her face peel away from it, wondering if blood was in the mix or if it the ground was simply wet.

Cassara could see Jesimae's back, which hid most of Shirina. She suddenly realized the dark night had been broken by a ball of light, hovering in the middle of the clearing.

That must be why the Eloms backed off, Cassara thought, wondering if they were simply waiting in the shadows and, if so, how Shirina had passed by them without using her magic. She wished she understood more of the magic they wielded.

"I've come to finish your job," Jesimae said, with none of the coldness Cassara had come to associate with the Circle. "It won't take long, if you'd just like to wait a bit."

Jesimae's hand shot back, the fingers wide apart and flexed. Her palm was aimed straight at Cassara, whose stomach lurched with dread for half a second before it felt like something twisted it from within. Cassara fought to hold the screams in, knowing it was what the woman wanted, but her insides felt like they were being torn to shreds. The metallic taste of blood filled her mouth as she bit down on her cheek, hard.

Her tears felt cool and fresh, the night wind chilling them as they streaked her face, the blood falling from her mouth like fire against her chin. Still, she did not scream.

She thought she heard Jesimae say something but paid her no mind, concentrating instead on not choking on her blood and keeping her screams locked away.

Then Cassara jerked and convulsed as she felt like a sword had pierced her body. Her eyes shot open and blood rushed out of her mouth. She would have now screamed if she could have, but the breath had been ripped from her body, leaving only pain and panic in its wake.

Then the pain stopped without warning and Cassara was left gasping for breath. After a few moments, she managed to move her right arm up to wipe the blood from her mouth. Her movements were awkward and broken, and she felt like lead had been poured into her veins.

She wanted to stand up and stare the woman down, but she could barely move her right arm. What she really wanted, she realized for the first time, was to be back home, sheltered and safe, warm and clean, without choice or danger. Lying on a strange forest floor on a strange mountain, her own blood and tears streaking her face, Cassara desperately wanted to return to the life she had once loved.

She heard someone move behind her, felt a touch on her back and tried to jerk away, only to be held back by a strong arm.

"Relax. It's me," Shirina said. Cassara moved her head slightly and saw that Jesimae lay on the ground, unmoving. The light she had created was quickly dimming. Cassara tried to detect the pungent odor, frightened the Eloms might attack again. She could only smell her own blood.

"Shirina," she managed to croak, wanting to warn her, but the sorceress did not answer. A warm, comfortable feeling began to creep into Cassara, and she feared she might be losing consciousness, only to soon she realized it emanated from Shirina's hand.

The sensation spread to her limbs, her left arm aching as she felt life returning to it, but she dared not move for fear of breaking the spell Shirina had cast on her. Soon her breath ceased rattling, and blood stopped trickling into her mouth.

Shirina removed her hand. Cassara slowly tested her limbs and finally sat up, turning around to face the sorceress.

"Thank you," Cassara said, her voice still shaking. Shirina nodded, her own features drawn and tired in the flickering light.

"We should go," Shirina said, glancing over Cassara's shoulder.

It was then that the spell of light died and the Eloms entered the clearing.

FOR A MOMENT, all that Cassara could hear was her sharp intake of breath, her eyes aching for light as an impenetrable wall of darkness smothered them. She felt Shirina move and heard the soft whispers of an incantation, spurring her into action. She reached up for her amulet, dread chilling her to the bones as she remembered it was gone, in the other Circle girl's hands.

She had to get the amulet to fight, but first she had to

reach the fallen Jesimae. They would be swarmed soon. If only she could see!

The rising cries of Eloms drowned out Shirina's soft incantation as they broke into the clearing, branches snapping in their wake. Cassara stumbled towards where she thought Jesimae lay, hoping she wouldn't run into an Elom instead. The damp ground was slick and uneven. She slipped and then tripped on something, falling hard to the grass.

Cassara ignored the shooting pain of her scraped palms, realizing she had tripped on a warm body. Frantically she reached for Jesimae and searched her body without shame as she looked for the amulet. She felt lightheaded as she found it clutched in the fallen sorceress' left hand.

She grabbed it, but just as she was pulling it away, the chain caught.

It's caught on her wrist! Cassara was growing frantic. The forest erupted in light and Cassara was blinded for an instant. Shirina had cast her spell. The Eloms, within an arm's reach of Cassara, moved away, the spell of light flickering above them. Cassara knew it was weak, guessing Shirina had used too much magic healing her.

She looked down and yanked at the amulet, her limbs growing numb as she saw Jesimae's eyes shining in the light, her hand firmly gripping the amulet's chain.

A tingling sensation worked itself into Cassara's hand and she quickly realized that it was not the familiar magic. Jesimae's eyes lit with victory as her lips chanted a spell.

"No!" Cassara clenched her teeth. The pain of the first attacks, although now dulled, was still vivid in her mind. She reached for her own magic and turned it towards Jesimae. Within seconds fires consumed her arm.

The hold on the chain was released and Cassara fell back, the smell of burnt human flesh clinging to her. She looked on with horror as Jesimae stared disbelievingly at her arm, the burnt, black flesh already peeling from her bones.

Jesimae's eyes grew wide, as though suddenly realizing what had truly happened, and she let out a primal scream. Winds slammed into the forest, the trees, eerily illuminated by Shirina's light spell, bent to its will as leaves flew up into the vast sky.

Cassara clung to her amulet and tried to stand, but the onslaught of wind forced her down. Her hair broke free from its restraints, the blond wisps flying towards Jesimae, and Cassara turned her head to see Shirina clutching the ground. The Eloms were nowhere in sight.

Jesimae screamed again and lightning crashed in the forest around them, the damp ground coursing with its energy, numbing Cassara's already-weakened body. She felt someone near her and turned quickly, the wind making her eyes water. Avarielle was beside her, dragging herself along the ground.

"Use your magic!" Avarielle screamed at the top of her lungs in Cassara's ear, the words muffled nonetheless.

"I can't reach her! Kill her!" Avarielle screamed again. Cassara looked towards Jesimae, protected from her own onslaught, her hair disturbingly calm. The limb was black and cracked.

I did this. I chose to use my magic.

I would choose and never look back. She swore she heard Kaden's words upon the winds, knowing it was only her tired mind playing games with her.

"I made her do this," Cassara said, remembering the pain Jesimae had caused her. "I've done her no better!" Cassara repeated louder, screaming at Avarielle, who screamed back: "Kill her before she kills us!"

Cassara held to the amulet, trying to convince herself it was like killing Eloms. But this was different and she knew it. She could not convince herself that killing a human was right.

Lightning struck near Avarielle, its power coursing through Cassara and making her skin tingle, the entire sky rumbling with low thunder and masking the words Avarielle still shouted at her: *Kill her!*

My older brother was killed by humans, she remembered Avarielle saying, and she couldn't help but wonder to whose family this woman belonged. She wondered who would grieve Jesimae and curse Cassara in the same breath.

The winds died faster than her indecision and Cassara looked up to see that Jesimae was gone. Avarielle stood up, giving Cassara a nasty look that made the princess blush, ashamed she had not acted. Her inaction could have easily resulted in their deaths.

"Teleportation spell," Shirina offered, already standing

and smoothing out her robes. "This was apparently planned well beforehand." The sorceress looked composed, her hair still almost perfectly set, only her squinted eyes betraying her fatigue.

"We have to move fast," Avarielle said, pointing towards the sky. Cassara then realized that the light was no longer coming from Shirina's spell, but rather from the red columns dancing against the night sky, flames consuming the fresh summer trees.

The forest was on fire.

And they were in the middle of it.

13

Within an hour, smoke covered the entire sky, reflecting the reds and oranges of the flames.

The three women hadn't spoken once during their escape, Shirina leading them, Avarielle bringing up the rear, sword tightly clutched, jaw firmly set. Cassara's amulet was back around her neck, knowing the Eloms had fled the fires and the magic could not beat back the flames.

Either Jesimae's original fire attack or the lightning she had invoked had set the fire, and the winds she had created seemed to have fanned it. The damp ground was proving to be a blessing, but the fire was growing from above, their entangled branches proving to be the old trees' undoing.

Winds were rising and a storm was brewing, but until the rain broke over them, the fanning gales hindered more than helped. Their one blessing was that the wind was blowing the smoke away from them.

"We're not far," Shirina called back. Cassara glanced quickly at Avarielle, who didn't even make a comment at the sorceress.

Despair swirled within her, not from the forest on fire around her, nor from the Eloms they had fought of late. Avarielle's silence struck her deeper than she would have imagined possible.

Trees cracked behind them as they walked and Cassara could feel the heat of the flames through her clothing, making her sweat even more than the fast pace Shirina was setting. Still, Cassara dared not glance back again to check on the fire's progress, for fear of seeing the anger and coldness in Avarielle's eyes.

The warrior had been the one constant since before Edoline had fallen. The one person she felt she could trust, and was beginning to consider a friend. Having disappointed and angered the warrior for the first time, Cassara was reminded of how little she knew of the woman. She was apparently much more than the wandering mercenary Cassara had imagined her to be. She was a hunter and a leader, and now that she was no longer in her good graces, Cassara was learning just how frightening Avarielle could be.

"Over here!" Shirina called out, glancing back once before jumping down a hole by a huge tree. Cassara looked down, seeing the hole clearly. Then she looked up, the wide branches and leaves of the tree a large canopy above them.

The winds were dying and the smoke began to fall, until she could no longer see the top of the tree. All she could see were the fires, swaying towards the leaves above them.

We'll be burned alive! Cassara looked up again, placing her hand on the giant trunk as she forced her eyes down, the hole in which Shirina had vanished thick with darkness.

"Hurry," Avarielle said as she stood by her, the orange hues reflected in her hair. She didn't meet Cassara's eyes, nor offer any words of comfort.

Cassara clenched her teeth and stepped into the hole, gasping as she began to fall. Then something stopped her fall and she was gently lowered to the floor.

"Come here to give Avarielle room," Shirina said from the darkness and Cassara walked towards her voice. Shirina cast a small light spell, glowing brightly on her pale features. Cassara could barely see their surroundings, but they seemed to be in a small room, perfectly enclosed. The walls were earth, lined with thick and thin roots, and the only break in the room was a huge root, jutting out from the wall to their right.

No insect or animal seemed to have claimed this place as sanctuary. Seeing Cassara's look of fascination, Shirina said, "Circle magic," a slight smile playing on her lips.

Cassara bit down a retort at mentioning the obvious, reminding herself that Shirina had saved her life.

She heard Avarielle land, and before she could turn, the warrior was already beside her, looking at her surroundings with squinted eyes.

"Another Circle trick?" Avarielle asked.

"It's a hideaway," Shirina said, walking towards the left wall, away from the giant root. She sat down in front of a fire pit, complete with some logs, her descent slow and painful. "It's kept with minimal magic, like that air chute, and the illusion spell that disguises the entrance, which I had to remove for you two to see." The last was spoken without accusation, which surprised Cassara. "But I doubt anyone will look for us with the forest up there burning." No remorse, no regret.

"Will the fires reach the village?" Cassara whispered.

"It might," was all that the sorceress offered in reply. She looked at the campfire, but seemed to think better of it and didn't light it. Cassara doubted the sorceress could currently use powers beyond her simple light spell at the moment.

"Is the Circle going to deny doing that, too?" Avarielle growled as she took a step towards Shirina.

"What do you mean?" Shirina said, looking up, her fatigue tempered by her rising anger.

"I mean that girl up there was from the Circle, or did you think I wouldn't notice that?"

"That woman's name is Jesimae, and we knew each other, once," Shirina said, leaning her head back against the root sticking from the wall. "But she isn't part of the Circle." Then she added as she closed her eyes, "Or at least, she didn't used to be. But things have changed since last I have been there."

Was that regret in her voice, or was it just the fatigue getting the better of her?

"I don't know which is worse," Avarielle mumbled as she crouched on the floor beside the fire pit, taking flint out from her supplies and striking it beside the small pieces of wood piled inside. "A secretive sorceress, or a suicidal princess." She looked sharply at Shirina.

Thankfully the wood was dry, and soon Avarielle had lit a good fire, Shirina extinguishing her light spell without making a sound or movement. Cassara sat down where she could see the two, Avarielle dark and brooding and Shirina still sitting up, hair hiding her face.

She wanted to thank Shirina for helping her, and explain her action, or lack thereof to Avarielle, but no words came to her. Here, in a dim pit trapped with two women she understood less the more she knew them, Cassara knew that she was alone, no matter how many she might travel and fight with.

She cast one more glance at Avarielle before lying down to try to get some sleep.

Above them, the fires raged.

Cassara woke with a start, the dark strands of a nightmare dissipating with the shy light of the dying fire. She took a deep breath, cold sweat clinging to her clothes, the room cooler than it had been when she had first fallen asleep.

Her throat was dry and water held the promise of quenching her thirst and washing her dark thoughts away. She sat up, quietly looking for her water skin, until it struck her. She had lost her supplies after encountering Jesimae. And she hadn't even noticed until now.

She coughed, the sound swallowed by the earth around them. Avarielle was right to be discouraged by her. She was a useless silly princess from a useless silly kingdom, and she should just go to Rashim and marry a prince who would take care of her.

She obviously needed it. She didn't feel better seconds later when Avarielle handed her a water skin, the warrior's eyes shining in the faint light. Shirina still slept soundly, her breathing slow and even, her chin resting against her chest where she sat, long raven hair shadowing her face.

Cassara hesitated to take Avarielle's water, since it was her fault that she had lost her supplies, but another dry cough changed her mind.

"I suppose you think I'm useless," Cassara said after taking a slow drink.

Avarielle stared at the dying fire, shuffling some logs with a stick before answering.

"I think you've got a lot to learn, but I don't think you're useless, no."

The warrior looked up towards the hole, lit by distant red and orange hues. "It might not have reached the village," she mumbled as she squinted down at their own fire.

Cassara barely heard her since she was carefully preparing her next words. "You told me your older brother was killed by humans," she whispered, and wasn't sure Avarielle had even heard her as she continued. "What would make me any better if I killed another human, Avarielle? Wouldn't Jesimae's family grieve her just as you grieved your brother?"

Avarielle's head snapped up, anger flaring in her eyes. She didn't bother whispering. "That's hardly the same thing. She attacked us with magic! And she hurt you, Cassara. I heard your screams."

Shirina shifted, but said nothing.

Cassara took a deep breath. "Did you kill the men who killed your brother?"

"No, but they didn't try to kill me, either," Avarielle said harshly. "And I don't mean that I didn't want revenge. I just mean that it would have been a waste of life, just like Rojon's death was, and just like your father's death was."

Cassara reeled back from the onslaught. Avarielle did not stop.

"Would you be hunting down humans had they done this, Cassara? If it was humans that had killed your family? Would you be seeking revenge like you are now?"

Before Cassara could protest, Avarielle continued, her voice crisp, biting off every word. "Don't fool yourself, princess," she spat out the title. "You don't know if Jayden is still alive, but you know that you'll find who did this to your family, if you hunt hard and long enough. That's why you continue on this journey. And definitely don't fool yourself into thinking there isn't a human at the end of this." She shot a look at Shirina, who did not respond, her face still hidden by her hair.

Avarielle stood up and looked down at Cassara. "Will you use your magic on them then? Will you be able to justify that, and yet not be able to justify your own life? If you'll only fight for the dead, Cassara, give up now. Go to Rashim and marry your prince. Otherwise, you'll just get yourself killed."

Avarielle turned around and began walking to the other end of the chamber, but Cassara shouted after her, unwilling to let matters rest this way.

"I don't fight for the dead, Avarielle! I fight because I know Jayden is still alive. That woman yesterday, she made an illusion of him, Avarielle. That means she must have seen him!" Avarielle stopped, but didn't turn around, as if not wanting to voice the fear that was growing in Cassara's heart since the night he had vanished. She swallowed hard and voiced the fears, hoping to exorcise them with the sound of her voice. "And if he isn't alive anymore," she paused, wondering how convinced she was of what she was about to say. "Then I'll fight for myself and my family and even for you if that's what it takes. I can't have this power and ignore it, but I also can't use it wildly! I'll fight, Avarielle, but I won't forget the dead either." She wished her eyes weren't watering.

Avarielle still refused to turn around.

"We'll see," she whispered as she walked into the furthest dark corner.

Cassara looked at the sorceress, but Shirina had not moved, and did not seem to intend to.

She wanted to follow Avarielle and explain more, wanted to understand her and be understood, but knew that the warrior wasn't interested in listening, and she wasn't even sure she had the words to explain. She wished she could see Avarielle as she had first known her, filled with belief in Cassara's abilities. She wasn't certain anyone believed in her anymore, least of all herself.

Uncertain what to do, she curled back down, the nightmares of her sleep more appealing than her waking ones.

THE STORM which had been lingering in the skies since the evening finally broke before dawn. The rainwater, although slowed by the wind magic at the entryway, dripped down the roots, not threatening to drown them yet, but making the previously warm atmosphere damp and cold.

"Great Circle planning," Avarielle mumbled. Shirina didn't bother answering, still sitting by the embers of the fire. Although awake, her face was taut and the darkness in her eyes was amplified by the dark rings underneath them.

Of all of them, Shirina was the one who had probably

slept the most. Avarielle had paced a great deal of the night away. Cassara wondered if the warrior would have left, had an exit been available to her.

Avarielle started out towards the entrance, looking up through the hole, which stood a good twelve feet up. The wind spell was apparently only for landing, and didn't translate into a spell that would help them exit.

"This should be fun," Avarielle mumbled. Cassara walked towards her, the water from the storm coming in a small waterfall by now, dragging with it charred remains of the forest. "At least the storm will stop the fire," Cassara said, not daring to meet Avarielle's eyes for fear of seeing disapproval in them.

"It should, if this lasts long enough," Avarielle said. "Mountain weather's so unpredictable. At least the woods weren't dry, so hopefully the fires didn't spread out too far." Avarielle took a deep breath and Cassara turned to look at her.

The warrior looked down at the fallen debris, charred beyond recognition, once part of a majestic landscape. "I guess," she said, a weak smile crossing her lips as she met Cassara's eyes, "that when magic is that powerful, it should be wielded more carefully."

Cassara was surprised for a moment at the veiled apology.

She returned the smile, and Avarielle shrugged.

"Guess I'm just not used to traveling with people anymore," she turned around and walked back to the smoldering fire and Shirina.

"How do we get out of here?" Avarielle asked, crouching on the other side of the pit from the sorceress.

Shirina didn't raise her head as she replied, her message clear yet delivered without the usual sarcastic tone. "Intent on finally getting clean, Avarielle?"

Avarielle cocked an eyebrow at her and was about to reply when she caught sight of Cassara's look of warning and closed her mouth again. She fell down hard on the ground, as would a bored child just reprimanded from having a bit of fun. Cassara ignored the reproachful look and crossed the pit, crouching down beside Shirina.

"Are you all right, Shirina?"

The sorceress turned her head to look at Cassara, blinking a few times, her brow furrowing momentarily before a slight smile crossed her lips.

"I'm just...tired," she answered, glancing sideways at Avarielle. The warrior did not miss the look.

"Don't worry, Shirina," she answered, lazily crossing her legs and leaning her elbows on her knees so that, although still on the other side of the fire pit, she was closer to the sorceress. "If I had wanted to kill you, I would have done so while you slept."

"How long will it take you to recover?" Cassara asked before Shirina could reply.

She leaned back against the earthy wall. "Usually it takes days to recover from a healing spell like the one I had to cast on you," she said, and did not meet Cassara's eyes as she spoke. "Jesimae was intent on killing you, you know."

Cassara had little doubt of that. She suddenly realized that since Shirina's loyalties to the Circle had been shaken, her confidence and self-assurance seemed to have been, as well. Not that she would ever agree to that. She would, in fact, be very insulted if she even heard Cassara's theory. She met Avarielle and Cassara's eyes all too infrequently of late. As though aware that they would see her fear and uncertainty.

"You healed her?" Avarielle asked as though the thought had never once crossed her mind.

Shirina shrugged. "I told you I needed your help. Besides," she added, some of her fire returning as she gave Avarielle a crooked smile, "the last thing I needed was a psychotic rampaging warrior coming to claim vengeance."

Cassara was surprised to hear Avarielle laugh softly. "You do have some wits left about you, then." Shirina seemed to be on the verge of replying when she thought better of it and let the temporary truce stand.

"How long before we can head out again?" Cassara asked, sitting near Shirina.

"I'm ready when you are," she replied, looking defiantly at Avarielle.

Avarielle ignored the challenge. "First things first. How do we get back up there?"

"It's a simple spell," Shirina replied. "But there's a bit more to consider."

Avarielle nodded. "If the rains continue as they have, the water will slide down from the mountain and eventually we'll drown."

"Or erosion from the freshly burned forest will begin from the rainfall and block the exit," Shirina continued.

"Of course, both of those things would be problems up there as well, but we might have more of a fighting chance," Avarielle finished, stretching her legs back out in front of her and leaning back on her hands.

Cassara looked at the accumulating water, the humidity pressing heavily on her lungs.

"I guess we'd better try our luck out there, then" she said, tugging her cloak tighter against her, her bones already chilled by the idea of walking into the storm.

"Sounds good to me," Avarielle said, standing and stretching. "I feel too much like a rabbit trapped in a hole down here. Besides," she added, looking at Shirina, who was struggling to her feet. "I think we could all use a bit of bathing."

"Next time we go to an inn, and may in Graydon's grace that happen soon," Shirina said, not complaining as Cassara took her supply bag and put it on her own back, having lost her own. "I vote that we make enough money to include a bath."

"You mean you're actually willing to go through that humiliation again?" Avarielle said, winking at Cassara.

"I'd do much more than that to help Tangia," Shirina whispered. With those words their harsh reality, held at bay by the fragile roots of the Circle's hideaway, came crashing upon them as strongly as the water flowing into the hole.

The three women, each brooding over their own dark

thoughts, stepped into the growing water and headed for the hole in silence.

"You should know she is beyond your help," a woman spoke behind them, and Avarielle had spun around and drawn Graysword before Shirina or Cassara had even turned.

Jesimae stood near the big root, what was left of her right arm covered by her cloak, her hand extended as she finished a spell. Avarielle ran forward, letting out a battle cry, but the spell ended before she could reach her. The warrior crumpled to the floor like a rag doll, Graysword falling uselessly from her grasp.

Shirina stepped in front of Cassara, chanting as she did, the words quick and urgent, and Cassara pulled her amulet free, the magic coursing through her arm stronger than it ever had.

Avarielle was too far for them to reach and she was in the path of any magic they might cast. Jesimae stood over the fallen warrior, her eyes gleaming with joy as she spoke.

"One down." She looked straight at Cassara, ignoring Shirina's presence as though she were a mere inconvenience.

"One more to go."

THE GRAYLOFT WAS in the way of any attack spell and both women before her knew it. Any spell to alter her body in any way, such as a sleep spell, would prove to be useless, a fact that Shirina soon acknowledged as she stopped chanting.

"I doubt you have the strength to use any spells anyways, Shirina," Jesimae said, feeling victory within her grasp, but still careful to keep the Grayloft between her and her enemies. She looked down quickly, to make sure her spell still held, pleased to see the strain lines on the warrior's face. She was trying to break free of the layers of sleep that had been thrown upon her mind, but Jesimae doubted she would succeed.

"How did you manage to affect her so?" Shirina asked, sounding genuinely curious. Of course she would be. Graylofts were protected from all spells by their ancestral magic, except for direct attack spells, in which case Graysword usually dispelled the magic before it struck its wielder.

She offered Shirina a secretive smile. "Not even Graylofts are immune to all magics." Shirina did not react to what she said and kept her cool, which angered Jesimae even more.

The spell appeared to her then, in the same way all spells came to her now with the new magic she had been given. Not through training and control, as the Circle had tried to show her, but rather through need and emotion. It was a less predictable system, but definitely one that Jesimae was quickly mastering.

The spell was still weak, but it would do, for now. Even if her orders were to bring both back alive, it would prove to be too much of a hassle, and that annoying soft-handed princess had cost her an arm. If she had been inclined to hurt her and not kill her before, she now felt the wisest course of action was to end her. She could simply convince Delora it had been an accident, just like the forest fire.

She grasped the spell and let it loose, her hand, more out of habit than need, aimed at the young princess. The princess' eyes widened in surprise, before they rolled back in her head and she fell uselessly into the water.

"Not very graceful for a princess, wouldn't you say?" Jesimae jested to Shirina, who had crouched down to see what spell had been cast. She raised the princess' head above water, propping it on a root.

"Don't worry, Shirina, it's just a sleep spell," Jesimae said, stepping over the Grayloft. With the princess' strong magic out of the way, Shirina was too weakened to pose a real threat. Jesimae took her right arm out of her cloak, showing Shirina the burnt flesh and bone, the unbending remaining fingers, all shimmering in the wake of her healing spell. The damage was so great, her magic could only halt the pain and hold the limb together. It would never see flesh again.

"I intend to repay her before I kill her," she whispered, fascinated by her own decaying flesh, fascinated by the strength of the human body to continue even after extreme pain and damage.

"How did you get back into Ravenhold?" Shirina asked as she stood up, ignoring Jesimae's last reply.

Jesimae looked at the raven-haired woman, mysterious and gifted with the very looks of nobility Jesimae had always wanted to have. She debated what to tell Shirina, wanting to reveal everything before she killed her, wanting to have one witness to the victories she had fought for, a witness who had known her longer than anyone else. But she remembered the pain and betrayal Shirina had dealt her, and her need for retribution was greater than any desire to be understood. It was power she longed for, and the Elite Shirina could never hope to even reach her strength and magic, no matter how many more years of sweat she poured over the old manuscripts and in the training halls.

But she did want her friend to die knowing that everything she loved was gone, not just Tangia. It seemed fair to her, somehow.

"Ravenhold is gone Shirina," Jesimae said, pleased to see the Elite's cool exterior fazed for an instant. "And I re-entered the Circle using something that you simply don't have."

She smiled and pointed her left arm towards Shirina, the attack spell fully in her grasp, the Elite too tired to counter her.

"Luck."

LAYERS UPON LAYERS, soft and warm, had been laid upon Cassara's mind and body. Dimly, she was aware that this was not desirable, but her comfort seemed more important. Memories were like a fleeting song, as insubstantial as the morning mists, as clouded as a stormy sky. There was light beyond her closed eyelids, a distraction to her dark slumber.

So heavy did she feel that she knew she must be sinking into the soft earth below her. At the edges of her body, where her skin met the world, she felt a chill grasping her, the deep warmth of her sleep barely enough to keep it at bay.

She heard voices around her, the words as impossible to grasp as her memories, but the tones tugged at her mind, commanding attention. Reluctantly she obeyed, her ears clearing only slightly, but enough for her to hear three things: two voices, one of which was very familiar, and water rushing into her ear. The latter jerked her free of some of the threads of sleep. Fear of drowning became alarmingly stronger as her senses returned and she felt the cool water on her right cheek, her neck stiff and uncomfortable.

Gone was the warmth, but still Cassara could not move her limbs. The veil over her memories lifted as her mind cleared, and she recalled the sensation being similar to her last encounter with Jesimae, except this time, it was not pain that was stopping her, but merely heaviness. Her limbs were too heavy to move, and her body would not respond to her commands.

She remembered seeing Avarielle toppling, her arms

not even breaking her fall, and realized that she must be under the same spell.

"I'm impressed you've managed to dispel my magic," she heard Jesimae say, her voice muffled by her covered ear and the sound of the water cascading into the cave.

"I'm not interested in your being impressed, Jesimae," she heard Shirina say, the voice as cool and controlled as it usually was, unless dealing with Avarielle.

"You should be, considering how much stronger I am than you now."

"You've always looked for quick solutions, Jesimae. I don't know which monster you had to make a deal with to gain your powers, but I'm certain it will be your downfall, just like it was in the Circle."

"My dealings were not my downfall in the Circle," Jesimae spat out. "My downfall was you. I thought of you as family!"

A long heartbeat passed. "The Circle is the only family I have ever had," Shirina replied, her voice unwavering and unrepentant.

In the silence that followed, Cassara imagined the calm look on Shirina's drawn face, and the anger seeping from Jesimae. Never would she have imagined the mad laughter that escaped Jesimae.

"Then consider yourself disowned, Shirina," Jesimae said, choking on a sob as she laughed.

So certain was Cassara that Jesimae was gathering her magic that she forgot for an instant that she couldn't see.

She realized her arm was cold, very cold, yet her hand was pulsating with warmth.

My amulet! The magic was still active and waiting for her to wield it. She wanted to open her eyes, to see where her magic would flare, but couldn't. Frustrated to the point of tears, remembering Shirina's warm healing hand on her back as she spent the magic that would have now saved her, Cassara squinted her eyes down, forcing them to become as heavy as possible. She then willed them to become as light as mist, and soon she could see, her vision cloudy but thankfully clear of the water.

From where she was, she couldn't see the two women and knew they were behind her. The silence was heavy, the dripping rain and falling burnt wood the only sound in the room. Cassara forced her arms to push her up, feeling the amulet's magic pulsate throughout her entire body now, its strength becoming her own.

Soon her ear was free from the water, wisps of wet hair clinging to her face. She slowly knelt, the water rising above her knees.

A movement caught her attention and she slowly turned her head around, the pain in her head growing to the point that she feared she might pass out. The two sorceresses stared at each other and Cassara was surprised to see waves of dark red magic passing from Jesimae to Shirina. A weak purple hue enclosed Shirina, its density lessening as each dark strand lashed at her.

Shirina's lips were pressed tightly, her features drawn as she pushed to maintain her defenses. Cassara's head throbbed heavily again, and the magic of the amulet responded.

She looked down, white mists spreading from it into her, her entire body cloaked in white. A violent throbbing at the back of her head made her heave and the mists surrounding her began to blind her.

Shirina fell then, her robes caught under her as both knees touched the ground, her head lolling forward and her hair hiding her chiseled features.

"You shouldn't have betrayed me and the Circle, Shirina," Jesimae said, and Cassara could see a dark cloud covering her fully. Shirina's own purple haze was gone, the sorceress clinging to consciousness.

"Because now, no one will grieve you once you've gone." The words struck Cassara hard, her eyes widening and the pain in her skull forgotten. *Who would grieve Jesimae when she was gone?* she had asked Avarielle.

No one will grieve you when you're gone

Cassara felt as though a sword had just cut through the shades of gray that had gripped her mind. The choices were now black and white, simple and easy. Jesimae had to die, or Shirina would. And the choice wasn't theirs. It was hers, kneeling in a puddle of water, a powerful talisman in her hands.

It was more than Jesimae's life that was in her hands. It was Shirina's.

Cassara invoked her magic, the white mists gently leaving her, picking up speed as they approached Jesimae. The sorceress only realized at the last moment what was happening. She flung her darkness out to protect herself, but it was too late, and the white mists sliced through her magical protection.

Jesimae did not even have the time to scream. The flames consumed her, the smell of burning flesh clinging to the dampness. The light was gone as quickly as it had come and Cassara's head stopped throbbing, only the memory of pain clinging to the back of her skull. Her vision had cleared. She did not look towards the ashes that had once been Jesimae.

Instead she looked at Shirina, who had gathered enough strength to raise her head and stare at Cassara, not with accusation, nor with gratefulness.

"I would grieve you," Cassara said simply, hesitating for a moment before putting the amulet back around her neck, its weight almost too heavy for her to bear.

14

Fanned by the winds, the fire had traveled a long way even in the damp wood, and Cassara strained to see how much its destruction had reached. She couldn't tell, the damage continuing well beyond her sight, the hills of the Maple Mountains keeping secret the extent of their devastation.

The small village might have been spared, but it was impossible to tell, and their journey was too pressing to backtrack. If the Circle was involved, and had possibly now fallen, there was no more time for hesitation or second-guessing. Whatever was spreading from the lands of the West had to be stopped before it claimed more lives, or all of the magic of Graydon.

The storm had already wasted its strength and was now a mere trickle of rain, for which Cassara was grateful. She was already wet enough.

"I say we go to Massir," Avarielle suggested after

hearing Shirina's unemotional report of Ravenhold's fall. "They're still expecting a princess down there," she said, waving towards Cassara. "And we know there's a council meeting in a few days, called by the Circle itself. If we're lucky, we'll catch a few Circle elders before they've all left."

Shirina crossed her arms and hugged her chest to ward off the cold and the fatigue. "It might also be walking into the den of the hungry wolf."

Avarielle nodded. She and Cassara were both being hunted by the Circle, and Shirina did not exclude herself from their company, meaning she would more than likely be considered a traitor to the Circle, her life merely an inconvenience to those she had called her family. Cassara wondered if the sorceress would ever allow herself to fully feel the sting of that loss.

"I can disguise myself and hide Graysword, and Cassara will be under the royal family's protection." Avarielle paused and looked at Shirina. "Could the Circle have gained control over Massir?"

Shirina deliberated for a moment before answering. "I really don't know," she said, meeting Avarielle's look without hesitation.

The warrior weighed the sorceress' honesty for an instant before shrugging.

"There's only one way to find out," she said, turning to Cassara. "What do you think?"

Cassara tried to imagine what could happen. For the first time since leaving Edoline, she truly understood just how easily her companions' lives could be taken, even with their skill and experience. And her own life seemed so fragile, as well. She had not believed death would claim her even when Jesimae had intended to kill her, so surreal had it all seemed. But now Cassara had killed another. She had inflicted death on Jesimae, who had been powerful, and it had been so easy. With a single thought, she had wiped her from this realm.

If someone of such power could so easily be destroyed, then would her own life not be just as easy to erase?

And by going to Massir, not only would she be putting her life in further danger from the Circle, she would also be trapping herself in marriage. She looked away from Avarielle and Shirina, towards the destruction that lay around her, and knew that it would only escalate. Since her encounter with Eloms in Edoline not even a month ago, they had become more frequent, and the destruction and dangers only increased with each passing day.

If they did nothing now, if she chose to run and hide and hope that she would somehow survive, then she would be just as responsible for the lives lost. She had the amulet and it could make a difference, if its wielder could make difficult decisions.

She did not reach up to touch her amulet, feeling the weight around her neck still, knowing its magic waited to be called upon, a white mist that might one day consume her.

Cassara took a deep breath, the fresh morning air

filled with the smell of campfire, which might have been pleasant in another setting.

She turned around, realizing her decision had already been made before she had even deliberated, having done so mostly out of habit than need.

"We head for Massir." Shirina nodded, Avarielle grinned, and the three were on their way. And for the first time, Cassara felt like she was now taking an active part of this quest, its necessity sharpening her mind.

And her two traveling companions, who at once intimidated and amazed her, seemed to have sensed this change in her, and now treated her as an equal.

It was amazing what saving one life could do.

THE WET GROUND made traveling difficult and with half a day's walk well behind them, they had yet to find a suitable break area. Amidst the burnt, fallen or falling trees, mudslides and newly-formed streams, the three companions hoped to reach some dry shelter soon.

Cassara was surprised to see some green patches under the black decay, where nature had survived the angry flames. She wondered if some of the older trees, so thick that they still stood despite being ravaged by the flames, would ever grow sprouts again.

The three slowly made their way down the Maple Mountains, although this portion required them to climb up first, to pass a small hill that should soon give way to a view of Solir, or at least what was left of it. If what they had heard at the last village was true, most of the country had been overrun in the past week, the invasion so quick, unforeseen and frightening that the leaders had fled to Rashim without a second thought, leaving their people to perish in the Eloms' wake. Cassara wondered how many villages already boasted a barricade, and decided it had to be few.

Walking on a fallen piece of wood, Shirina, now to the point of exhaustion, lost her footing. She would have fallen had Avarielle's arm not shot out and caught her.

"Curse those reflexes," Avarielle mumbled as she let Shirina's arm go. The sorceress, despite her fatigue, still managed to tease the warrior.

"Thank you, o mighty warrior. You've saved my robes from needing to be cleaned."

Cassara sighed and shook her head.

"You two enjoy arguing entirely too much," she added with a smile. "It would be with ease that one would mistake the two of you for a couple."

Avarielle and Shirina immediately turned to Cassara, denial and insult clear on their faces. Cassara could not help but laugh at their distraught expressions. She passed them both, surprised by Avarielle's control when the warrior did not trip her, and reached the top of the hill before either one of them.

"I swear, I'm starting to consider picking up regicide as a hobby," Avarielle mumbled as she came up beside her.

Shirina, who had regained some energy with the exchange, was not far behind.

"Then I'm safe because I'm no king, and look at that!" Cassara said, laughing as she looked down the hill. The fire had reached the top, but had failed to fall back down, only a few burnt trees scattered within the upcoming tree line. The mountains gracefully sloped down, and past the forest stretched the valley. Several rivers crisscrossed farms scattered as far as the eyes could see. Cassara wondered how many people had stayed, and how many had died.

"Is that a village down there?" Avarielle asked, pointing to the bottom of the hill, where they could see the ends of a wall. Cassara imagined the warm food and beds they could find there.

"Shall we go before Avarielle and I continue our verbal sparring and Cassara dies from a cold?" Shirina said coolly, although some urgency slipped into her voice as well. Spurred on by the promise of food and warmth, and surrounded by the life around them, the three companions set a faster pace down the hill.

Although they all understood, no one mentioned the fact that the Eloms that had scattered in the fire would probably be lurking, waiting until nighttime to emerge.

By then, they would be ready.

15

Gragor, youngest guard of Edoline, forced himself to walk and not just stumble into the throne room of the king of Rashim. His queen had sent him on an urgent mission and he would not fail her. He would not fail to keep the oath he had sworn, nor fail to repay the kindness of the queen, who had spoken comforting words to him after all of his companions had been slaughtered or robbed of their courage.

Only two years older than the youngest daughter of Edoline, he still considered he had much to learn, but without Klar's tutelage, he doubted he would ever get much better. And after all that he had witnessed, he was convinced this was no longer his calling.

Speeding down the roads on various horses, during all weather and even braving the monster-infested darkness, Gragor had decided that after he had seen his queen safely out of the clutches of the invading army, he would find himself a wife and maybe a farm. He was certain the queen would grant him land for his courage and hoped she would offer him some riches as well.

"Announcing Lieutenant Gragor Gramid of the Royal Protectors of Edoline," he was clearly announced across the court. The various ladies and lords present for today's proceedings looked back with minor interest, some resuming their quiet chatter as the ladies fanned themselves to escape the rising summer heat.

Gragor barely noticed them, raising his chin as he began walking towards the king, proud to have heard the title lieutenant, even if he had mostly earned it because of the death of his companions. Still, today he was an important man, and he intended to speak clearly and be heard.

The king looked up with mild interest. Beside the king, a proud man who could only be Dayshon, heir to the throne, looked at him with dark, searching eyes. Gragor looked away, unable to keep eye contact with him, only halfway to the throne and already feeling the weight and power of the kingdom of Rashim. He heard a court lady whisper an inappropriate, although flattering remark about his body, and felt himself blush, feeling younger and younger with every step he took.

The court of Edoline and its royalty did not demand much, and even the few formalities seemed casual now besides the grand, gold-splattered halls of Rashim. He reached the beginning of the carpet that led up to the king's throne and, as instructed earlier, he stopped a step shy of stepping on the carpet. He was now flanked on both sides by six guards, all armed to the teeth, the six of them bearing more weaponry than all of the guards of Edoline had owned.

Someone cleared his throat loudly. Gragor quickly bowed, having forgotten the formality, knowing his face reddened for it, wishing he didn't have to look up at the king and the heir to the throne. But he had to, and so he did, facing the cold, calculating eyes of the king.

Gragor wasn't certain how to begin, or in what way to address the most powerful king of Graydon. It had never occurred to him that he might not be familiar with the etiquette of the court, and he had never imagined anything else but a flawless presentation of the problem and a quick rescue. Now, he didn't know how he would convince the king to help Altessa, nor how he would find Princess Cassara in all of this, and inform her she was now free to change her mind. He didn't think they would take kindly to that.

Someone giggled behind him, deepening his blush. His tongue was pasty, words not able to form on his dry lips. He couldn't imagine the kind Princess Cassara dealing with this cruel pretension day after day, and he gained strength in the knowledge that he could save her as well as the queen.

Before he could speak, however, Prince Dayshon addressed him.

"I was well-received in Edoline," he began, his voice warm and welcoming, which surprised Gragor. "And I wish to extend the same courtesy to one of its trusted guards." Gragor hadn't thought it was possible for him to blush more, and he was really glad he wasn't facing the ladies of the court now.

"Thank you, Prince Dayshon," Gragor managed to mumble, and he bowed slightly to him, hoping to buy himself time to compose his thoughts.

"Tell us, what news of Edoline?" the prince asked, his voice hopeful, momentarily confusing him. He decided to first enquire on Princess Cassara, convincing himself he wanted to make sure she was safe, even if in reality he only longed for a familiar face.

"I have come to speak to the Princess Cassara," Gragor said with a pedigree that would have made the queen proud. Instead of the simple answer he had expected, he was surprised to see the prince's eyes narrow.

"We did not know we were expecting her," the king said, not looking towards his son, his deep and piercing eyes destroying whatever slight level of comfort he had managed to achieve.

"But," Gragor began, the confusion and urgency he was beginning to feel pushing his lack of comfort aside. "We sent word through the Circle. Have you heard nothing of what has happened?"

"What do you mean?" Prince Dayshon demanded as he took a step forward.

Gragor was overheating again and he wished he could control his blushing more. He tried to answer the prince but found that no words were coming. He was so hot. His vision was becoming blurry, and he felt himself sway, surprised when Prince Dayshon was suddenly by his side supporting him. Then that vision became blurry as well and he slipped into darkness, wondering what Queen Altessa would think when she heard that he had fainted before the King of Rashim himself.

***

DAYSHON CROSSED the floor and reached the fallen Lieutenant before the six guards flanking him had even moved a muscle, their weaponry clanging awkwardly as they tried to follow him. The heir to the throne kept his hand close to the jewel-encrusted knife on his belt as he reached Gragor, in case a trap should lie in wait.

"Take him to the healers' quarters," Dayshon ordered Jiles, the captain of the guards as he joined the prince at the front, his weathered face troubled as he met Dayshon's face, indicating with his eyes the left of the room. Dayshon gave a slight nod. He knew Jiles wasn't pointing out a current threat, for he and his father would have been whisked away, but rather a potential threat or disturbing coincidence. He hoped it was the first of the two possibilities, for that could be resolved more quickly.

Dayshon stood up as Jiles ordered two guards to follow the prince's orders, he himself choosing to stay behind with the king and prince. Dayshon looked around briefly to the ladies and lords of the court. Their self-focused conversation broken for a few moments to see what had befallen the newcomer had resumed, all the latest gossip of the kingdom leaving lips faster than sailors abandoning a leaking boat.

Carefully Dayshon glanced around the room as he resumed his position by the throne, hearing the lady as she spoke, knowing immediately why Jiles had warned him of her presence.

"I trust the guard will recover well?" the lady Delora, Elder of the Circle and current liaison to Ravenhold said as she approached the throne, keeping a respectable distance away.

"Lady Delora," King Darmir acknowledged her, which was more than he did to most of the guests of the court. Dayshon had not yet been made privy to whatever thoughts or worries had forced the king to withdraw. But that would soon change, as it always did.

Dayshon focused on the woman before them, tall, dark and beautiful, around his mother's age, with an air about her that could freeze the most passionate of hearts. She smiled warmly, infused the right tinge of concern into her words, but her eyes were as cold and calculating as on the first day they had met a few months ago, hard granite in pools of white.

"You honor us once again with your presence, Lady Delora," Dayshon spoke when it was clear his father did not intend to do so. To an outsider, it would seem that the king of Rashim was stricken by an illness of the mind or of the body, but Dayshon knew his father well enough to see that only dark thoughts had grasped his mind. Or so he hoped, at least.

"I came as quickly as I could to give you news from the East," the lady said, no hint of urgency in her voice. Dayshon felt his mouth go dry as he spoke.

"News of Edoline," he whispered, his voice echoing throughout the court, everyone suddenly silent at the mention of the small kingdom, only a few ladies still fanning the summer's heat away.

"Tragic news, I fear," Lady Delora said, lowering her head respectfully. Dayshon gritted his teeth as he waited for her to continue. A lady whispered something to another, only to blush lightly as she realized how much the noise carried in the quiet hall. His impending betrothal to the Princess Cassara had come as a shock to the court, who would see him wed the much richer and well-known Princess Malir of the Southern kingdoms. Dayshon knew that more than a few of the court hoped to hear of Cassara's refusal or death, so that the activities could resume, with many of them having already forged strong allegiances with Princess Malir.

As though enjoying the slight moment of suspense but knowing enough not to try his patience any longer, Lady Delora continued.

"An army of dark monsters swept through the kingdom of Edoline one night a few weeks ago. And few were spared. I am saddened to report that, despite the valiant efforts of his guards, King Alexavier perished in the attack."

What of the princess? Dayshon wanted to ask, his mouth completely dry, visions of gold and laughter pounding his mind. Before he could betray his rising emotions, his father spoke.

"So Alexavier is dead," he whispered, his voice still commanding the attention of the entire court. Dayshon could not recall the last time the lords and ladies had stood so quietly and with such anticipation.

Delora stared at the king openly, as though waiting to see his reaction. Dayshon thought he glimpsed rare indecision in his father's face before it became clouded with anger.

"Out with it, woman!" the king said rudely, everyone in the court taken aback except the Lady Delora. "What of my son's promised princess?"

Delora performed a short curtsy as though acknowledging her disrespect, but Dayshon was taken aback by the obvious tactic at not responding right away, as though a child enjoying a last moment of disobedience. Although she was a respected Elder of the Circle, when in Rashim, she too was expected to follow the king's orders.

"The Lady Cassara lived," Delora answered, her tone flat as she answered. "And was on her way to join your son in Rashim when we believe her carriage was attacked. She has not been seen or heard from since."

"When and where was she attacked?" Dayshon asked immediately, his father once more motionless in his throne as he watched Delora with passing interest.

"In Kosel, about two weeks ago. She should have

reached Rashim by now," she finished. No other words were necessary. Dayshon heard some noise in the back of the court, looking up to see Malir was amongst those present, angry with himself that he had not noticed the princess before now. He could feel her vulture eyes search his out, but he refused to meet hers, seeking out Delora's instead.

"The guard said that they had sent word through the Circle. Why had we heard nothing of this until now? Is the Circle's power so weak?" He spoke the last with some venom, expecting to get a reaction from his father. None came, and Dayshon refused to look down from the dark, angered eyes of the Elder before him.

"Our initiates," she spat back at him, and for the first time Dayshon felt he was finally seeing her true colors, "are busy keeping your borders safe from the demons, your highness." The last words were strained and Malir shuffled uncomfortably closer, as though she meant to diffuse the situation, but uncertain how. Dayshon admitted he admired her courage, and for the first time thought maybe she could make a good queen, though not nearly as interesting or genuine as the princess of Edoline.

He felt a pang of regret that he would not get to know her better, but he would have to let go of her after some searching. And although Delora's last words were spoken with anger, the truth in them still stung. Dayshon knew well enough that Rashim needed the Circle right now, but he strongly suspected the opposite to be true as well.

"An effort we appreciate," Dayshon said, tilting his

head in acknowledgement. Delora smiled gratefully, baring perfect teeth he was surprised did not drip venom. "But if you will excuse me, I believe that a search party needs to be organized." He skipped the two steps leading away from the throne, landing on the floor and sprinting across the back of the hall to reach the private chambers, the gossip in the court resuming with vigor. Only Princess Malir's eyes followed the graceful strides of the heir of Rashim.

16

Even though sheltered by trees, the three knew the village would soon be spread before them and their quick pace slowed. Avarielle took the front, the warrior's red hair catching the few rays of sun as she looked around them. Cassara stood by Shirina, the sorceress stubbornly refusing to ask for help, even if her feet seemed heavier with each new step and her shoulders were not as high as her proud bearing usually demanded of her.

The wind blew gently in the trees, several leaves losing their grip and falling silently to the ground. At first, Cassara thought very little of it, but when a billowing wind struck and leaves fell all around them, she looked up to the highest branches of the trees, and found most bare.

The wind was fresh and warm, an early summer breeze. The grass and bushes were green and yet, it seemed that high above them, someone had mistakenly patched the leaves of the wrong season. Another wind struck and Cassara watched the leaves fall, but with them fell something else.

A wooden arrow shaft was sticking out of the ground before Cassara had even realized what had flown past her vision. Avarielle began walking back towards them, her hand on the pommel of her sword when a voice shot out from the forest.

"Don't move, any of you, or it'll be a deathblow next." The man spoke with the loose accent of Solir, where words tended to blend together.

"We don't mean you any harm," Avarielle said, as she slowly removed her hand from the pommel of her sword.

"Neither do we," the voice answered softly. Cassara heard the rustling of leaves behind her but dared not move. "But we will harm you, if you don't listen to us."

A man walked out from within the trees to face them, and three others surrounded them, bows drawn. Their ages ranged from younger than Cassara to the middle-aged man who led them. He took an instant to observe them, his quick brown eyes barely pausing as he absorbed every detail.

"Aren't you an odd traveling party," the man mused, furrowing his brows as his eyes continued their travel from Avarielle's western looks to Shirina's chiseled, proud features, to end on Cassara's light hair. "Why exactly are you in this area, dare I ask?"

"We are heading to Massir," Cassara said, her body

easily regaining the confidence and bearing that had been trained into her since childhood.

"And why is that?" the man asked suspiciously, not trusting the sudden shift in Cassara, who suddenly seemed in control of the situation.

"I am to meet my fiancé there," she offered as an explanation, wondering if he would question her further or simply accept her story.

"And these two?" he asked, casting a quick glance at Shirina and Avarielle.

"My maids," Cassara said, forcing her lips to remain still and not curl up. She was surprised and disappointed not to hear any protest from either of the women.

The man's eyebrows shot up again. "Two maids in this area is a rich lady's game. Why are you traveling without guards?"

Cassara looked down momentarily, hoping he would see it as a young woman's hesitation or repression of emotions. She had wanted to test their story before reaching Massir anyways, and this seemed like a much less dangerous audience. Even if their bows were still aimed at their hearts, she doubted they would kill them.

"We were attacked by these dark creatures." She let a bit of distress seep into her voice, an act that didn't take much effort to pull off successfully. "The rest of our party was killed, and we've been running from the fire ever since." She paused, feigning hesitation. "We were hoping for a warm bed and food." She let the thought linger in the air, the leader of the men still regarding her with suspicion.

"Your blood looks red enough," he said as he regarded their wounds.

"I'm Arlos," the man said, offering his hand, which Cassara gratefully took, trying not to wince at the strength of his grip.

"I'm Cassara," she offered in return and then, waving dismissively at the other two, she said, "and this is Ryle, and Rina." At that Shirina did grunt.

"You can have a room for all three of you," the man said, motioning for the other three men to lower their weapons. "And a warm meal. But you'll have to work for them. What skills do you have to offer us?" he asked with hesitation, as though fearing the useless answer she would give him.

Cassara offered him her sweetest smile, winning a sigh from Shirina and a grin from Avarielle.

"I'm willing to guess that your village could use some entertainment."

***

BEYOND THE WOODEN walls of the village of Rockor lay a besieged people, a fact evident despite the laughter escaping the surrounding buildings. The walls had been reinforced several times, huge trunks holding together the old falling sections, some houses torn apart to gather the precious lumber. Archers patrolled the wall even though no monsters lurked in daytime. Cassara couldn't help but wonder what else haunted the small hamlet.

"The monsters, Eloms, you say, came maybe three weeks ago," Arlos said as he walked beside Cassara. Avarielle and Shirina, having assumed their roles as maids, followed behind them. "Maybe more. Time seems to flow differently, now," he added with an apologetic smile. "At first, we thought they might be wolves, but there were soon so many that it was impossible to ignore their presence. Or their cravings."

Cassara was surprised to hear the laughter of children coming from some homes, the only people in sight being the few archers currently patrolling the streets.

"We were luckier than most, with our walls," he said, waving at another villager as he passed by. The man's eyes scrutinized the three newcomers, his hand nervously fidgeting with his bow. "We haven't seen or heard anything from any of the other nearby villages, but a few farmers who came here seeking sanctuary told us many people had already been killed by the passing Eloms."

"You say passing?" Avarielle asked, moving closer to them. "Which way were they headed?"

"West, we think," Arlos answered, glancing back at her. "Towards Massir. But not all of them. Some of them seem to be staying in the area." The last was spoken very softly and he looked around to ensure that they were alone on the small road.

"I take it you can fight?" he asked softly, the words more of a statement than a question.

Cassara nodded, wishing she still had some weapons. "Our scouts report that there are more Eloms in the area than ever, and our walls aren't as strong as they once were," Arlos said, glancing around them, his voice so low Shirina and Avarielle crowded Cassara to hear him. "Sometimes we're lucky. We find some hiding and we burn them out. But, well, we just don't have the manpower to hunt in the day, and our people aren't fighters, and they grow hungrier and more tired with each passing day." He gave them a crooked smile. "There's even been talk of having to eat their corpses soon for food."

"You mustn't do that," Shirina immediately said, her voice ringing clearly across the empty road before she lowered it to continue. "They're tainted, and would do you no good. Besides," she added with uncharacteristic gentleness, "how good could they taste?"

Arlos smiled at her and laughed softly. "Wise words for a simple maid," he said, winking at her.

"The Lady Cassara only hires the best," Shirina replied flatly.

We'll have to work on this act before we reach Massir, Cassara thought before speaking again.

"With the fires over the Maple Mountains," Cassara said, amazed at the steadiness of her voice, remembering the hot flames from Jesimae that had streaked by her. "The Eloms have probably come down this way, to find shelter. It accounts for their increased numbers," she ended softly, wishing she had more wisdom to impart.

"No matter how many we kill, it won't stop, will it?"

Arlos asked softly of Cassara as they resumed walking. The inn came into view, a well-sized establishment with a creaking sign above the door that read the Mountain Path Inn.

"No Arlos," she answered as softly as he had asked as the four reached the door. "It won't stop." In the silence that followed her answer, Cassara wanted desperately to say something, or better yet, to have Shirina or Avarielle correct her, or even argue about it together. But no sound came save for the creaking sign and a door banging off in the distance.

THIS WAS by far the biggest crowd Cassara had ever played to, and she was amazed at their cheerful faces and rambunctious laughter.

"Looks like strong drink is the one thing that's still widely available here," Avarielle said, winking at Cassara.

"Not for long at the rate they're consuming it," Shirina said with a sneer. Pitchers of ale and bottles of wine were freely passed around, washed glasses too great a luxury in a village that was trying to preserve its well water, for fear Eloms had contaminated nearby water sources.

As Cassara brought her flute to her lips to play an old ballad of Rashim, unwilling to challenge her tired friends, she decided that it was more than a few sips of ale that kept their spirits high. Seeing the easy camaraderie they shared, everyone familiar with each other and happy to share what little they had left, she decided that what kept them going was the feeling that they weren't alone in this world, no matter how dark and frightening.

As the first note escaped her flute, she found herself wishing she could be one of them, understood and accepted by the friends around them, knowing that no matter what you chose in life, you would never walk down that path alone.

The first song ended and the room was filled with cheers and applause so loud the floor above them creaked in protest. Cassara quickly began the second song, Avarielle and Shirina following her lead, and the inn was quiet again as the sorceress' voice reached for notes that seemed to be a gift from Lady Fate herself. By the end of the song the sun was already low in the sky, signaling the end of another day, and the beginning of another nightmare.

"We should eat soon, and get ready," Avarielle shouted to be heard above the cheers. Cassara nodded, but her fingers still covered the holes of her flute, her lips aching to feel the soft wood.

"Go ahead," Cassara said to Avarielle, turning around to tell Shirina the same. "I think I'll play one more for them."

Shirina went to sit down immediately, still fighting the exhaustion that had been devouring her all day, the few cheerful patrons who would have joined her quickly discouraged by her withering glances. Avarielle's eyes refused to break from Cassara's for a moment, as though searching for something she couldn't find. Then she nodded and slipped her boots back on, looking thoughtfully at Cassara one more time before exiting the inn.

Cassara watched her go before taking requests from the crowd.

"The Lost Lovers Duet," a man shouted, and Cassara looked at his young, wistful face, surprised to hear the request. A few grunts of agreement were heard in the inn and Cassara nodded, accepting the request. The last rays of the sun shone dark yellows and oranges into the inn as the patrons grew quiet.

The song itself wasn't complex to play on the flute, but the full melody could never be reached without a male and female singer to play Elihor and Graydon's roles. Softly Cassara played the first note, one of many long notes, held captive longer than necessary to set the mournful air of the tune.

The music came easily to her and she let it take over, from the meeting of Graydon and Elihor in what used to be the Midlands, to the war that broke between their peoples, tearing them apart. The music soared as Graydon sent word to his beloved that they would try to unite their magic and end the war, the light and the dark living as one, his hopes to be with her sent in the one final word he gave to her—*come.*

And she would have, had she not been betrayed by her very own, intent on keeping the powers for themselves. The notes fell as she had in the sea, as Graydon's tears of rage had upon feeling her death, ripping his soul from deep within him.

The song ended with rage and anger, but Cassara strung it to a tune of Edoline, one of mourning, of prayer and of hope. The music hissed, the angry, quick notes becoming long again, soft and soothing, and she felt like she was holding Graydon, the man she was told was her ancestor, as she lead him through his grief. But history was never far, as she knew he had created the Wall that still stood on this day, to keep the treacherous forces of Elihor away, to let them die in their darkness, before Graydon threw himself into the very sea that Cassara had always heard striking against the shores of her youth.

The song brought her beyond Graydon's mourning and another face came to her, not her father's, nor her mother's as she might have imagined, but Jesimae's, dark, frightening and painful. She gagged as she remembered the smell of the burning flesh, her numbed fingers and breath tripping on a few of the notes. No one in the room seemed to notice except Shirina, who looked up at Cassara for a brief moment before concentrating back on the growing darkness around her.

The last light of the day vanished, the new darkness hiding the tears on Cassara's face, the smell of cooking filling the inn and hungry stomachs.

She closed the song to some applause, the few candles in the place making it impossible to see whether the song was enjoyed. Soon the laughter resumed, breaking the darkness, but Cassara felt too removed from it to partake.

Whatever closeness she had felt with these people had vanished with the last note of the song. She felt just as she had after playing in Edoline: alone.

The Eloms would be here soon and she felt hot and smothered in the inn. She cast a glance at Shirina, but the sorceress, from what little outline she could see, was looking into the distance, lost in her own thoughts. Cassara held the flute in her hand for a moment longer, bringing it closer to her face to see some of the detailing, before putting it slowly away and securing it in the pouch on her belt.

She needed to get out, to feel the fresh night air. She stepped out into the night, the moon shining down brightly, the storm that had ended the fires long gone, only a few puddles remaining as proof of its passage.

Cassara had barely taken ten steps when Avarielle called her name. The warrior jogged down the road, Graysword's pommel still covered and Cassara wondered how often the sword would need to flash this night.

"Thought you'd need this," Avarielle said as she handed Cassara a bow and a quiver of arrows.

"Thank you," Cassara said as she took the weapon, the weight of the arrows on her back and the feel of the bow's string pressed against her clothing reassuring. "But I'm still not very good at it," she added with a slight smile.

"You're better than you think, and you'll just get better. Besides, you'll get plenty of practice tonight," Avarielle said, motioning for Cassara to follow her. "Their defenses aren't bad," the warrior said, pointing towards the wall that surrounded the village. "For mostly farmers, it's actually quite good. Apparently on the first few nights they tried fighting the Eloms one on one, but quickly gave up on the idea after they lost the few individuals who knew a thing or two about swordplay."

Cassara heard distant voices and she could see young men standing by the wall, recognizing some of the archers from this afternoon.

"Now they just use archers. Thankfully, with all the hunt around here they have quite a few good ones," Avarielle continued, waving at the young men, already acquainted with them. "They stand on the rooftops closest to the end of the wall, sometimes with makeshift towers for increased height, and shoot at the incoming Eloms." Avarielle pointed enthusiastically to an old house, which was covered by a pile of wood planks, what Cassara skeptically guessed to be a makeshift tower.

"I told them the two of us could help, and maybe even Shirina, although I'm not sure she knows how to hurl much else than her magic and insults."

"No magic tonight?" Cassara asked. They had used their magic on fewer Eloms than they would be facing this night, and had barely escaped with their skin intact.

Avarielle shrugged. "The only thing they know about magic is the fact that the Circle's Elite come by every eight years and collect children they claim have powers. So it's not very well looked upon, and I don't think it's in our best interest to reveal our powers, especially since they're so good with their bows."

"I suppose you're right," Cassara reluctantly agreed, wishing she felt more confident with the bow. She had, after all, just gained more control over her powers, and yearned to explore its possibilities.

Avarielle waved towards the wall. "The wall will protect us," she said. "And tomorrow we leave for the borders of Rashim. Tonight should be the easiest part of that journey." Cassara failed to be comforted by the warrior's words, but she was ready to accept them for now. There really wasn't much else they could do.

"Food is ready!" The scream came from the inn, followed by loud cheering.

"Not a particularly subtle bunch, are they?" Cassara said. "I suppose it wouldn't make much of a difference, since the Eloms already know where they are."

Avarielle nodded slowly, deep in thought. "I find it odd, though. Some of them are staying here, hunting the humans, while others are converging towards Rashim. It's like there are two types of Eloms, the ones that are wild, only hunting for food, and the other ones that seem to think and plan." Avarielle looked off in the distance. "I never thought I'd say this, but I wish we knew more about them."

The warrior shook herself free of her own gloom and grinned at Cassara. "But first, to more important things. Food! Go ahead and eat with Shirina, and I'll keep checking their defenses. I want to make sure I'm comfortable with our safety."

Cassara nodded and started walking towards the inn

before she hesitated and called after Avarielle. "Did you ever kill someone?" The words seemed to be the only sound left in the village. The laughter, the rustling leaves and the creaking sign all part of a reality Cassara felt she no longer belonged to.

Avarielle stopped and slowly turned around to face Cassara. She nodded. "I was younger than you, and acted out of fear," she said, the words heavy with the weight of memory. "It took me a while to understand that it would have been them, or me." She seemed to be grasping for words that would not come, but then gave up and simply shrugged. Still, she did not walk away.

I didn't act out of fear, Cassara wanted to say. *I made a choice, not by instinct, but by what I felt was needed.* But she did not speak, choosing instead to try to understand what that fully entailed, and if she still felt the same chill she did every time the word describing her actions danced around her mind. *Murder.*

Instead of speaking of her true fears, instead of asking the warrior's advice, Cassara simply stood, resisting the urge to hug her jacket tight against herself, despite the warm summer night. But one question would not lay silent.

"Does it ever go away? The memories, the smell? The feeling?" *Burnt flesh. Magic.*

Avarielle hesitated for a moment before answering.

"I'm sorry you had to do that," she answered. "I'm sorry you had to go through that."

"But," Avarielle added, her eyes hardening, "it's

something you're going to have to deal with yourself." Her eyes gained a bit of the cold steel Cassara had only witnessed when Shirina pushed her luck too far.

Cassara nodded and turned around, walking back towards the inn to fill her body with food, so that part of her wouldn't be as empty as her spirit felt.

17

*T*he villagers had done a decent job of securing the town. *Otherwise, they'd all be dead by now,* Avarielle thought as she examined the ramparts. Still, the wooden fortifications had been hastily reinforced and she guessed that with the mounting attacks they would only hold for a few more nights. If even that.

Well, it didn't matter anyhow. She just needed them to hold for one night.

"Should we even bother feeding it? What a waste." Two men walked by Avarielle, their weapons clutched tightly.

"One of us should stay," the taller of the two said, his eyes darting back and forth.

"I hear they had a show at the inn!" the other guard moaned, his eyes flickering towards Avarielle.

"What are you gentlemen talking about?" she asked sweetly, smiling at them.

The tall guard glanced at her suspiciously, but the

other guard smiled and answered. "That odd Elom. At least, that's what we think he is. He certainly didn't seem to have any problems with the dark creatures."

"He?"

The guard smirked. "You want to see him? We've got him caged in the back of that chicken coop." His eyes wandered up and down Avarielle's body. "I'd be happy to show him to you."

Avarielle narrowed her eyes and smiled coldly, squaring her shoulders back as she looked down at the shorter, bolder guard. "Tell you what," she hissed, the guard blanching visibly. "Why don't you two enjoy the inn for a short while, and I mean short, and I'll keep watch over your prisoner for you?"

The taller guard shifted his feet. "I don't think Arlos wants us to leave him alone."

"He'd hardly be alone," Avarielle snapped before lowering her voice. "And if you're unsure of my skills with weapons, feel free to test me."

The taller guard swallowed hard and the shorter one took a step back. "Let's eat."

Avarielle watched them go for a few seconds before turning her attention to the small desolate building. An odd Elom was something worth investigating. She wondered if "he" was one of the new Eloms Trevon had described to her, but doubted it. If the new Eloms were as powerful and deadly as Trevon had said, then a chicken coop and some villagers hardly seemed enough to hold one.

She fought back her worries for her people and took a deep breath. The air was oppressively humid, like most of the cursed eastern lands seemed to be. Not dry and comforting like her land.

"Enough," she mumbled and curled her hands into fists. She walked towards the small building and pushed open the door, one hand firmly clutching the pommel of her sword. She peered in, letting her eyes adjust to the darkness inside, though some light from the full moon filtered in through the slits in the wood.

She ducked and entered, feeling some magic coursing in her sword. She looked towards the back instinctively, spotting chains secured to the wood. A man sat on the floor, his head lowered to his raised knees, his arms held up by the chains. His shirt was in tatters, his arms fully exposed as they stretched upwards, muscles bulging under the strain. His hair was dark and at least shoulder length. He didn't raise his head to see who had come. Beside him, out of the reach of his bound hands, the guards had left food and water.

Avarielle examined him, her hand tightening on the pommel. She could feel Graysword react to him, but only with a shadow of its usual might.

"Who are you?" she asked without whisper or formality. The man's head shot up immediately. His eyes focused on her, and Avarielle's breath caught in her throat. His eyes were wells of inky black, moist and unblinking. No white graced them.

His face bore the scars of a warrior's life, his jaw

strong, but his skin slightly gray, as though he had not often seen the sun. He looked at her for a moment before standing, his movements slow and calculated. Avarielle wondered how long they had kept this man in captivity. Her magic still whispered but her instincts told her he meant her no harm.

Now that he stood, he was taller than her and she thought she detected curiosity in his dark eyes.

"Who are you?" She repeated the question, her voice steady. She kept her stance relaxed but ready. And she met his gaze unflinchingly.

He stared at her but didn't answer.

"Can you even understand me?" she suddenly asked, wondering if a language barrier had kept him in here longer than necessary. Still, the man did not answer.

"Never mind," she said, removing her hand from her sword, feeling the emptiness in her hand where the magic had flowed but moments before. An odd noise escaped the man's stomach and he scowled. Avarielle grinned.

"Here," she took a step forward, picked up some food and the jug of water and stood before him, out of reach. Tied or not, he was still big and probably much stronger than she was. The man stared at the food and then at her, and she smiled encouragingly. She didn't know what he was, exactly, but a grumbling stomach seemed human enough to her. She would speak to Arlos about this.

He hesitated for only a second more before grabbing the stale bread and eating it slowly, keeping a careful eye on her. Avarielle waited patiently, feeling as though he was testing her. Once the bread finished, he took the jug and drank slowly, his eyes closing as he leaned his head back. He looked very human to her in that instant.

Then his midnight eyes opened again, and he passed her the jug, purposefully not extending his arm so she would have to reach for it. Avarielle didn't flinch as she reached in, took the jug and pulled away slowly. She wasn't about to be intimated by an unspeaking lout chained up in a chicken coop.

He grinned at her, his white teeth as square as her own, and not the pointed teeth of the Eloms. She smiled back. She would definitely speak to Arlos.

"See what we mean?" the guard said from behind her, making her jump slightly. The creature's smile vanished, and he caught her eyes for a second before lowering himself back down, his sore muscles slow and awkward. He put up his knee and his head lowered again. As she had found him.

She looked at him for a moment more before turning to face the guards, handing them the jug and plate.

"No, I don't."

She stepped back out into the night air, Graysword's magic awakening more with each new star appearing on the dark canopy above.

SHIRINA SAT IN THE DARKNESS, the shadows around her a protective veil against the loud surroundings. Her hair was freed from its restraints, the straight black mane hiding her features as she bent over what they dared call food in this area. Although she couldn't find fault with their generosity, Shirina felt it would hardly be difficult parting with food that looked and tasted like old shoes cooked with some onions. Old, worn leather shoes, at that. At least they had onions.

Cassara joined her at the table, the princess wise enough not to address the brooding sorceress. She was glad that no candle had been spared for their table, lest Cassara see the pale, drawn features of the sorceress. Sleep had been too rare of late, and her own thoughts, torn and betrayed, did not allow her the rest she might otherwise find.

Cassara left and Shirina remained silent, waiting for that annoying warrior to come tell her to get ready for battle. Why would she bother fighting for a little village in the middle of nowhere that no one cared about anymore, not even their own rulers? She sighed, wishing the fatigue that had set within her was simply physical, and not the dark treachery that had grasped her mind as well. Both were her fault, she knew, one for overextending her magic and the other for her wavering, uncertain loyalties.

A cup, possibly the only clean one left in the entire country, was placed before her. She was about to argue that she didn't drink ale when the smell of bitter tea soothed her senses, her body already perking at the promise of the reviving drink.

Shirina glanced up to see Cassara vanishing through

the door, probably to meet the warrior. She had no doubt that the princess was the one who had convinced them to give her a clean cup and then part with some of their precious water. She didn't think the princess realized just how good she was at convincing others to do her bidding. *A skill for a queen. Or a sorceress.*

She brought the warm liquid to her lips, not caring that the cup was metal and hot, her hands long numb from having wielded too much magical fire. The tea was stale, but it was strong and hot, and Shirina felt her spirits grow lighter. Cassara would be loyal to her, this she knew, as evidenced by her killing Jesimae. Shirina took another long, slow sip from her tea, cradling the cup between her two hands and enjoying the steam from the drink on her tired, cold face. Cassara didn't seem to have yet realized how much her actions had amplified her already dangerous situation, so concerned was she with the taking of another life.

She closed her eyes, letting only the sensation of the hot steam on her skin remain, pushing back the weary, aching pain of her body.

For Shirina, Jesimae's death had represented two distinct opportunities. One involved Cassara, the other the Circle, and both the hope that Tangia would see the light of Graydon once again.

You should know she is beyond your help. Jesimae's words haunted her, for she knew they were true. Even one hour in Siabala's Rage was too much for most to bear, and it had already been so long. She opened her eyes, focusing on the empty chair before her, draped in shadows.

She chased a foolish hope, she knew, one of the only emotional pursuits in her life. But it involved the only family she had ever truly known, and by the time she finished her tea, she had convinced herself that Cassara, following her own foolish hope of finding her little brother alive, would understand the path that Shirina might be forced to take.

Even if it meant betraying them all.

THE VILLAGERS SHOT their first arrow just past midnight, to their relief. They were beginning to get jittery. The Eloms usually arrived shortly after nightfall, but for some reason they had waited a long time this night.

A cheer went up as the first spotted Elom went down, the moon full and generous, the monster falling to the ground and moving no more.

"Prepare arrows!" Arlos cried, having just joined them after getting some rest. Cassara and Avarielle had not rested, the lust of battle too great for one, the nightmares too frequent for the other. Shirina was nowhere to be seen, but neither one had expected her to show up, considering she could not use her magic and did not wield a bow.

Upon hearing Arlos' command, Cassara nocked her arrow, waiting to spot an enemy before pulling the bowstring tight, in order to preserve her strength. She did not have to wait long, an Elom staggering into her line of sight. She pulled the string back, spotted the Elom following the shaft of the arrow and let it fly. The Elom fell silently. The hungry beast was followed by another, which Avarielle, who stood on a nearby roof, quickly downed with her arrow.

"Nice shooting!" Avarielle called at Cassara, grinning at her. Cassara smiled back, glad that so far it seemed she remembered how to aim.

All around the village arrows went flying, the twang of the strings more often than not followed by a cheer. The archers, all twenty-one of them, seemed to be in good shape so far, and the backup archers would be coming to relieve them in two hours.

Within an hour, Cassara had lost count of the number of Eloms she had downed, her misses fewer than her hits, her right arm aching in protest every time she pulled the string.

She had refilled her quiver five times and the latest arrows, which accounted for most of her misses, seemed to have been cut too quickly by the villagers. Or possibly while they were drunk. The shafts were all slightly crooked and most of the heads unbalanced.

"Elihor's blood!" Avarielle cried out after another miss. "Doesn't anyone know how to make arrows anymore!?"

The villagers below scrambled to find another batch of arrows while others continued working on the weapons near the campfire located in the middle of the village.

Cassara was grateful that the Eloms were at least manageable, and in fact their number seemed to be dwindling. The smell of the dead creatures was overpowering at times, the stench hanging heavily in the still night, most of the archers tying rags over their mouths and noses.

She was envisioning a nice comfortable bed when thick clouds covered the moon. Darkness smothered them, only the small fire at the center of the village still casting light, but not enough for the archers to see their targets or each other.

"Hold fire!" Arlos screamed. Cassara kept her arrow loosely nocked, comforted by Avarielle's soft cursing. She dared not move, afraid of reaching the end of the roof and plummeting off. Even if the houses weren't that high, two short stories in all, she could still easily break her neck, which struck her as a silly death after everything they had gone through.

She strained to hear something below, anything, and a few times she thought she heard some scuffling. Moments passed in darkness, the sound of her own breath heavy in her ears.

She thought she heard some leaves rustling even though there was no wind, seconds before the stench of rot struck her hard. She knelt carefully as her head spun from the stench and she feared falling off the roof.

She heard scratching all around them, quick and urgent and even more disorienting. *Claws. Teeth!* The moon finally broke through and the villagers gasped in fear as they looked below.

Surrounding the village, so thick none of the grass or rocky patches could be seen, was an army of Eloms, pushing each other to get through the wall, which buckled heavily in several areas. If it did not give way to their claws, it would succumb to the pressure of their bodies.

"Fire! Fire! Fire!" Arlos screamed, until he lost his breath. Cassara didn't even bother to aim, letting the arrows fly, assured a hit every time. The spare archers were called out, but still there were too many, and the arrows were running out faster than their supplies could be replenished.

"Fire!" Arlos managed to wheeze again, but in the chaos, it was Avarielle that Cassara heard.

"Bring everyone to the front gate!" Avarielle's voice was steady as she shouted the order.

"All archers flank the main gates from the rooftops! Bring the rest of the villagers to the farthest point away from the gate!"

The villagers, knowing they were fighting a losing battle, quickly followed Avarielle's orders, the warrior's voice authoritative and calming in the chaos.

"Cassara, come with me!" she shouted up, and Cassara quickly scrambled down, dropping all of her arrows as a result.

"Leave those," Avarielle said when Cassara began picking them up. "We'll need your other fighting talents tonight." Cassara followed, leaving the arrows where they lay scattered, but keeping the bow and quiver with her, for comfort, if nothing else.

"Split yourselves up evenly!" she shouted up as the villagers scrambled up the roofs. "And not too many to a roof! If you're as good at building roofs are you are arrows, the whole thing could collapse!"

Cassara met Avarielle's stride and Arlos quickly caught up to them. "What are you doing?" he demanded, although he sounded more relieved than annoyed that Avarielle had taken charge of the situation.

Avarielle did not break her pace as she replied. "We're going to open the main gates."

Arlos stumbled, the sound of clawing growing louder as they approached the gates, the wooden fortification buckling under their weight.

"You're going to let those monsters in?" he asked, his voice loud enough for a few of the archers to hear and repeat the words, their horrified voices ringing over the sound of the Eloms. This time, Avarielle did stop and turn to face him.

"We're not letting them in, Arlos. They're letting themselves in. All we're doing is deciding where they come in, so that we can have a welcoming party," Avarielle said sharply and crisply, making sure the archers would hear. "You and your archers take down as many as you can once they get in. The houses are tightly built here, so they'll only have only one place to go. And Cassara and I will take care of any that get through."

Arlos opened his mouth but closed it as the wood of

the gates cracked loudly. Other smaller cracks could be heard in other areas of the wall.

"Your choice," Avarielle said, shrugging.

Arlos' face lightened for a moment as he grinned at her. "You sure you're just a maid?"

Avarielle smiled back. "I am, but a bloody good one. Now get moving and tell your people to open those gates before the whole wall comes crashing onto us!"

Arlos scrambled up one of the ladders, ordering his people to pull the ladders onto the roofs with them after casting one last look at Avarielle and Cassara. At the back of the village, they could hear the cries of children as all the remaining villagers were being brought together. Cassara looked back once to try and see Shirina amongst them, but she couldn't spot her.

She reminded herself that Shirina was currently too weak to help them, anyhow.

"Open the gates!" Arlos shouted.

For a second the world stood still as everyone, even the Eloms, held their breaths.

Then the gates flew open, three houses from where Cassara and Avarielle stood, a wave of Eloms heading for them, claws and fangs the only things she could easily identify. Three short houses away.

"Get ready," Avarielle said, pulling Graysword free from its scabbard, the blade lit with moonlight and magic.

Cassara nodded and pulled her amulet free, her hand numb except for the comforting presence of the magic pulsing through her arm.

"I won't be able to use my flames too close to the homes," she said urgently as Eloms were felled by arrows. She cast an uneasy glance at the three small wooden houses.

"Do what you have to," Avarielle said, planting her feet firmly on the ground, one behind the other. "But stay behind me, and far enough back that I won't chop you."

Cassara quickly complied, backing up as the first Eloms reached Avarielle, Graysword easily taking them down. If the archers hadn't been so busy protecting themselves and their homes, they might have been impressed and frightened by the powerful magic of the sword. Too busy fighting, Cassara doubted any of them had noticed.

More Eloms broke through as the archers tired.

"Eli!" Avarielle swore as six Eloms stormed the tired warrior. Cassara summoned her fires, taking down four of the Eloms, the other two easily handled by Avarielle.

"Thanks!" the warrior called back as she hacked the last one. Cassara was about to remark how well the battle was going when she heard another crash beside her, and turned to her right as the wall fell down, Eloms scrambling over each other to reach the humans.

"Eli's blood!" Avarielle gasped as she downed two more. Cassara turned towards the new attackers, throwing her magic into their midst, knocking them down, burning. A few of them did not die immediately, their blackened skin catching on fire like old dry wood.

They shrieked and ran around in a panic, setting one of the wooden homes on fire.

The flames shot out, red and angry, the other Eloms shying from the light, backing away as the wall caught on fire as well.

"They're afraid of the fire!" Cassara called to Avarielle, who was losing ground fast. Quickly, she called her magic, breaking the strand into two so that it would go around Avarielle and reunite in front of her to attack the Eloms she currently blocked from her aim.

Avarielle looked back, stunned at seeing the white fires go around her and reunite to knock the Eloms dead. Before the warrior could ask questions that Cassara wouldn't know how to answer, the princess repeated herself, pointing at the burning home and wall.

"They're afraid of the fire!" Cassara repeated. Avarielle looked without surprise at the destruction.

"Well, so am I, Cassara!" Avarielle answered as she downed another Elom. "What are we going to do, set the whole town on fire?"

Cassara felt her magic rise within her, and she held out the amulet towards the burning building, willing the flames to become tamer. A small sweat broke out on her brow as the fires began to recede, her powers answering her quickly and easily, without smoke or glowing embers.

"I think I can do this, Avarielle!" Cassara shouted at the warrior, who began to falter from fatigue.

"How many of these are there?" she grumbled as Cassara approached her, the side of her face covered in blood from a gash at her hairline. "Order the archers to retreat and come to the center of the village, where the fire pit is!"

Avarielle's eyes sparked to life as she began to see Cassara's plan.

"Arlos!" she shouted, just managing to be heard over the sounds of the charging Eloms. Cassara summoned her fires to protect Avarielle, practicing as she easily formed a wall before the warrior.

"Order your archers to retreat!" Avarielle shouted, unfazed by Cassara's magic. Arlos stared open-mouthed for a few moments at the wall Cassara had created, before turning back to his men, ordering them to make their way to the third roof, where they could easily climb down behind the line of Eloms and the fire created by Cassara.

Without the archers slowing them, the Eloms came furiously, a few dying in the white fires before they stopped, as though they had just noticed the light.

"They're all down, and everyone's in the center," Avarielle said, and Cassara jumped at the voice beside her. Last she had noticed, the warrior was in front of her and none of the archers were down. Cassara nodded, wondering how easily she would pull this off.

Frustrated from the lack of movement from the two open sides of the walls, the Eloms struck the other failing portions of the wall with renewed intensity. Some of the monsters were pushed into Cassara's flames by their kin's anticipation of the blood and flesh of humans.

Cassara backed up, keeping an eye on her wall of

magic, the white fires easily staying strong. Avarielle put her hand on her shoulder, stopping her, and Cassara realized she was in the center, in front of the gathered villagers. She hadn't seen that time pass, either.

She shook her head, feeling as though she was sleepwalking, unable to control her movements and not fully grasping the situation.

Even the breaking of the wall to her left didn't elicit a reaction from her, only numbness existing where fear should have been. She heard the villagers scream behind her, and reached out, calling her wall of fire around her, imploring it to surround them. It did, with unnatural ease.

She felt the fires surround them, felt the Eloms burn within it before she even smelled their flesh. The amulet grew hot, hotter than even the strongest fire, yet it did not burn her.

All that she could see was fire, white flames accented by pinks, purples, yellows, sometimes even black. She wanted to turn around and make sure that everyone was within her wall, that Shirina was with them and safe, and that none of the Eloms had made it through. Visions of Avarielle's bloodied face turned the fires around her red for an instant.

But she couldn't. She couldn't turn around, couldn't make her body obey her, her mind only a witness to what she was creating.

She realized her arm was raised, holding the amulet. Pain shot up at the lack of blood, the arm having kept that position too long. She wanted to unclench her fingers from around the amulet, the crescent shape biting deeply into her hand, but she couldn't even remember what it felt like to move her hands.

She felt warm, and light, and lost, without control, only her wall remaining, only what she had created to protect them still before her. But she could no longer remember why, and through her numbness she was beginning to feel the fear, like an old friend come to greet her. Still, it could not force a reaction from her.

Her body and her mind were each forgetting the other existed.

She thought she heard her name but couldn't be sure, until she felt sharp pain on her cheek, and then on the other, stronger, sending her head reeling back.

The warmth vanished and her eyes flew open. The colors of the world all looked stark and dim, as though its palette had run out of bright colors long ago. She could hear soft murmurs around her, the sound seeming so far away, people sharing secrets in the depth of the night.

"Cassara, are you all right?" Avarielle asked, and Cassara focused on the warrior's face. Dry blood had been poorly cleaned from the side of her face and her red hair seemed a bit duller than before. She realized that the sun shone off of it, and looking to the side through the burnt, fallen fortifications, she noticed that the sun was rising.

"What?" she barely managed to ask, her dry throat choking on the word, the metallic taste of blood making her gag. Avarielle helped her sit up, grabbed her water pouch and removed the top with her teeth before handing it to the princess. Cassara drank slowly and deeply, the water feeling as cool as the fires had been hot, the blood cleansed from inside her cheeks where her own teeth had cut her.

"I didn't think she'd hit you," Avarielle said apologetically, shooting a nasty look at Shirina, who stood above Cassara. The sorceress ignored the warrior and looked at Cassara instead, with the same dark, searching eyes that had intimidated Cassara the first time they had met. Only this time, Cassara did not shy away.

"I think," Shirina said so softly Cassara barely heard her. "That we should begin some magic training for you, before you kill yourself with your own powers."

The village stood as silent now as it had been noisy when it had seemed like the screams of the Eloms themselves would tear down the walls. The air had grown stale, even the gentle morning breeze unable to remove the smell of decay and fear. Cassara tried to get up but her body still felt strange to her, her numb, cold legs refusing to unfold from under her, her tired, aching arms unable to support her weight. Avarielle reached down and Cassara grabbed the warrior's callused hand gratefully. Avarielle easily pulled her to her feet. She swayed as gently as the breeze but managed to stand on her own, her numb feet now aching as the blood rushed back to them. The veil that shielded her from the world lifted as a thousand needles pricked her body.

Avarielle stood near but asked nothing, her eyes as calculating as Shirina's as she stared at Cassara, the only difference between their gazes being the concern that marked Avarielle's. Shirina's bore no such kindness and Cassara found she could not meet either stare, nor address them, still disoriented from her magic. Instead, she looked around at the village. She was wary, uncertain she was ready to witness the destruction she had caused. But once her eyes began scanning her surroundings, she could not stop, slowly rotating, the pinpricks and needles grounding her as firmly as the sight around her.

She knew that destruction had been inevitable to save the villagers, but still, she could not believe that the now-cool amulet would be capable to imparting such disaster. It was even more difficult to believe that she could have been a part of it. Around her, the houses were mostly incinerated, only a few walls still standing. Most of the buildings were gone, only dark, black marks on the ground showing where they had once stood. The wooden wall that had protected them so poorly was mostly gone as well. There was no sign of the Eloms, aside for the stench of decay.

Scorched body parts littered the ground. Cassara swallowed hard. *Those must belong to Eloms.*

She continued slowly turning, unable to look at the villagers yet, for fear of what she might find, for fear that Jesimae had not just been a warning or an accident, but rather a shadow of what was to come in her own future.

A gentle breeze lifted the hair from her sweaty neck, the fresh air reviving her. It was then that she noticed that nothing around her seemed to be burning. No building smoldered, no wood smoked, and the earth seemed as calm and fresh as though no fire had ever struck it.

"There's no fire," she whispered, her tired mind struggling to understand. Surely there should be some fire? Had she truly even used her magic? Why had the time passed so quickly? She sought in her memories, trying to grasp what exactly it was she had done, but she could remember nothing except the white fires, and the hopes, and the fears. She was so disoriented that she swayed for a moment. Shirina's voice grounded her again.

"You kept your magic in check," the sorceress whispered, so close to Cassara that the princess jumped. "And drew it back into you."

Drew it back?

"How...?" Cassara began asking, but she was withdrawing again, trying to see within her what it was that she had done, and how she could have done it. Still nothing came to her.

"I didn't know you could do that," Avarielle said. Cassara snapped to attention again. She turned around to face the warrior, seeing the villagers standing behind her, their beleaguered faces casting wary glances their way.

"I didn't know either." Cassara heard Shirina speak, but the sorceress' annoyed voice seemed so far away, as far away as the cool metal of her amulet as she placed it back around her neck.

Part of her wanted to know what Shirina meant, why an Elite hadn't known what seemed like such basic and necessary knowledge. But she was too concentrated on

Arlos, who was walking towards her, each foot slowly planted in front of the other, his eyes never leaving her, yet never meeting hers.

"My Lady," he said, bowing awkwardly to Cassara. She blushed furiously, wishing he didn't feel the need for such formalities. Wasn't she the one who had destroyed their village after all? Moving quicker than she believed would ever be possible for her again, she bent down and grabbed both of his arms and forced him to stand and face her. There was such wonder in his eyes that Cassara wanted to cry.

I could have killed you. So easily.

"Thank you for saving us," he said gruffly, his words repeated by the villagers behind him. She looked beyond Arlos, towards the villagers, seeing the children in their mothers' arms and lovers still holding hands. Everyone she remembered from the village was here, everyone who had cheered them on last night, the innkeeper, the archers...she simply couldn't tell who was missing.

"How many didn't make it?" she whispered, her voice distant in her own ears.

"We all made it," Arlos said as he stood beside her.

Cassara swallowed hard and nodded. Slowly she counted the villagers once, and then twice, not able to speak, the colors around her regaining some of their earlier light. The breeze felt so fresh it dried her eyes before any tears could escape. She dared not blink, for fear the sight of the villagers might be lost as easily as she had been lost last night in the fires of the amulet.

"Where will you go now?" Avarielle asked Arlos. Cassara could still not tear her eyes away from the living before her.

"Up the mountains is too dangerous, with the woods still settling after the fires, and we don't even know if there are any villages left," Cassara heard Arlos say, the words slowly breaking through the last of the mist left behind by her magic, forcing her to pay attention. "Ravenhold won't welcome us, and I doubt Rashim will either. I guess we'll head south, towards Kosel, and hope someone will take us in."

"We've just walked from there and it's fairly infested," Avarielle offered. "Make sure to keep watch and your bows handy."

Cassara looked away from the villagers and snapped at Avarielle. "You can't seriously be thinking of letting them try that on their own?"

Avarielle furrowed her brow and smiled at Arlos. "Excuse us a moment, please." She linked arms with Cassara and dragged her away, Shirina trailing not far behind.

"They're too much luggage for us to bring, Cassara," Avarielle said matter-of-factly.

"Avarielle," Cassara said, interrupting her. "Aren't you the one who said you wanted to defeat the Eloms and learn more about them? Aren't you the one who put yourself in danger, night after night, for years, to save villagers around you? Can you really leave these people to their deaths now, after all of that?"

Avarielle raised her eyebrows for a second before bursting out in laughter. "I wish I'd never told you anything about my past! You have entirely too good a memory, my Lady," she ended with a bow.

Cassara felt flushed from her tirade, but she kept her gaze cool as she looked at Shirina, simply raising an eyebrow questioningly.

Shirina replied flatly. "Who am I to question a princess' orders?"

"Shirina, please," Cassara said, feeling the sorceress drift away from them again, farther than Cassara herself had been drifting but a few moments earlier. "I want your opinion."

Shirina gave a half-smile, although by no means did it warm her face. "I'm afraid I have to agree with the Grayloft. They will only be extra baggage. And I would add," she said, without hesitation, "that saving them will not bring back Jesimae."

Cassara stepped back as though she had been struck. "Shirina," Avarielle growled in warning.

"Shelter her as much as you'd like, Grayloft," Shirina said, her eyes and words steady. "But mark my words, she will be our downfall if she doesn't grow up faster." She walked away without another word.

Avarielle shook her head, a slight grin on her face as she addressed the silent Cassara. "I vote we bring the villagers, just to annoy her, if nothing else."

"Do you think we can protect them?" Cassara whispered, looking back at the hopeful faces.

Avarielle shrugged. "There's what, seventy of them?"

"Seventy-two, actually," Cassara replied softly.

"Seventy-two then, and over half of them can use a bow, and the other half, including the children, are quick to obey orders, from what I could see last night." She looked pensively towards them. "A lot of it depends on what type of Eloms we'll be facing. Last night it was just the wild type, the hungry type that simply wants to eat flesh. But it sounds to me like those heading for Massir are the smart ones, the more dangerous ones."

She paused and looked back at Cassara. "So I really don't know. I'd feel more confident if it was just the three of us, but I think we can handle whatever comes our way, especially with the way you handled your magic last night."

Cassara nodded, glad to have the warrior's support, although it all seemed to be more of an experiment of interest to Avarielle than a genuine desire to save the people.

"Just don't lose yourself in the magic again, Cassara," Avarielle warned sternly. "You might not find your way back next time."

Cassara nodded again. Avarielle grinned at her and began walking towards the villagers.

"Well, are you going to give them the good news, my Lady?" the warrior said teasingly.

"We're definitely going to have to work on the whole maid act before we reach Massir," Cassara mumbled as she walked towards the villagers.

As Cassara spoke to the villagers, the only solemn face was Shirina's, and despite her best efforts to forget the sorceress' harsh word, Cassara could not help but feel like a child again.

Except this time, they were letting her make the choices.

AVARIELLE DID a final sweep of the village to see what could be salvaged during the journey ahead. Cassara's magic had done a fine job of destroying all of the buildings and supplies.

She was just about to head back to the group when a burnt building caught her attention, the roof collapsed on itself. It was the chicken coop from earlier. One post remained standing through the carnage, chains dangling from it. Empty chains, without a burnt corpse attached to them.

Avarielle took a deep breath of ashes, placed her hand on the quiet Graysword and wondered what had happened to the prisoner. She knew of only two options. He might have escaped on his own. The second, less favorable option was that he had escaped with the aid of Eloms. She hoped that wasn't the case.

A brisk wind whipped through the forest, the trees dancing and leaves falling all around her, ashes scattering at her feet, the burnt remains of Eloms clinging to her boots and legs. She scowled at the sight and headed back towards the others.

She sincerely hoped he had escaped on his own and doubted she would forget his haunting eyes. She hoped she wouldn't regret allowing him to live.

19

———————

"Almost forty archers, and not one bit of hunt in sight," Avarielle mumbled as she stared across the bleak terrain. Cassara followed her gaze across the plains of Solir. All she could see were a few dry farms that had once defied their surroundings by surviving despite the rocky terrain. She already knew that the farmhouses would be deserted, some empty, some with corpses.

Her stomach, despite its emptiness, still reeled at the memories of the farms they had encountered on their first day out of Rockor. No matter how much Avarielle tried to shelter her, Cassara had still seen more in the past few weeks than she had in all of her years.

Parched waterways spidered before them, once giving the farmland much-needed irrigation. Now their dry beds mocked the weary, thirsty travelers. They were seventy-five traveling without food and barely any water, Cassara's magic having destroyed their storehouses.

"How could the destruction spread so quickly, and yet I'd heard nothing of Eloms until just over a month ago?" Had it really been only a month?

Avarielle's eyes narrowed as she continued looking towards the horizon.

"Because they were contained in the West for a long time, and then the Circle decided to get involved." Cassara cast a look to where Shirina sat by herself, leaning against a tree, autumn leaves falling around her despite the summer breeze.

"What did they do?" Cassara asked. The warrior didn't turn to face her as she replied.

"They wanted to study the magic, to see what types of creatures they were," Avarielle said with a soft yet harsh laugh. "We told them what they were, and the only proof we needed that they were from Elihor was the fact that Graysword was so efficient against them. But still they took a few."

"You let them?" Cassara interrupted, surprised. Avarielle's face darkened.

"They sent a diversion. Some of their younger students, I guess the least promising ones."

She let the matter drop and Cassara did not ask for more information. She didn't really want to know how old the students were, how many there were, and what had happened to them.

"And then I guess the Eloms escaped," Avarielle shrugged.

"With all of the powers of Ravenhold to keep a few

Eloms in check, I find it difficult to believe that they simply managed to escape," Cassara whispered, in case Shirina might hear them from where she sat.

Avarielle turned her head and gave Cassara a quick grin. "That was my problem with the entire theory. I thought I could find out more coming into the East, but between staying out of sight in the areas where Westlanders are still very much frowned upon, avoiding capture by the Circle and destroying the ever-growing number of Eloms, I guess I didn't do that great a job." She ended with a whisper, her hand absently going to Graysword's hilt.

"Why did you really leave the West, Avarielle?" Cassara asked softly, meeting Avarielle's eyes as she turned to face her. "I just find it hard to believe that you would leave your people in the hands of monsters, when you have the power to help them."

Avarielle pondered for a moment, as though deciding whether or not to tell a lie. Finally, she seemed to think better of it, her eyes gleaming a bit as she answered.

"What Shirina said was true, that my family was keeper of the West, and its leaders for a long time. But...it hadn't been that way since the wars, not since my family was nearly destroyed. And the Westlanders themselves, my people... Cassara, they turned against us. Not all, but some." She paused and swallowed hard, looking back towards the horizon before continuing.

"I did some things I'm not proud of, and some people paid the price. I thought it would be best to leave for a while, and with the Eloms on the loose, it gave me the perfect reason to go. But, I don't think I ever really, I mean, I never really decided what to do about all of this, except for traveling from area to area, and then the Circle came for Graysword. There were more at first, but I guess they grew tired of our little games. I just didn't want to bring them back to the West. My people have had enough of their magic, enough of their white and green flames."

"Green flames?" Cassara asked, remembering Kaden's fires and his stories about the Western Wars. On their special role, and their special magic.

"Green flames that consume all." Avarielle clutched Graysword tighter. "It's my earliest memory, and even then, it's really more of an impression, like a dream."

Cassara waited, not wanting to break the silence, not really wanting to know why the green fires elicited such angst from Avarielle. She didn't want to know what darkness haunted the men that had protected her in her youth. But she already knew, remembering what Avarielle had told Carsyn on their first encounter. Remembering how each of Avarielle's family members had been ripped from her—brothers, father...and mother.

"Your mother," Cassara whispered softly, and Avarielle nodded, the simple gesture confirming what she had feared.

Why would the Circle need a special unit with different magic if not to wash their hands clean of more blood, blood shed simply to spur on a war?

It wouldn't have made a difference, she had told Kaden, to ease the old man's pain. His wrinkles and his strong hands, the laughing face and comforting presence of her youth were assuming a new shape, yet she still couldn't associate Kaden, Carsyn, Klar and so many others with the horrors of killing a woman, while her young daughter was in the room with her. But she knew there was no other answer.

The Circle must have ordered the assassination of Avarielle's mother, to ensure the Westlanders would continue the useless war.

"Avarielle, I..." Cassara began, not certain what she would say, only knowing that she could not betray the old man who loved her as a daughter still.

"We should head out soon," Avarielle interrupted. She headed towards the few archers who were gathering wood to carve into arrows and rocks to knap into arrowheads.

She walked with purpose, not once breaking her stride. Cassara watched her go, her mouth still open, glad the warrior trusted her enough to share that much. Yet Cassara was sad that she didn't trust Avarielle enough to tell her what she knew. And probably never would.

Standing in a land of rocks and withering trees, heading towards the land of her future, Cassara vowed never to betray her past, including Kaden and Carsyn, and the horrors they had endured and inflicted.

AVARIELLE SET a quick and unforgiving pace, the warrior wanting to cross all of Solir in three days and reach Rashim's eastern border, and they hoped some safety. The capital of Solir, small by Rashim's standards but big by Edoline's, lay two days' walk to the west. Strong rumors indicated that it had been evacuated.

From the Eloms passing through, Cassara thought, thinking of Avarielle's people as the Eloms swept through their lands as well. They had no escape, the borders to the east closed for the past twenty years.

"This is as much of the countryside as a lot of us will ever see!" Arlos exclaimed as he walked beside her, holding his two-year-old grandchild.

Cassara smiled at his remark, gaining a giggle from the toddler.

"Young Arlos likes you," Arlos replied, a proud smile on his face as he gazed at his grandson.

"And I like him," Cassara replied, smiling widely at the child and eliciting more laughter.

She looked around her at the many villagers, very few carrying toddlers and babies.

"Your village doesn't have many children, does it?" Cassara remarked, wishing immediately she hadn't as Arlos' face darkened.

"I'm sorry. I didn't mean to pry."

Every line on his face was marked by an old weariness and, for the first time since having met him, Cassara wondered if he might not actually be well over fifty years of age.

"A few years ago, well, sixteen, to be exact, Rockor didn't even exist," Arlos began, speaking softly as to not alarm the child, whose eyes were drooping. "The Circle's Harvest took place that year and children were taken from Solir, as usual. Some of us who had lost children gathered from several villages, but Ravenhold's stand was clear. The children were theirs, as was agreed in a treaty signed a thousand years ago. A thousand years ago, before most of our countries were even formed. Can you believe that?" he asked, his voice raising a bit, the child stirring unhappily. He lowered his voice again.

"Anyways, we'd heard of several villages who had escaped Harvests, because the Circle's power and influence wasn't what it used to be. We built a new village, at the edge of Solir, hoping the next Harvest would miss us, and our children would grow old in peace. Of course, most of us had lost a child or a grandchild, so it was a quiet village, at first."

"And then?" Cassara asked, wondering if Shirina was close enough to hear.

"Eight years after the first Harvest, the Circle found us." Arlos smiled, the gesture defying the sadness in his eyes. "We fought back, but lost many adults, and then a few children were taken, again."

He gently kissed the top of the toddler's head. "They will return, soon. By then, we will have scattered in Kosel, if necessary. We will no longer lose our children to their magic, no matter if it is in their blood." The determination in his voice amplified the soft words.

I would have been one of those children, had the Circle's Harvest reached Edoline when I was a child. Cassara wondered how different her life would have been.

"You have magic," Arlos stated as he narrowed his eyes.

"Yes, but I'm not with the Circle."

"I knew that. Or hoped, at least. But how did you learn to wield magic so expertly without the Circle's help?"

"People learn, Arlos," she said softly, looking ahead at Avarielle, whose mastery of Graysword was in no part due to the Circle. Unless you considered the motivation she had gained through her need to escape them. "Maybe they don't learn because they want to, but they learn. Magic isn't something only the mind and knowledge control, after all."

Arlos smiled sideways at her. "That's not something the Circle would like to hear you say."

She smiled back, noticing that Shirina was closer to Arlos. She wondered what the sorceress was thinking, and what Arlos would do if he found out she was from the Circle. She decided it would be in all of their best interests to end the conversation now. "We all have our own paths to follow, Arlos. And I wish you the best on yours."

Arlos nodded, his eyes distant as he held his grandson closer.

Cassara looked towards Shirina, the sorceress' face as stony as the terrain around them. She wondered if the remaining children of Rockor would one day claim the Circle was their only family, as Shirina had to Jesimae.

20

It was the most beautiful and frightening sight Cassara had ever seen. Even Shirina and Avarielle, both knowledgeable and well-traveled, seemed speechless as they looked upon what had once been the most legendary lake in Rashim. Named the Hunter Lake for the bounty in its waters, it was the largest trading network in all of Graydon, between two of its main powers, Rashim and Solir.

"I was hoping we could take a boat from here to the capital," Avarielle said. To the left of Cassara, Arlos whistled. The villagers chattered nervously amongst themselves while the sun set on their second day of journeying.

"It would cut tomorrow at least in half," Avarielle continued, shifting the quiver of arrows on her back.

"We have bigger concerns than that," Shirina said, her voice rough. "If Hunter Lake is drying up, that means that most of Graydon's water sources must be slowly doing the same, at least in this part of Graydon. And that would definitely explain why all of the small rivers of Solir were dried up."

Cassara nodded, remembering their fear as they reached the narrow that would have provided them with the necessary water to survive the oncoming journey, and the silence that had followed the rough walk ahead, as everyone tried to conserve what little water remained.

Avarielle shrugged. "They can dig for their water then, and that might be cleaner than this boat-filled, over-bathed and sewer-ridden water. In the West we use wells, and I'm sure we're not the only part of this land that has underground water sources."

"That's what we use in Edoline too. I wonder if the two waterways are connected at all," Cassara said, looking down in the deep basin of the lake, its ridges dried earth, moss clinging to some rocks, the smell of dead fish lingering in the air like a heavy fog. Paths made of stale water muddied the bottom, far out of their reach.

A shiver ran up her spine as she noticed some unearthed shipwrecks. Rotting broken masts and hulls sprinkled the edges of the lake and clung to rocky spikes which shot out of the crater's bottom.

"Some of those ships could be as old as Elihor and Graydon's time," Cassara whispered as she squinted her eyes, trying to find others.

"Perhaps even older," Shirina said, her battered Circle dress beating in the wind. The fabric was torn in several places, the once-white cotton now encrusted with mud, dirt and blood.

"We need to get you a new dress," Cassara mumbled, shaking her head as she imagined the entrance they would make in Massir. Her own clothes needed far more than a simple wash. She'd been wearing the same pants and shirt since having lost her pack.

"Neither one of you looks or smells like a springtime daisy," Avarielle said as Shirina shook her head. "But right now, we have more immediate concerns. First of all, it smells disgusting here, present company included, and second of all, we're not going to make it to Rashim on our current water supply, not with all those villagers in tow." Cassara was ready to argue for the safekeeping of the villagers, her mouth pasty from the little water she had ingested in the past few days, but was relieved when neither the warrior nor the sorceress argued with her.

"So we need someplace safe to set up camp. And some water to carry us through the rest of the journey, which should end tomorrow night, when we reach the borders of Rashim."

"If that section of Rashim hasn't been evacuated as well," Shirina said.

The setting sun steadily stretched the shadows of the lake bottom.

"Well, we have water here," Avarielle said, waving towards the bottom of the lake.

"You expect us to climb down there and somehow

bring back water from the bottom?" Shirina deadpanned, not even rising her usual eyebrow.

"I'm open to suggestions," Avarielle shrugged.

Shirina stood quietly for a moment, analyzing the land around her. Cassara, who was looking straight at her, noticed for the first time the tree near the edge.

"The tree," Cassara said, pointing behind Shirina. "It still has leaves." The maple tree displayed the red and orange hues of fall they had seen spreading throughout their travels. But unlike the other withered trees in the region, it still bore some of its leaves and its bark was not withered.

Avarielle and Shirina understood immediately and the warrior peered down the edge of the lake.

"I think I see a cave below, maybe twenty feet beneath us," Avarielle said, crouching to secure her balance. "There must be a puddle of water trapped there."

"We could set up a pulley system, with the containers we have and the few ropes available," Cassara continued, starting to feel excited and energized by the idea. A few of the villagers, including Arlos, began pulling out the necessary supplies. Some children laughed as they sensed the excitement in the adults, the young ones not as parched as the adults, the precious liquid having been preserved for the youngest and weakest.

"There could be Eloms down there, far enough that Graysword's magic can't alert you of their presence," Shirina said, her arms crossed on her chest. The word rippled through the villagers, spoken in hushed and frightened tones. Many of the archers clutched their bows protectively.

"Then we send someone down with magic, and leave another here to protect the villagers, just in case," Avarielle said, taking some rope from Arlos and tying a few lengths together.

"I'll go," Avarielle continued as she tied the last pieces together. "Since it was my idea." She turned and offered Shirina a grin. "And you're coming with me."

Shirina gave a dry laugh. "Still don't trust me with your ward, do you, warrior?"

"Not for one moment."

Cassara took a step towards them, wanting to reprimand them for so easily forgetting the plan they had forged on the burnt grounds of the Maple Mountains, where they would be her two maids with which to enter court. Did they not realize that these villagers would be entering Rashim, and perhaps even Massir with them?

"Very well," Shirina replied amicably, and Cassara sighed in relief. The air between the warrior and the sorceress was still thick with unspoken words, but at least they remained unspoken for now, until a better opportunity came along. Cassara was suddenly glad she would be remaining on the surface, even though that meant she was the only one to defend the villagers should trouble arise.

Avarielle secured the rope to the tree, tugging on the knots to make sure they would hold. Satisfied, she threw down the other end, the rope uncoiling and striking the dirt and rocks lining the lake.

"Think you can make that climb?" Avarielle asked Shirina. The sorceress refused to answer as she grabbed the rope and swung herself over the edge with relative ease. She was gone in an instant.

"Once we're down, bring the rope back up and tie the containers to it and lower them down," Avarielle said to Arlos as she removed her bow and arrows and placed them by her pack. "We'll fill them up and send them back to you, as often as necessary. Don't drink the water without boiling it first, so get a fire started."

Arlos nodded, wished them good luck and turned to the villagers to get them moving on building a fire, instructing the archers to keep watch. Satisfied, Avarielle looked down the rope, sounding slightly disappointed as she said, "She made it."

She grabbed the rope.

"You shouldn't run into any problem up here, and we'll be back before it gets too dark," Avarielle said. "And don't worry, I promise I'll try to bring Shirina back alive. Wounded, maybe, but alive."

With a wink, Avarielle was over the edge, expertly climbing down, leaving Cassara alone and relieved to still be in the fading sunlight.

She had had enough of caves for one lifetime.

"It's clear," Shirina said as soon as Avarielle landed, the sorceress' light spell dancing gently in the air above them, casting an eerie light on the walls of the cavern. Avarielle looked around, the cave not too deep, but filled with roots. A large brown puddle filled its bottom.

"Not too attractive, but it'll do," Avarielle said as she put her hand on Graysword's hilt, the magic silent. Satisfied that they were alone, Avarielle took the lead into the cave, trying to keep her footing on the unstable rocks. Shirina followed. She slipped a few times, each time standing back up without complaint.

"Tell me something, now that we're alone," Avarielle asked casually. Shirina eyed her suspiciously, not fooled by the friendly tone. "How long were you hoping it would take me to realize that you're useless to us now?"

A bitter smile crossed Shirina's thin lips, the sorceress' features etched by the shadows of her magic, her dark hair contrasting her pale skin to perfection.

"I thought you were always of that opinion and simply kept me around because Cassara was of the opinion that I could be of use."

Avarielle stopped shy of the muddy water and turned around. Arlos would soon be sending the containers and Avarielle preferred not being caught down here during the night.

"I was always of that opinion. But before, at least, you were a way to access the Circle," Avarielle said as she faced Shirina. "Now with Ravenhold fallen and your betrayal, I'd say that you're no longer useful that way." Shirina did not react, which pleased Avarielle to some degree. If there had been one constant in her life of late, it was Shirina's stubbornness to remain the same.

"On the other hand," Avarielle said as she resumed walking towards the entrance, the first containers already dangling in the cave mouth. "We're of use to you. Cassara, in particular. You need her to get into Massir, under guise of being a maid."

To Avarielle's surprise, Shirina had come with her to help her untie and carry the containers. Once all freed, the two women walked back inside the cave, carrying quite a few skins and some ale bottles, which had all been lowered in a blanket.

"But what worries me," Avarielle said as they crouched to fill the containers, "is what happens once you reconnect with your old friends? What happens if you find someone for whom you still hold loyalty?"

Avarielle let the question dangle, watching the bubbles escape the skin she was filling.

"Tangia was the only one I was loyal to," Shirina whispered. "And since she's no longer there, it's hardly an issue anymore."

Avarielle sealed the skin and grabbed another one as she ungracefully fell from crouching to sitting, keeping a close eye on Shirina. The sorceress seemed concentrated on the waterskin she was filling, but Avarielle noted that no more bubbles escaped the container.

Avarielle guessed what Shirina was thinking. When she was first being hunted by the Circle, she had been naïve enough to think it had been because she was killing Eloms, their little experimental subjects.

On the day Shirina had saved her life when she could have easily taken Graysword, Avarielle had understood that they needed her alive, and in possession of her ancestral blade. The Circle now also wished to claim the amulet of Edoline, although Cassara's life seemed to be expendable. And the woman from the Circle that Cassara had killed wielded a magic different from theirs, one that could affect the heirs of Grayloft. And her family's ability to resist the magic of Graydon had come from Graydon himself.

Which meant the magic had not been from the Land of Light.

"Would you accept it?" Avarielle asked. "Would you accept the dark magic of Elihor, like your little friend did?"

Shirina's head whipped up, her eyes blazing with fury. "Jesimae was a power-thirsty fool who sold her soul for a chance at greatness. *If* that magic was even from Elihor," Shirina added, the murderous look in her eyes only serving to confirm Avarielle's theory. "I would never accept the darkness."

Shirina did not break eye contact, even when Avarielle whispered the last words.

"Even if accepting those powers meant saving your old teacher?"

Shirina's eyes flickered for an instant, not with uncertainty, but with grief. Slowly she pulled the skin out of the water and sealed it. Her face looked strained under the light.

"Even if I did," Shirina said, shrugging a bit as though to make light of the situation. "Tangia would be the first to kill me after I rescued her." She met Avarielle's eyes again.

Avarielle held her gaze for a few moments, wishing she understood more of the sorceress and thinking, although she would never say so, that Tangia sounded like a good woman. But one that was gone.

"She's probably dead by now, or at least beyond your help," Avarielle said, looking back towards the lake. "Why don't you just forget it and go back home? You must have spawned from some parents, no?"

"Is this your new way of getting rid of me, now?" Shirina spat. "By being the sympathetic friend? By encouraging me to find a new path now that all my old plans have crumbled around me? Do you think me fool enough to believe that you have my best interests at heart?"

Avarielle shrugged, a slight smile gracing her lips as she replied. "I was hoping. I unfortunately promised Cassara I would bring you back to the surface alive."

Shirina's eyes flashed. "Same problem I faced for months of hunting you?"

Avarielle stood up and gathered the cloak holding the filled water skins. She gave Shirina one last glance as she shrugged. "Except you're the one sticking around. I'm starting to think you just enjoy my company."

Shirina scoffed and stood up, walking past her to reach

the exit, unconcerned that her back was to the warrior's. The rope was pulled up and the cloak had just vanished over the edge when the cheers of joy turned to screams of fear.

"Eli's blood!" Avarielle barely had the time to curse before the sky above them erupted in flames. The tree holding the rope plummeted down towards them, its leaves on fire.

By sheer instinct she grabbed Shirina and pulled her in, the two landing painfully on the jagged rocks of the cave as the tree landed on the ledge, blocking them in, the smoke from its burning leaves filling the cave at an alarming rate.

The two sat silently, stunned and uncertain what to do next, and Avarielle wished that someone above them would at least scream.

21

Cassara smiled as the villagers cheered when the cloak was pulled clear of the edge of the cliff. Two of the archers grabbed the cloak when a scream shattered the cheers and heat flashed by Cassara, the fires swallowing the two archers before striking the tree behind them. It plummeted over the cliff.

She wasn't given time to react before the next attack came. She threw herself to the ground and covered her head as the smell of burnt flesh surrounded her.

It's not night yet! She fumbled for her amulet, the magic warm against her.

"Arlos!" she screamed, hoping the man would hear her. "Tell everyone to take cover!" She stumbled to her feet and tried to locate the Eloms, but couldn't spot them. She heard whimpering, but couldn't stop to identify the dead and wounded. She hoped no one would get in the way of her attack.

Where are they! Dusk had comfortably settled on the dry land but the day still offered plenty of light, the rocky terrain providing very little cover or places to hide.

White fires danced about the amulet in her hand, but she could see no assailant into which to hurl it. Loas, one of the youngest archers, looked up and drew back his bow, and Cassara followed his aim.

She gasped at what she saw.

Flying above them were two obsidian-skinned creatures, their chests jagged as though carved. Their backs were adorned with two large feathered wings, their span twice as long as Avarielle was tall, and their motions as graceful as the arms and legs were stiff and unnatural. Loas let his arrow fly, missing the lowest creature by a few yards, the arrow falling into the empty lake.

The creature soared in a graceful arch and straightened its wings once it faced them. Its arms and legs dangled as though merely an inconvenience.

Then it moved its arms and dark fires glowed from its fingers.

Loas yelped and fell to the ground, the fires heading directly for him. Cassara screamed and threw herself in their path as she grasped the amulet and held it high, summoning her magic. Her white flames erupted before them, but they weren't strong enough. Cassara felt the dark fires break through and turned her face as some of her hair singed. She screamed in pain as the fires hit her outstretched arm, the dark magic thankfully retreating.

Biting her lip, she quickly examined her burns. Her

blackened shirt revealed angry red skin underneath. Her arm was singed, but it was still usable and would heal in time.

She looked back up. The creature was gone. She searched frantically and screamed when the creature landed right in front of her, grabbing the front of her shirt and pulling her off the ground. Furiously she kicked, the shirt digging deeply into her armpits, the worn seams ripping at the shoulders.

Her hands came up and she grabbed her assailant's two hands, trying in vain to pull them free. The hands, so human and yet so cold and immovable, held firm. Like stone. Even her fingers could not dig into the skin to inflict any sort of damage.

Dark eyes looked at her, red fires burning the pupils to life, as though the flames of Siabala's Rage dwelt there. Her amulet throbbed in her hand, but she feared that using it would mean her death as well.

Loas screamed as he attacked the creature, only to be brushed aside as its giant wings extended, sending dust flying into Cassara's eyes. One of the arms let go of her front and wrapped around her waist instead.

He was going to take off with her in tow!

She whimpered and grew lightheaded as the creature's wings flapped strongly and its feet left the ground. Her heart in her throat, she clung to the creature, terrified of falling. Her legs were heavy and dangling below with her heart and stomach somewhere still on the ground. The arm around her waist cut her breaths short and dug into her ribs.

Faces clouded her mind...Avarielle, Dayshon, Kaden, her father. The faces of the people she knew would protect her. But now she was alone and had only herself to rely on.

Closing her eyes, she whispered a small prayer to fate and released her fires on the creature, and herself.

***

"GET US UP THERE, SHIRINA!" Avarielle demanded, her voice a growl in the back of the cave, where they had retreated to ward off the smoke.

"I don't know how close I'll be teleporting us to Eloms," Shirina said, not arguing with the warrior. Avarielle was surprised, knowing that teleporting two individuals, even over such a short distance, required much concentration and energy. If she had wanted, the sorceress could have easily left the warrior to die in the smoke-filled cave.

Avarielle looked closely into the dark eyes of the sorceress, seeing no deceit. The warrior kept her voice low as she said: "They're not Eloms. Graysword isn't reacting at all. We're not so deep that it wouldn't react to their presence."

Shirina's eyes grew wide for an instant, the eerie glow of the mage light reflected in them.

"Get close to me," Shirina said, taking a step towards

Avarielle. "And don't activate Graysword's magic until we teleport safely. You could kill us both, otherwise."

Avarielle swallowed and nodded, the two standing much closer than Avarielle had ever intended or wished to be. The mage light flickered once and died as Shirina gathered all of her energies.

Avarielle held her breath. She felt energy rising all around her, as though stuck in a strong gale that moved no clothing or hair. She heard Shirina whispering and Avarielle moved a bit closer as the mists gathered, afraid the spell might miss part of her, afraid that she had walked into a trap after all.

Shirina's whispers never stopped, never hesitated, never stumbled or slowed in cadence, nor did they quicken or pause, as though her very need for breath was obsolete, a need born of humanity, not of magic.

The mists surrounded them and Avarielle felt disoriented, not knowing what was up, down, or where she was. She resisted the urge to reach out and touch Shirina to find some grounding, still scolding herself for having moved closer in the first place.

Suddenly, her feet touched solid earth again, and the mists receded, to lead them into fire.

WHILE STILL IN THE MISTS, Shirina's senses came to life, and she knew that she was leading them to their doom. Quickly she cast a protective spell, easily spun from the already invoked magic around her. As the mists dissipated, Avarielle swore. Fire surrounded them.

Thankfully the warrior did not have the reaction to back away from Shirina. Avarielle pulled Graysword free from its scabbard and placed herself in front of the sorceress.

"How long will your spell hold?" she asked, not turning to face Shirina.

"A few minutes, at most, but I doubt anyone could sustain fires of this strength for much longer."

Avarielle nodded, the warrior looking around, obviously trying to pinpoint the origin of the onslaught, unable to do so in the white fires.

Shirina waited patiently, concentrating on the shield, making sure it would not dwindle before she meant it to. The shield magic, like the mage light and unlike teleportation, was self-sustaining for a time after being cast, but even the strongest magic eventually faded. That truth seemed to also apply to the Wall separating Graydon from Elihor, or so it seemed from the invading Eloms.

"Is that Cassara's magic?" Avarielle asked, and Shirina could have hit herself for not recognizing the distinctive white fires surrounding them.

"It would seem so." She wondered what had incited the princess to cause such an onslaught. Shirina regretted that, due to fatigue and constant travel, she had not taken the time to teach Cassara more about the immense potential she wielded. If Cassara failed to control her powers again, she could be lost forever.

Shirina gazed into the fire, wishing to see beyond it, lured by the white beauty, her shield shimmering a slight purple as she waited for the magic to end.

THE FIRES RAGED all around her and she felt herself fall, landing heavily on her feet and rolling on the sweet ground, surprised to feel no pain from the fires. Stunned, she remained seated, her legs aching where the fall had been absorbed.

She slowly looked around. The white fires still raged around her. She caressed them with her hand, the fires enveloping it and then breaking to grant her safe passage.

Looking down at the amulet clutched in her hand, she was surprised to find it cool, the metal peacefully resting. A noise caught her attention and her head jerked up. She wondered how many people were caught in her fires. The protective blanket of magic suddenly seemed deadly to her. Would it protect others as it had her?

She bit her lower lip, her breath caught in her throat as she called the fires back, fearful of what she might see, of what she might have caused while selfishly trying to save herself. The white fires died slowly, and in them she saw people, imagining some burnt and dead on the ground, others writhing as the fires consumed the last of them. But when the fires were gone, when at last she could see the colors of the earth and the sky once more, she was greeted by Loas' wide-eyed face, barely ten feet from her own. The youth seemed unharmed.

She took a deep breath of relief, smiling widely at Loas and laughing a bit, when suddenly the dark-winged creature landed beside her again. Its glowing eyes now seemed alive, its unmoving human features animated by the shadows from the dancing flames.

The obsidian arm came down in a quick motion, grabbing Cassara by the wrist and pulling her up. She kicked hard, hurting her foot as it met unyielding stone.

A battle cry sounded and Graysword came slicing down on the arm, sparks flying as the blade struck, surprising the creature enough that it released its prey.

Cassara threw herself back. Graysword's magic flared to life under Avarielle's bidding, and she struck hard at the wings, cutting one in half.

The creature barely seemed to notice, continuing its advance on Cassara. Avarielle spun around and landed another magical blow on the second wing, severing it at the back joint. This time, the creature stopped and turned to face Avarielle.

Cassara held her amulet. She pleaded for her magic to give her the strength to destroy the creature. The amulet flared to life just as the second creature, forgotten until now, landed right beside the princess. Avarielle swore but Cassara was too concerned with escaping to turn to the warrior.

The creature was barely an arm's length away from her

as she backed away, trying to summon the fires. *Please!* Her amulet lay dormant in her hand.

Shirina's fires flew into the creature, sending it to the ground, its wings burnt and smoking. After a few moments it stood again, and without the feathered wings, it looked more like a statue than a living thing, its stone skin reflecting the last of the sun's light.

"How do you kill stone?" Avarielle screamed as Graysword struck another blow.

"They're just animated, soulless creatures," Shirina hissed, the sorceress planting both feet firmly on the ground as she raised her hand to the creature approaching Cassara, her eyes unbelievably still as she recited a spell.

Her second hand came up, aimed at the one Avarielle was fighting.

"Try to keep them in the same spot, to make it easier for Shirina to do whatever she's doing!" Avarielle screamed at Cassara.

The creature walked towards her still, but Cassara stopped backing away, calling forth a small wall of fire between the creature and herself. She was relieved when the amulet obeyed her.

As she had hoped, the creature stopped and hesitated. It observed the wall, turned its head slowly, and Cassara resisted the urge to run. Then the monster began walking forward through the wall. Cassara took a step back, her magic failing.

It took another step, but suddenly the red fire in its

eyes faded into the same dark stone as the rest of its body. It lowered its head and stopped moving.

"Eli's blood and guts, that's unnatural," Avarielle swore behind her, striking the creature one last time just to make sure it wouldn't move.

"What did you do?" Cassara asked Shirina, turning around to look at the sorceress when she didn't answer.

Shirina stood quietly, her feet still firmly planted, her arms now lying peacefully by her sides, her eyes dark and wide.

"Maybe you should sit down," Avarielle said as Cassara approached Shirina. Gently the princess laid a hand on the sorceress' arm. Shirina blinked.

"I'm fine," she said flatly.

"I'd expect no less from an Elite of the Circle," a soft voice rang across the plains. Avarielle clutched Graysword and stepped in front of Shirina and Cassara. A woman appeared, the air crackling with her teleportation spell as she stepped through its mists to stand before them. Her dark hair and blue eyes were familiar to Cassara, but she couldn't place her in her memories. The only thing that mattered was that she was obviously from the Circle and therefore their enemy. Shirina tensed beside her.

"Who are you?" Cassara demanded, the amulet growing hot in her hand.

The woman took on an exaggerated air of sadness. "What's wrong, Cassara? Don't you recognize your own aunt?"

Cassara reeled back at the words, suddenly seeing the

resemblance between her and Altessa, recalling a day that now seemed like years ago when she had seen this woman, and mistaken her for her sister. In their father's study, looking down as she left behind everything she had ever known.

"You were in Edoline the day I left," Cassara said weakly, the magic throbbing in her hand. Cassara didn't unleash it, haunted by Jesimae's last cries.

"Yes, I was. But if I had known you had the amulet with you, I wouldn't have let you get away so easily," the woman said, seeming pleased that Cassara had noticed her. "But, it all works out in the end. Here you are. Here I am."

Cassara fought not to take a step back, forcing herself to hold her ground. "Why do you want this amulet?"

The woman gave a short, dry laugh. "Because it's mine by right. I was your mother's older sister, and much more gifted in magic. But she would not give it to me in the end, even when I was an Elite of the Circle, and very powerful." The woman cocked her head and looked questioningly at Cassara. "Don't you remember, dear? Don't you remember the first day you met your auntie Delora? It was the day your mother died, I fear."

The last words were spoken with such hate that Cassara took a step back, shaking her head. *What was the woman talking about?*

"Poor Alexavier. Losing the love of his life and having to continue raising the child that killed her."

The words sliced through Cassara and the magic of the

amulet danced about her wrist. She remembered the warmth, from a time before Eloms lurked in Edoline. The memories came quickly, hidden by magic and pain a long time ago.

Cassara was back in Edoline, in the Courtyard of Travelers, playing the travelers' song for her mother as she prepared to leave for destinations lost forever from Cassara's mind. The music had flowed easily and without the same pain and regrets that usually grabbed Cassara now whenever she picked up her flute. They had laughed. Cassara had stared in wonder as her father had gently helped her mother mount her horse. Why hadn't she remembered this before?

Delora, her mother had said, her breath catching in her throat.

I've just come to say goodbye. And her father was on the ground, and Cassara was afraid, and the amulet her mother had just given her burned. And she had unleashed the magic. Badly. She couldn't control it, barely understanding it was hers.

And her mother's horse had reared in fright. And the fountain of stone had caught her mother's head.

Cassara blinked away tears, the magic of the amulet withdrawing as she stared at it in horror. She had killed her own mother. Not the Circle. Not the horse. It had been her all along.

"It took me years to heal, and I had to make deals with forces I would have preferred never meeting," Delora continued, and the next thing Cassara knew, Delora stood right in front of her.

"And now, this is mine." Delora pulled on the amulet. Cassara refused to let go, and Delora pulled so hard the chain cut in to her already-burnt flesh. She screamed in pain, seconds before her throat closed, blocking air from reaching her lungs.

"Be a good girl, now, Cassara, not like your sister was?"

Altessa!

Cassara felt despair engulf her, and the air Delora was not blocking from her throat was being blocked by her sobs. She had brought this destruction on her family. Her, and no one else.

Delora screamed in pain and let her go, her spell losing its grip on the princess' throat. Cassara gasped for fresh air as Avarielle and Shirina stepped in front or her, the two women blocking Delora's path to her. Through her tears, Cassara could see the land had grown red, fire breaking behind Delora, red and wild, feeding off of thin air. She hoped the villagers had taken shelter.

"You dare betray me, Shirina?" Delora spat out.

"I never owed you any loyalty," Shirina hissed back. A funnel of noise ripped the air from around them. The red fires grew and gathered, forming a crimson portal behind Delora, perfectly oval-shaped, yellow fires licking its edges. "How convenient that you brought them all here anyways, Shirina. Just like you were ordered to."

Shirina did not answer, though her fists tightened.

"I have one piece," Delora said, dangling the amulet

nonchalantly from her hand. Cassara gasped as she realized that she had lost that too, just as she had Jayden, Altessa, her mother, her father and Edoline.

"Now I need the other." She smiled evilly and held out her hand. Avarielle lurched back and then was thrown forward, Graysword falling from her grasp. The warrior crumbled to the ground by Delora. She jumped back to her feet, only to have Delora's hand tighten around her arm and twist it, snapping the bone like a twig. With a yelp of pain, Avarielle buckled, but refused to fall to her knees, eyes filled with hatred.

"Avarielle!" Cassara shouted, rising but not knowing what to do, her only weapon in Delora's hand.

"Oops," Delora said, flashing a grin as she extended her hand towards Graysword, the blade beginning to move. Cassara leapt sideways and grabbed the hilt of Graysword, convinced she had to keep the sword from Delora's grasp. She was certain that it was the only way to save Avarielle.

"Shirina! Help!" Cassara screamed as the blade continued moving towards Delora, despite Cassara's efforts.

Shirina looked at Cassara slowly and turned back to Delora, black hair flying around her face as she raised her hand and chanted a single word. Delora's eyes widened, obviously not expecting this move, and in a flash of light Delora, Avarielle and the portal were all gone. The pull on it gone, Graysword fell with a loud clatter on the ground, dragging Cassara down with it.

"What...?" Cassara could barely word the question. Silence smothered everything.

Shirina stood still for a moment, not looking at Cassara as she answered. "Delora needed both the Grayloft and Graysword, as well as your amulet, to do what she planned to do. To lower the Wall of Loss."

Cassara looked back towards where Avarielle had been but a moment before.

"Where is she, Shirina?" Cassara whispered. "What did you do with Avarielle?"

Shirina hesitated again, answering slowly. "I pushed them all through the portal."

A villager grunted on the ground nearby, making Cassara start. She could hear their whispers from where they cowered. The rising wind cooled the sweat on her face.

"Shirina?" She implored. "Where's Avarielle?"

"Go to him, Cassara. Go to your prince, get married, and forget all of this," Shirina said as she slowly began walking away.

"Shirina!" Cassara screamed, her hands tightly clutching Graysword. "Tell me what you've done to Avarielle!"

Shirina flinched a bit at the words, but this time she did turn around and faced Cassara as she answered.

"I've sent them all to Siabala's Rage."

EPILOGUE

$\mathcal{A}$rlos had been amongst the first killed. The second wave of fire had come for him, and he had scooped his grandchild up and hurled him out of the way, the fires catching the old man in their passing. The witnesses said that he had smiled at young Arlos to comfort him as he had vanished into the flames.

There was little left of his body, or of the eleven others who had been killed in the attack. Six others had been badly wounded and might not last the night, a fear heightened by the loss of their water.

Cassara swallowed hard, keeping her tears in check, knowing that she simply couldn't afford to lose more hydration. She was tired and lightheaded. Her lips were cracking and her skin felt like sandpaper. The magic and battle had sucked out whatever energy she had left, and for the first time since leaving Rockor she feared not reaching Rashim. Not because of enemies, but because of her own weakening body.

I'm not the only one who feels that way, Cassara thought, forcing her thoughts away from her growing thirst, from her heartache, from her fear.

The villagers cast glances her way, sometimes frightened, sometimes hopeful. One thing became increasingly clear as the night wore on and they kept close to her. They now looked to her for guidance.

Cassara sat well into the night, unable to sleep, feeling numb even where her skin was burnt and cracked. She had lost her allies and friends. And her magic.

She fought back a sob as she thought of Avarielle in Siabala. *Siabala's Rage.* Where even Elders of the Circle stood little chance of survival.

Graysword was cold in the night air, yet Cassara kept a firm grasp on it. This was hers to safeguard for now, but she had to return it to Avarielle's people. They needed her. They needed their leader, but she was gone, and Cassara was just a princess from a little kingdom barely anyone remembered. And she had lost her magic, the only thing that had made her useful in this quest.

Her grip tightened on Graysword. *No.* She wasn't just that, not anymore. She had to become more, whether she was ready for it or not.

She looked around her at the freshly dug graves and at the sleeping, huddled villagers, and knew she had to reach Massir. She might not be able to save Avarielle, but she could help her people by becoming a leader in the East.

She imagined the Wall of Loss shimmering in the distance, and wondered how long it would be before Delora sent more of her demons to claim the lost sword of the heirs of the West.

To be continued in the Heirs of a Broken Land 2:
Warrior of Darkness